- HERGÉ -
★

THE ADVENTURES OF TINTIN

THE BLACK ISLAND

L B

Little, Brown and Company
New York   Boston

www.casterman.com
www.tintin.com

Little, Brown and Company
Hachette Book Group
237 Park Avenue, New York, NY 10017
Visit our website at www.lb-kids.com

First Edition: December 2011

ISBN: 978-0-316-13387-6
2011921034
SC
Printed in China

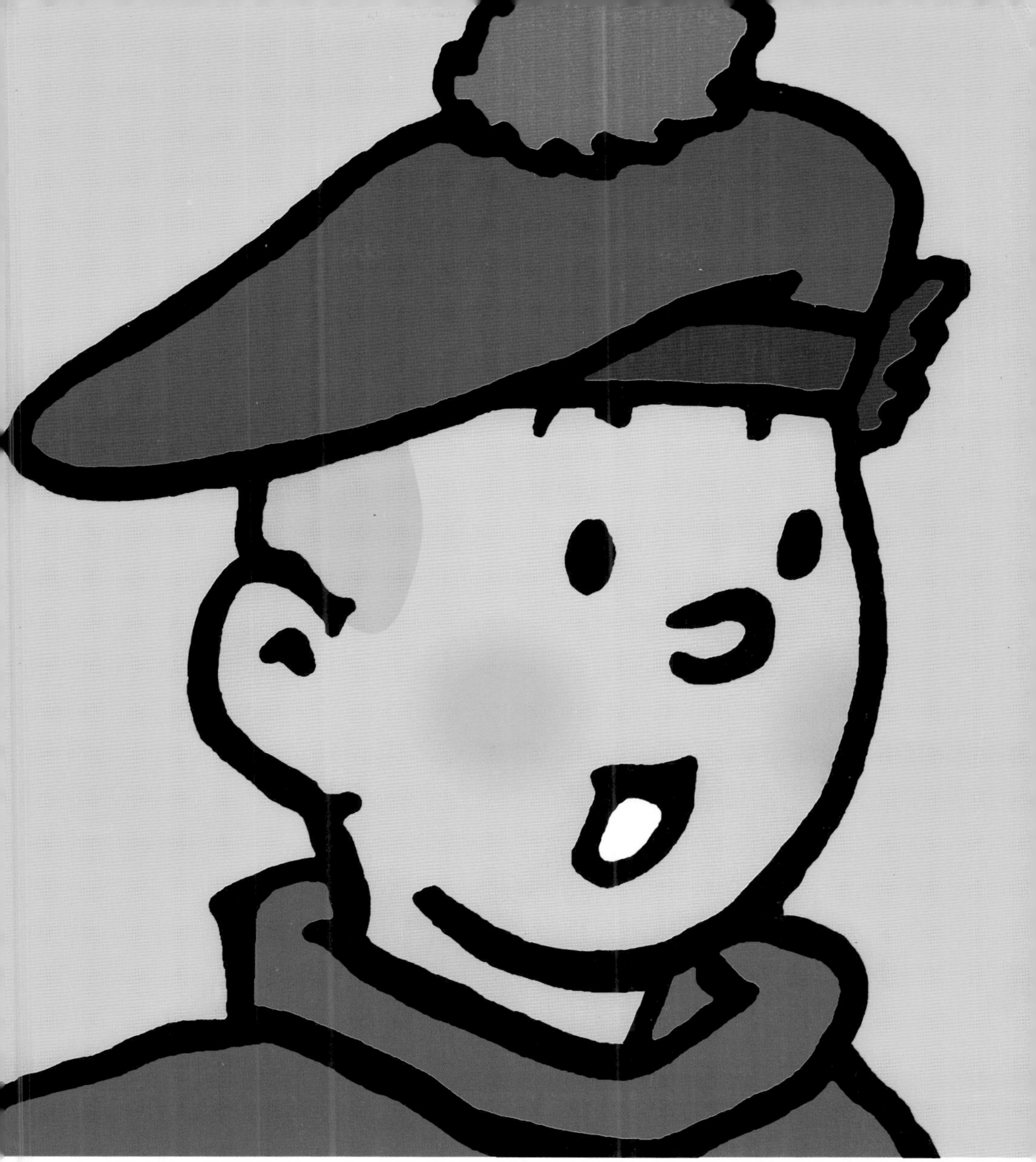

Tintin

Nothing—not even doctor's orders—can stop brave reporter Tintin when he senses a new adventure!

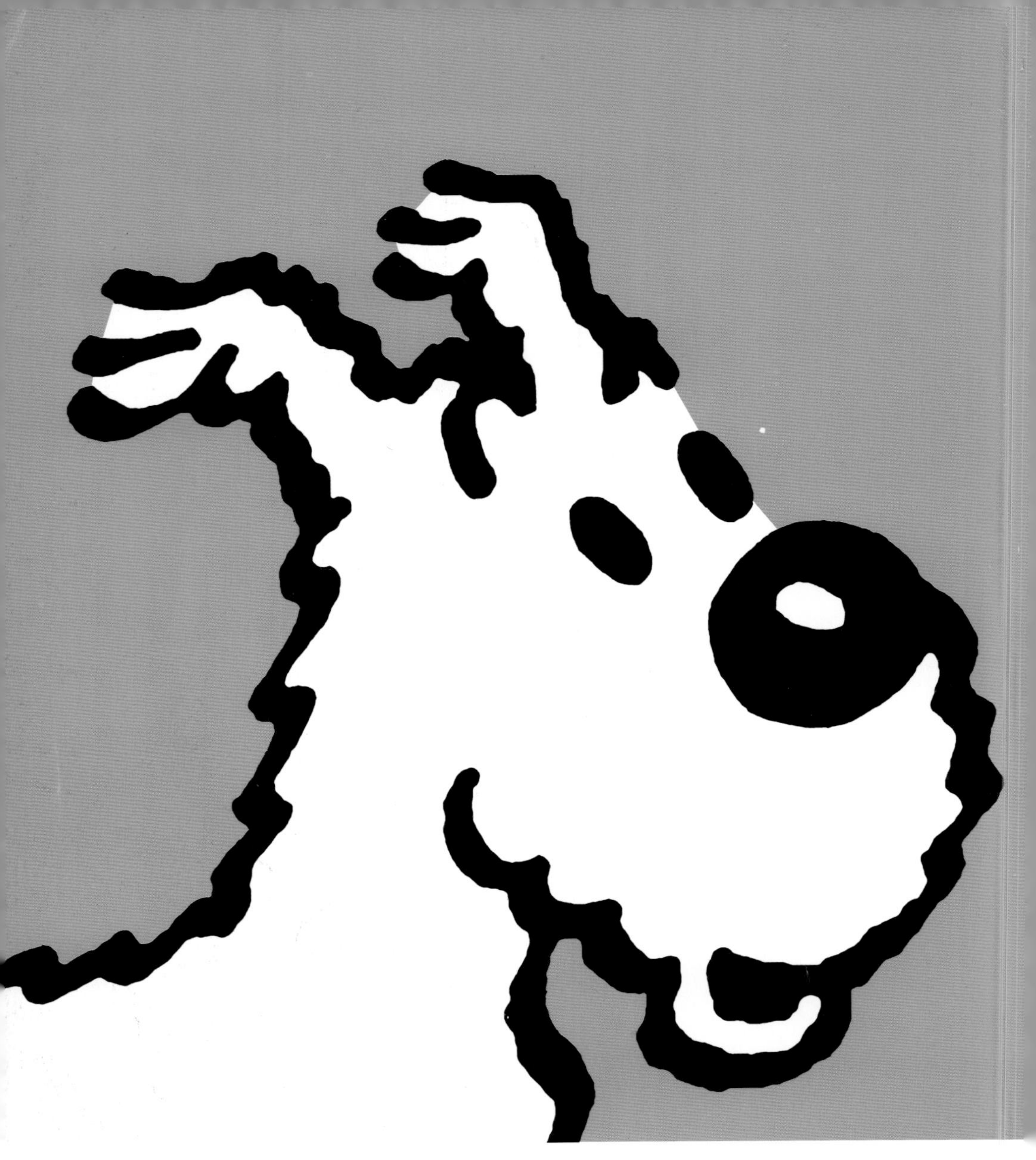

Snowy

It looks like Snowy is invincible: he even has the beast of the Black Island running scared! But Snowy's not so brave when he comes face-to-face with a tiny spider!

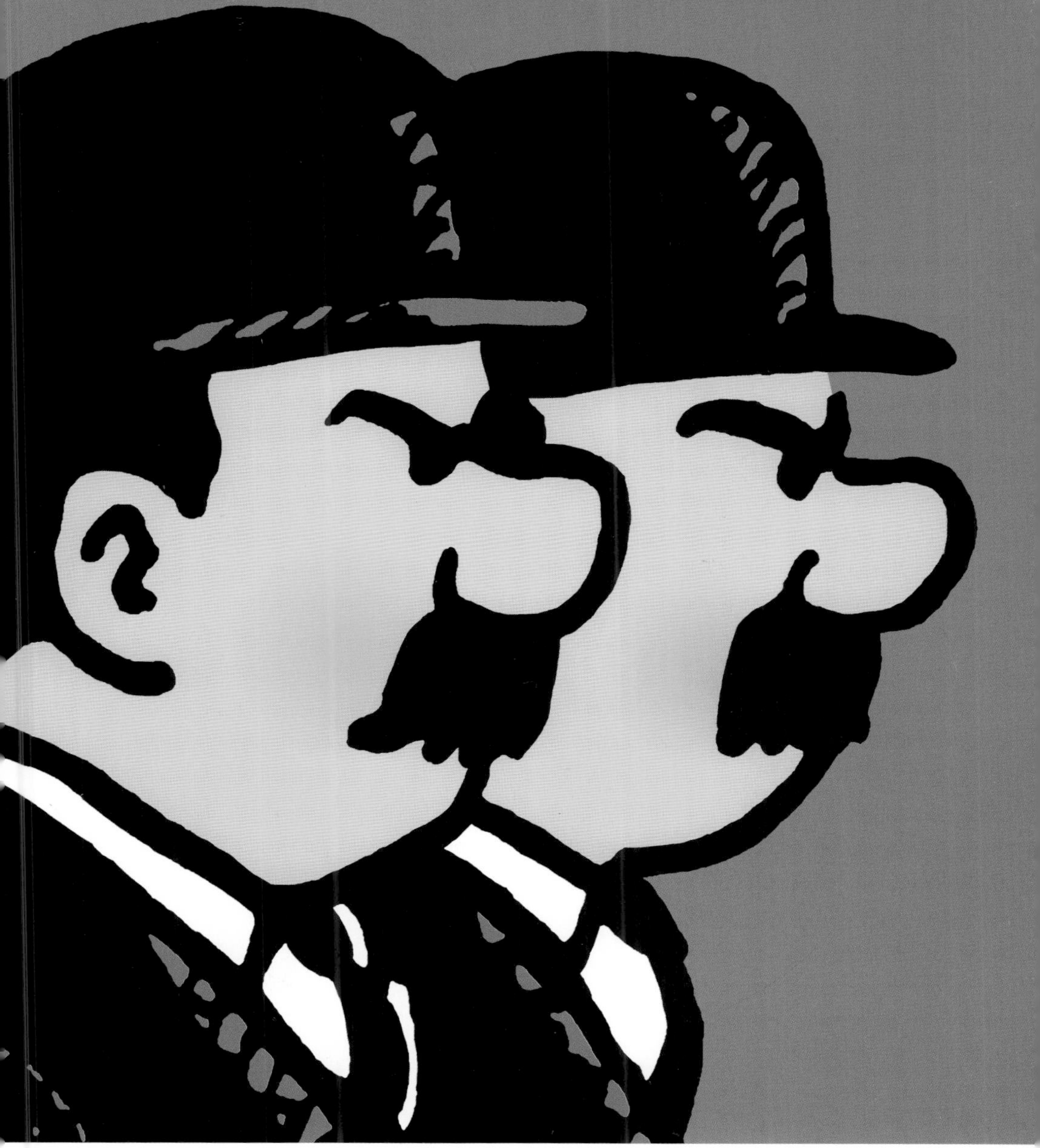

Thomson and Thompson

The two accident-prone policemen are determined to see "justice" done...
and make life difficult for Tintin in the process.

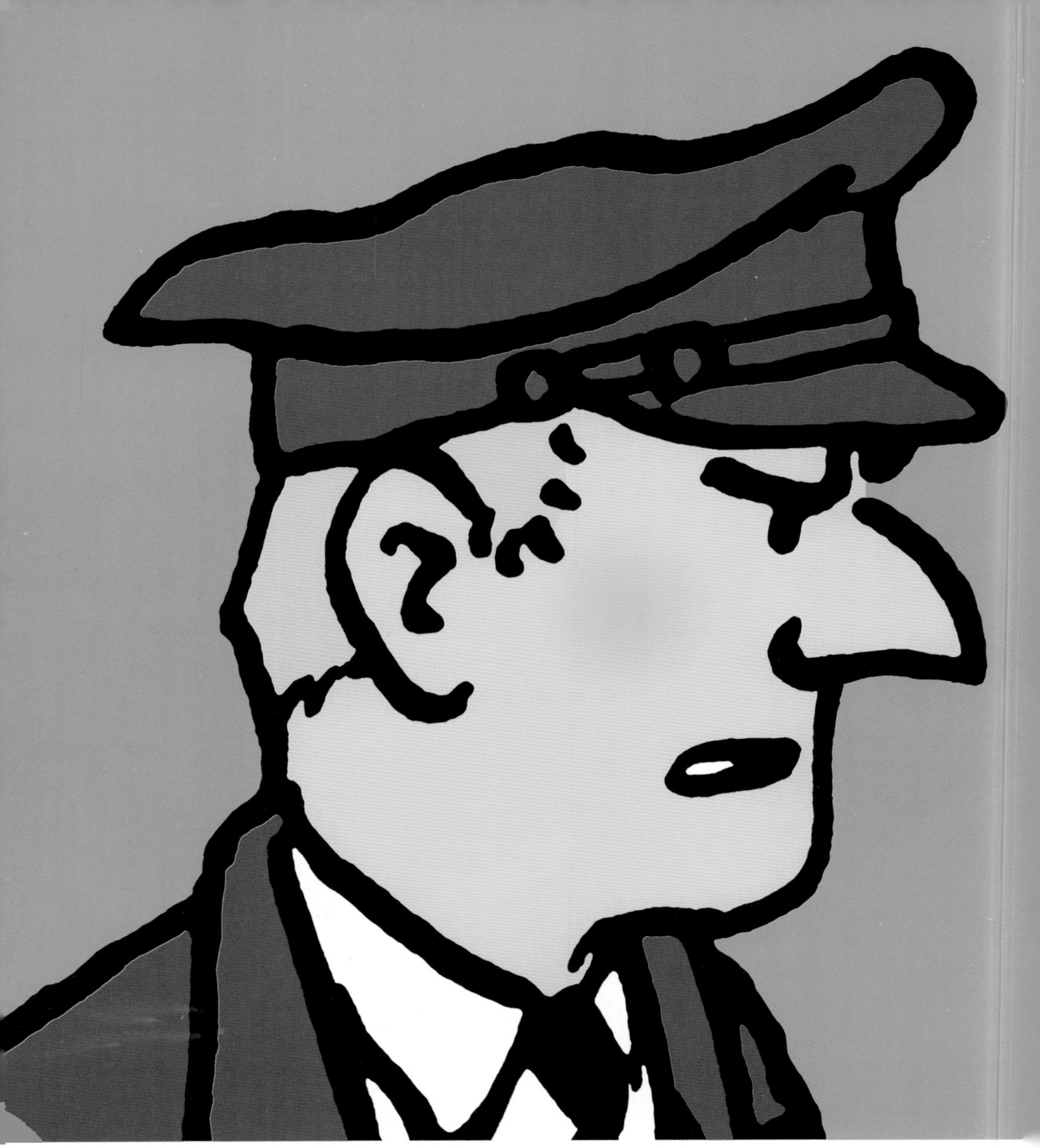

Ivan

Ivan is not just the chauffeur for the bad guys—he also does some real dirty work on his own.

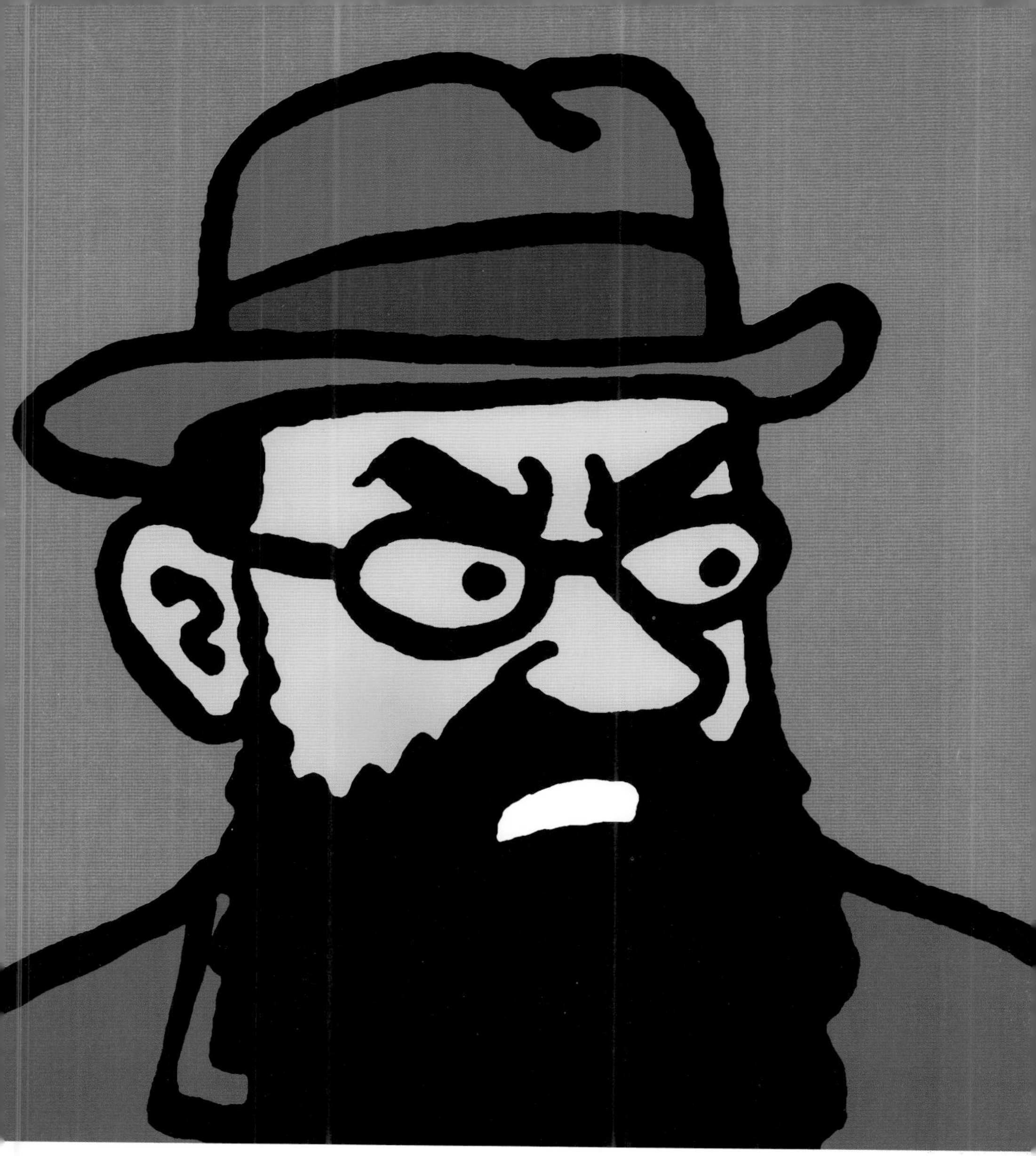

Puschov

Puschov is a member of the criminal gang that Tintin hunts down.
The villain tries to convince Tintin to practice diving…off a cliff!

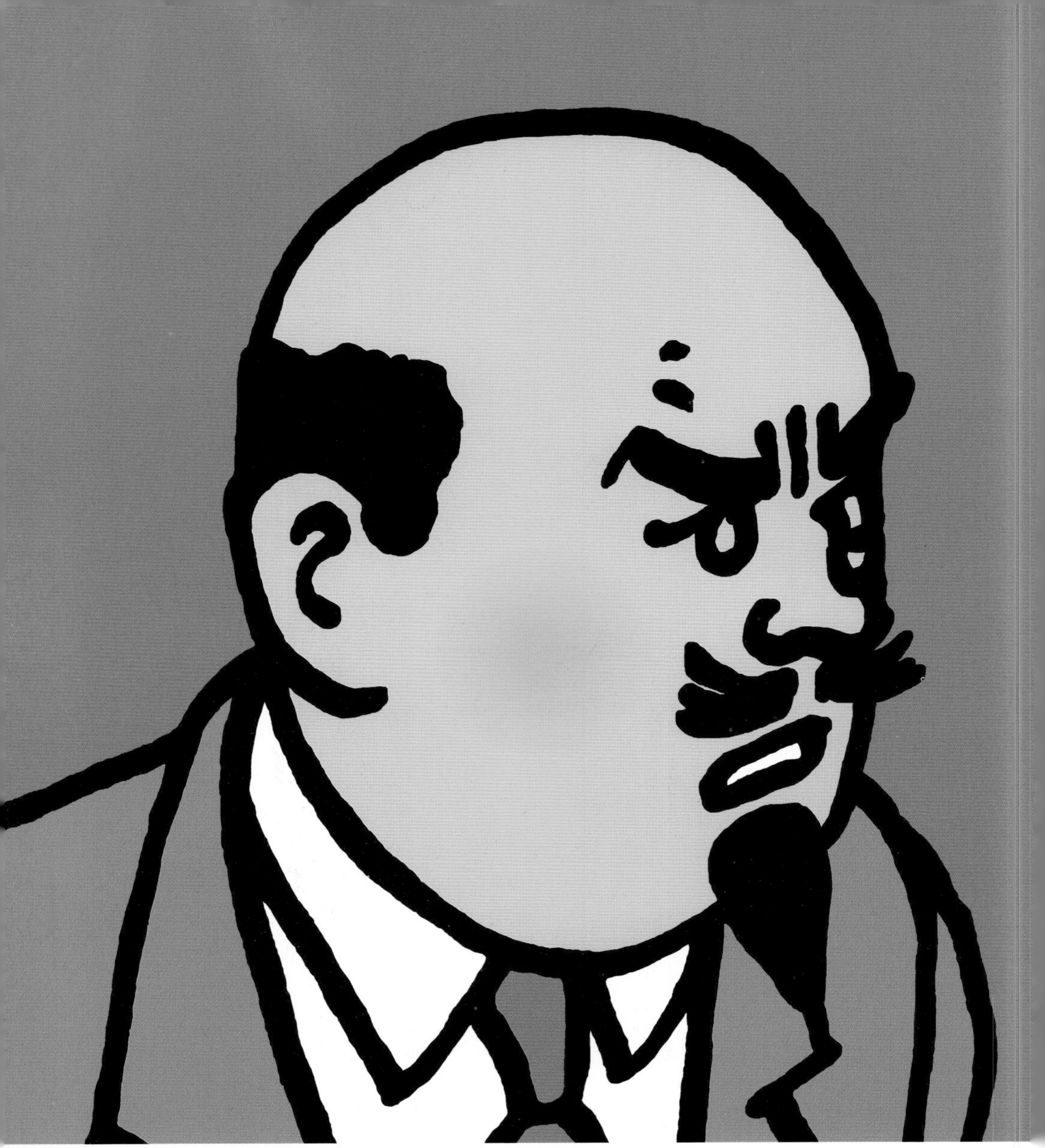

Dr. Müller

The evil mastermind behind the illegal operation that Tintin investigates, Dr. Müller won't hesitate to use his medical training for harmful ends.

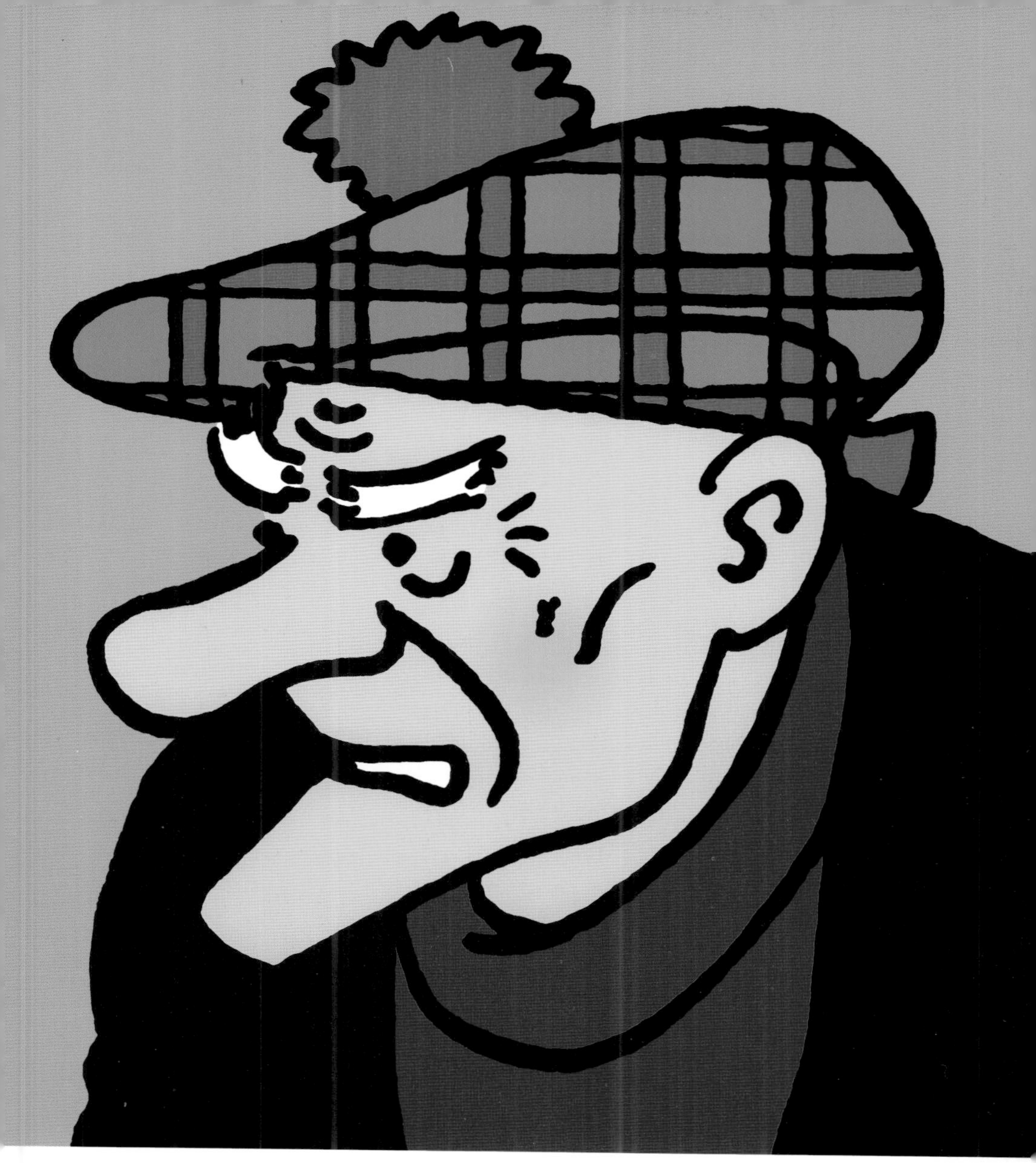

The old Scotsman

The straight-talking old Scotsman has only one piece of advice for Tintin: beware the beast of the Black Island!

THE BLACK ISLAND

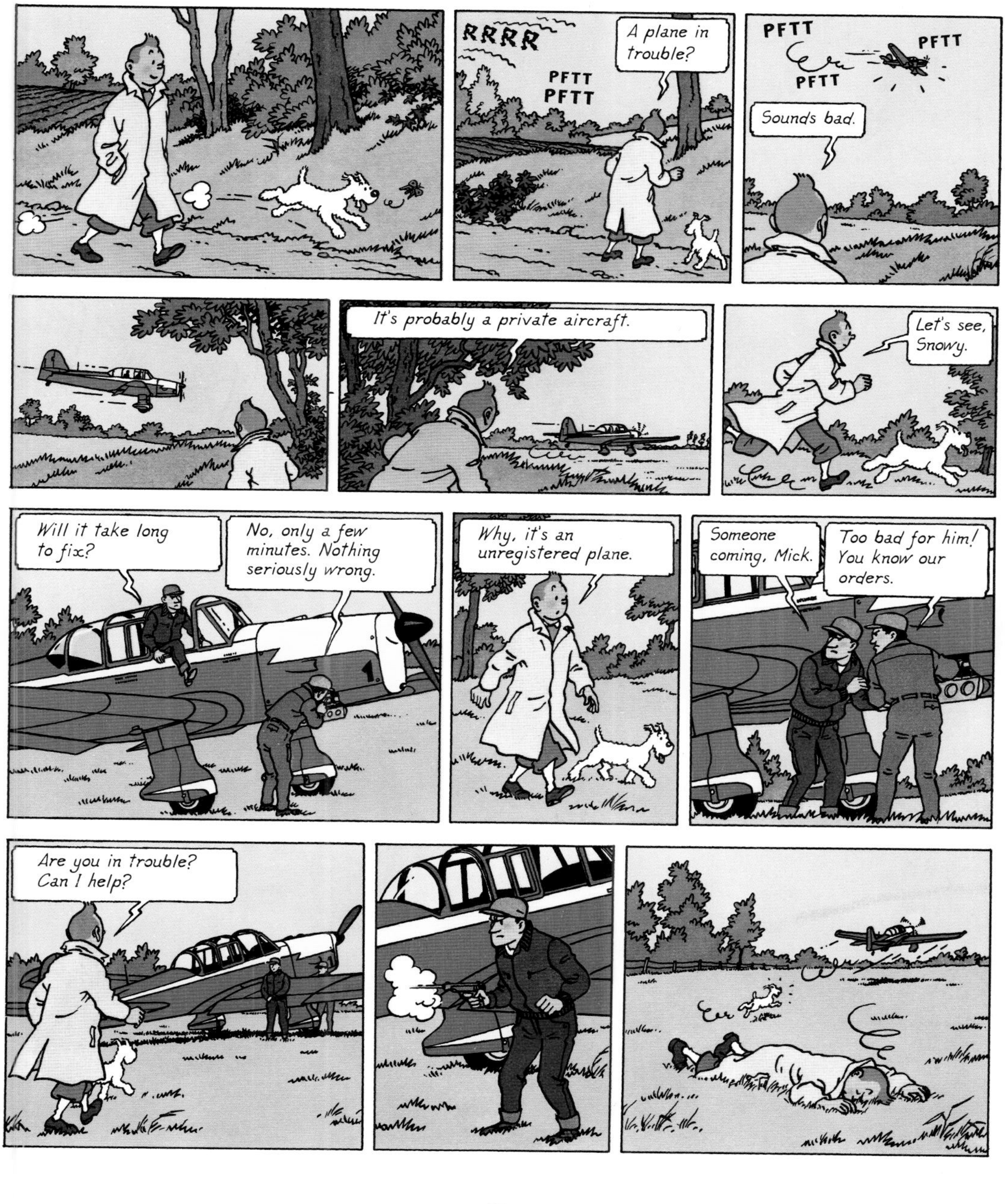

RRRR
PFTT
PFTT
A plane in trouble?
PFTT
PFTT
PFTT
Sounds bad.
It's probably a private aircraft.
Let's see, Snowy.
Will it take long to fix?
No, only a few minutes. Nothing seriously wrong.
Why, it's an unregistered plane.
Someone coming, Mick.
Too bad for him! You know our orders.
Are you in trouble? Can I help?

Next morning...

Well, doctor?

He was lucky. The bullet only grazed a rib. He'll be up and about in a couple of days.

Excuse me, nurse.

Can we see Tintin, please?

You can go in.

Look here: are you absolutely sure the plane had no registration marks?

Quite certain.

It all looks very fishy to me.

To be precise: the whole thing looks like me, very fishy.

Telephone, please, for Mr Thomson or Mr Thompson.

Hello? ... Yes ... Interpol? ... Yes sir, Thompson, with a p, as in psychology ... From Scotland Yard? ... Eastdown? Last night? ... Yes sir, I understand. We'll leave at once.

We're going back to England. An unregistered plane crashed last night near a place called Eastdown, in Sussex. Goodbye.

Goodbye, and watch your step!

Thanks!

CRASH

?

Why can't you look where you're going?

To be precise: speak for yourself.

Eastdown ... If only ... It can't be helped, I simply must go. Never mind doctor's orders!

Goodbye, nurse. Many thanks!

Ach! The silly fools! Who d'you think they shot at last night? Tintin himself!

Pity they didn't finish him off while they were about it.

Look!!

KÖLN
BRUXELLES
LONDON

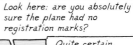

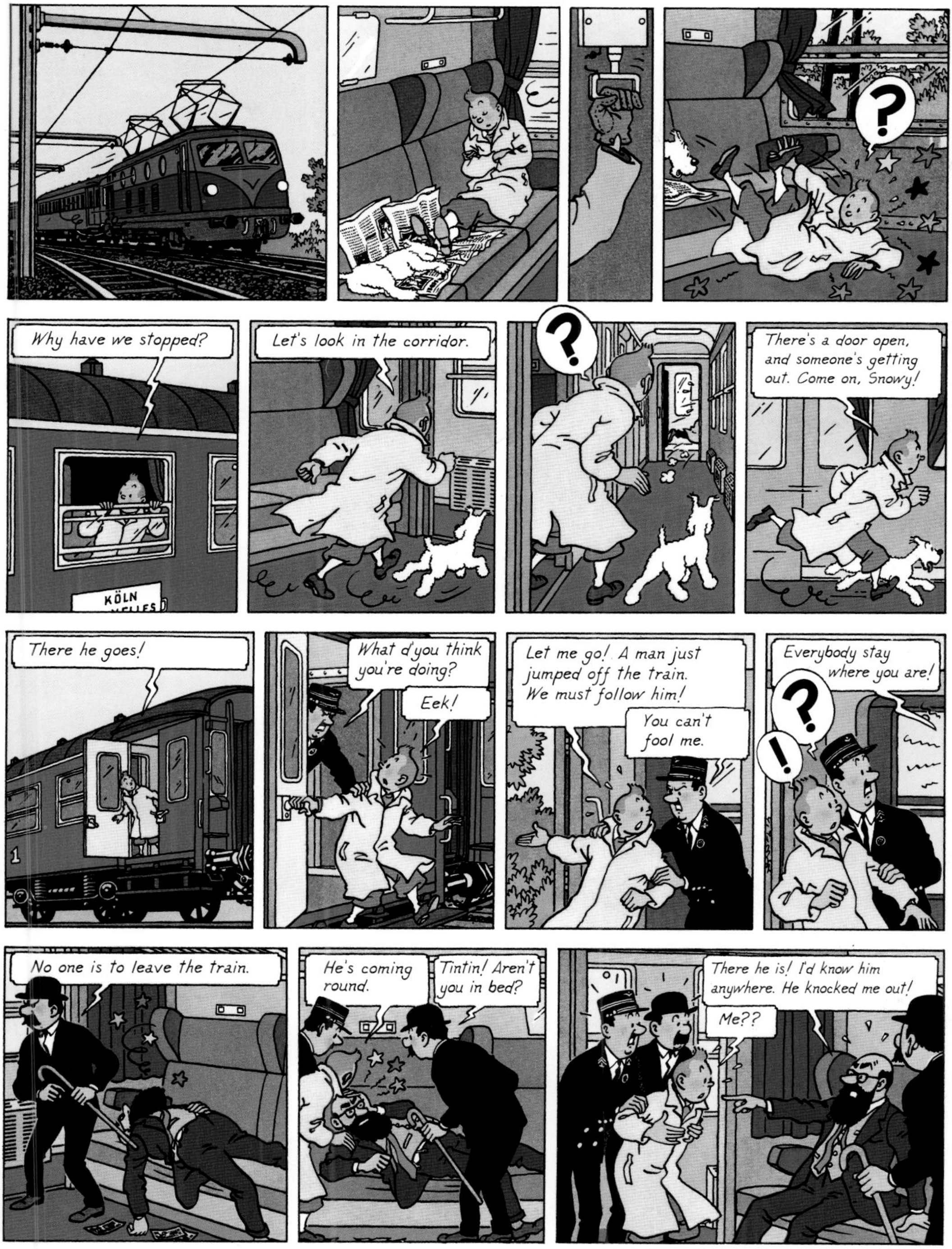

?
Why have we stopped?
KÖLN
Let's look in the corridor.
?
There's a door open, and someone's getting out. Come on, Snowy!
There he goes!
What d'you think you're doing?
Eek!
Let me go! A man just jumped off the train. We must follow him!
You can't fool me.
Everybody stay where you are!
?
!
No one is to leave the train.
He's coming round.
Tintin! Aren't you in bed?
There he is! I'd know him anywhere. He knocked me out!
Me??

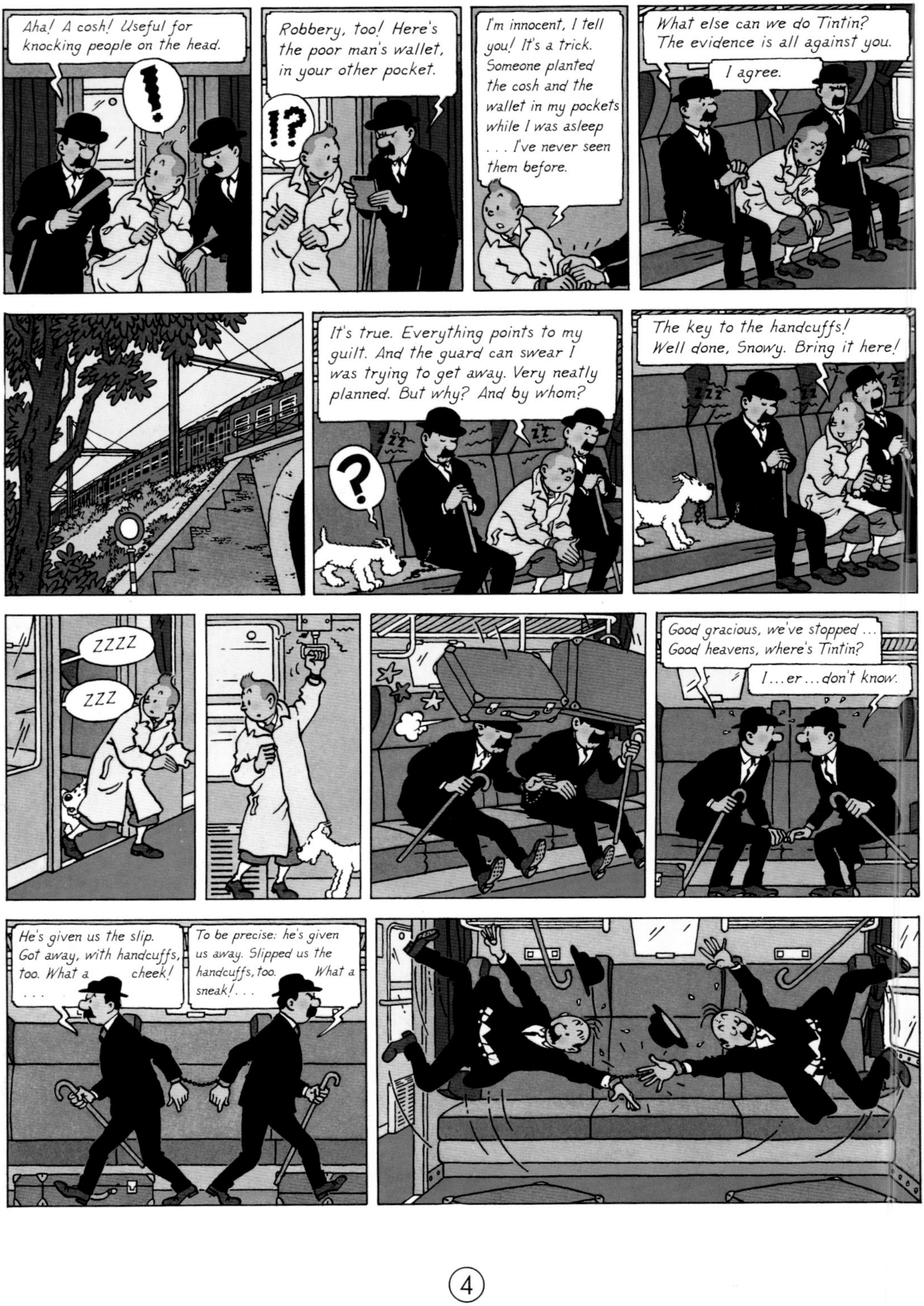
Aha! A cosh! Useful for knocking people on the head.
!
Robbery, too! Here's the poor man's wallet, in your other pocket.
!?
I'm innocent, I tell you! It's a trick. Someone planted the cosh and the wallet in my pockets while I was asleep . . . I've never seen them before.
What else can we do Tintin? The evidence is all against you.
I agree.
It's true. Everything points to my guilt. And the guard can swear I was trying to get away. Very neatly planned. But why? And by whom?
?
The key to the handcuffs! Well done, Snowy. Bring it here!
ZZZZ
ZZZ
Good gracious, we've stopped ... Good heavens, where's Tintin?
I ... er ... don't know.
He's given us the slip. Got away, with handcuffs, too. What a cheek! . . .
To be precise: he's given us away. Slipped us the handcuffs, too. What a sneak! . . .

An hour later . . .

Good! A village. Perhaps I can hire a car to take me to the coast.

CLINK

CLINK

CLINK

Just wait till I get my hands on him!

To be precise: . . . er . . . just wait till we get our hands!

Hello!

Tintin!

!

You!

Hey, stop!

That's what they call putting your head in the lion's mouth!

Stop him! Stop him!

Where's he gone?

Excuse me, sir. Have you seen a young man running past your house?

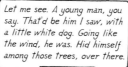

Let me see. A young man, you say. That'd be him I saw, with a little white dog. Going like the wind, he was. Hid himself among those trees, over there.

Aha! We've got him!

Snowy!

WOOAH WOOAH

!

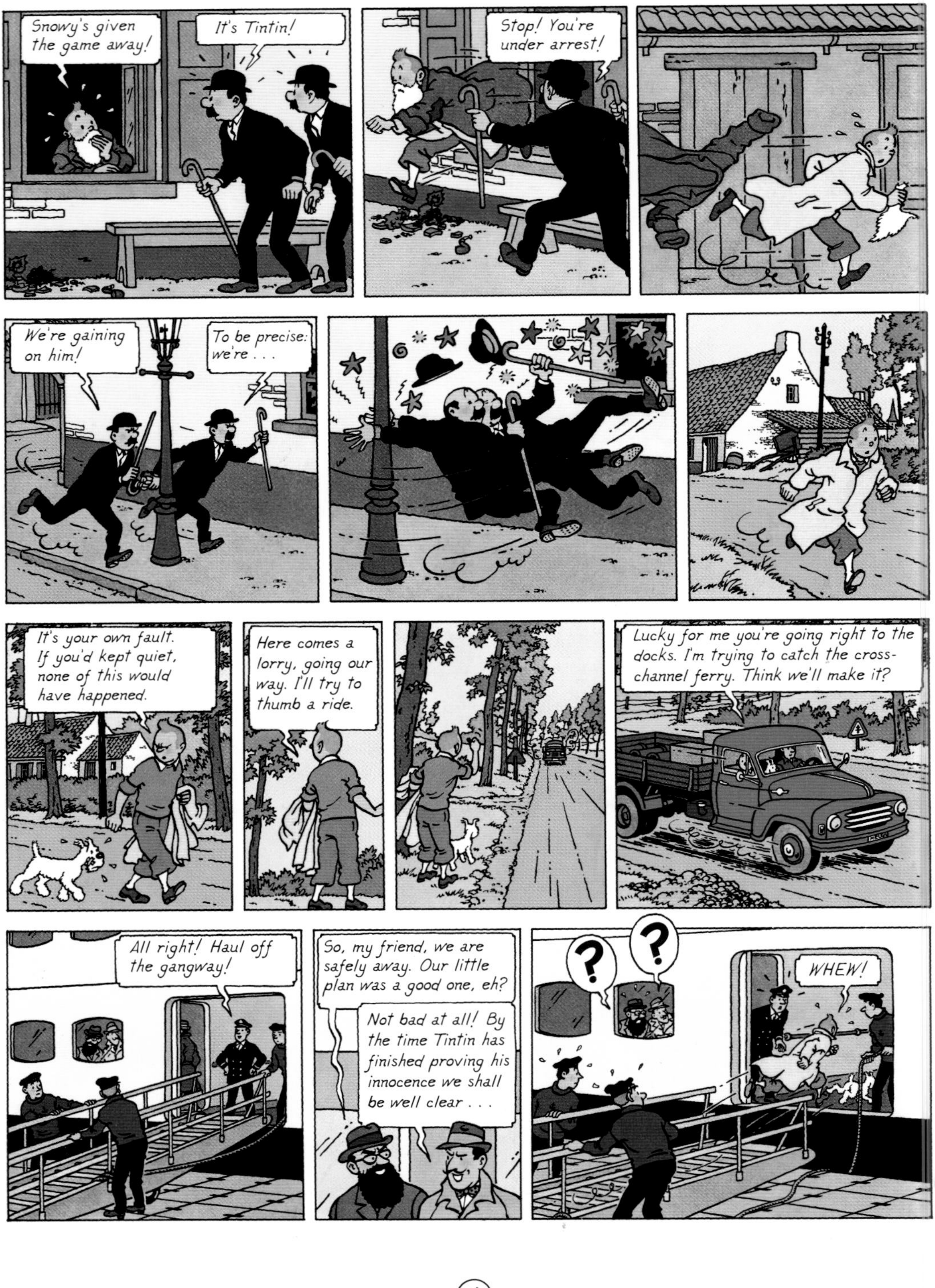
Snowy's given the game away!
It's Tintin!
Stop! You're under arrest!
We're gaining on him!
To be precise: we're . . .
It's your own fault. If you'd kept quiet, none of this would have happened.
Here comes a lorry, going our way. I'll try to thumb a ride.
Lucky for me you're going right to the docks. I'm trying to catch the cross-channel ferry. Think we'll make it?
All right! Haul off the gangway!
So, my friend, we are safely away. Our little plan was a good one, eh?
Not bad at all! By the time Tintin has finished proving his innocence we shall be well clear . . .
?
?
WHEW!

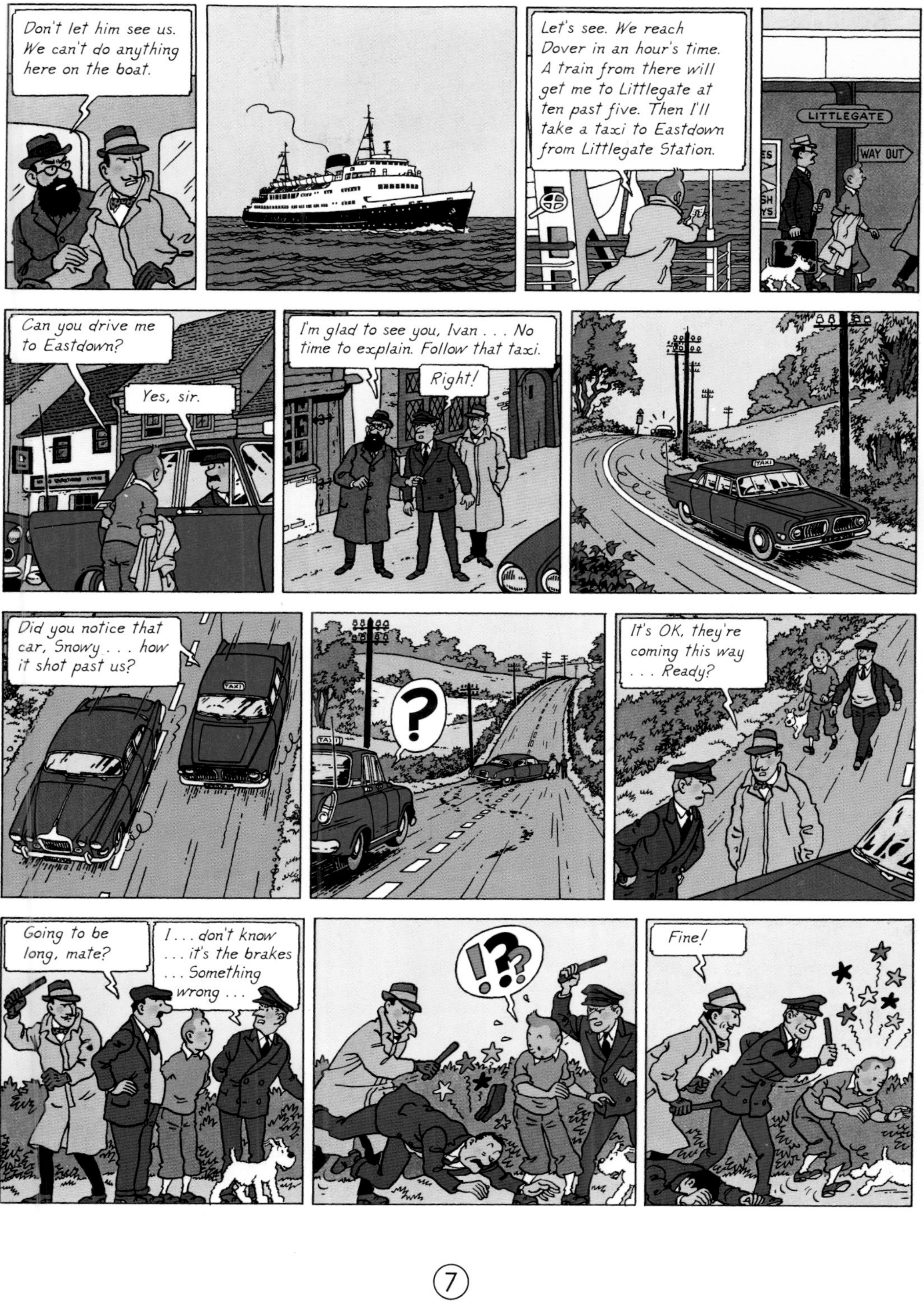
Don't let him see us. We can't do anything here on the boat.
Let's see. We reach Dover in an hour's time. A train from there will get me to Littlegate at ten past five. Then I'll take a taxi to Eastdown from Littlegate Station.
LITTLEGATE
WAY OUT
Can you drive me to Eastdown?
Yes, sir.
I'm glad to see you, Ivan . . . No time to explain. Follow that taxi.
Right!
TAXI
Did you notice that car, Snowy . . . how it shot past us?
TAXI
?
TAXI
It's OK, they're coming this way . . . Ready?
Going to be long, mate?
I . . . don't know . . . it's the brakes . . . Something wrong . . .
!?
Fine!

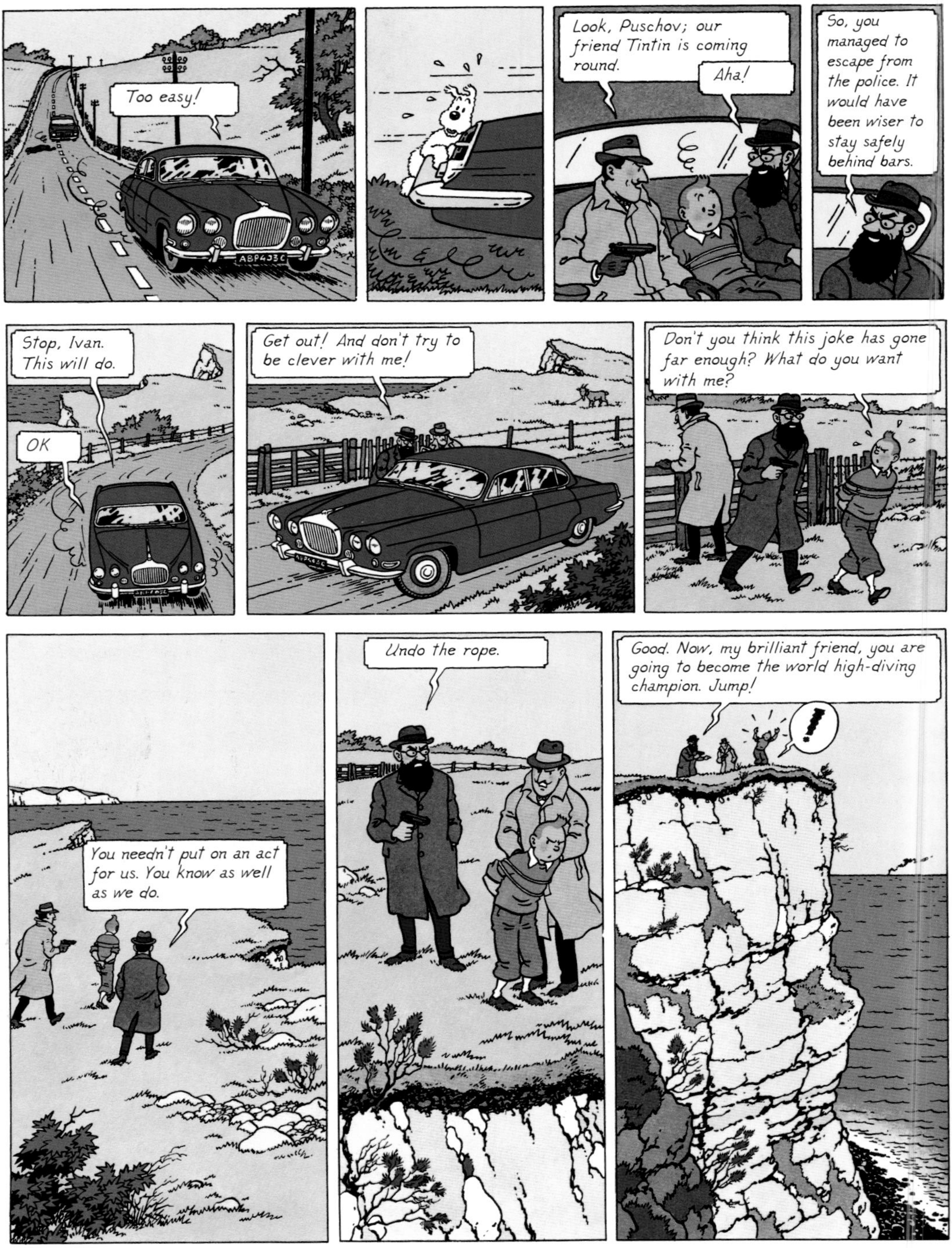
Too easy!
ABP 413 C
Look, Puschov; our friend Tintin is coming round.
Aha!
So, you managed to escape from the police. It would have been wiser to stay safely behind bars.
Stop, Ivan. This will do.
OK
Get out! And don't try to be clever with me!
Don't you think this joke has gone far enough? What do you want with me?
You needn't put on an act for us. You know as well as we do.
Undo the rope.
Good. Now, my brilliant friend, you are going to become the world high-diving champion. Jump!
!!!

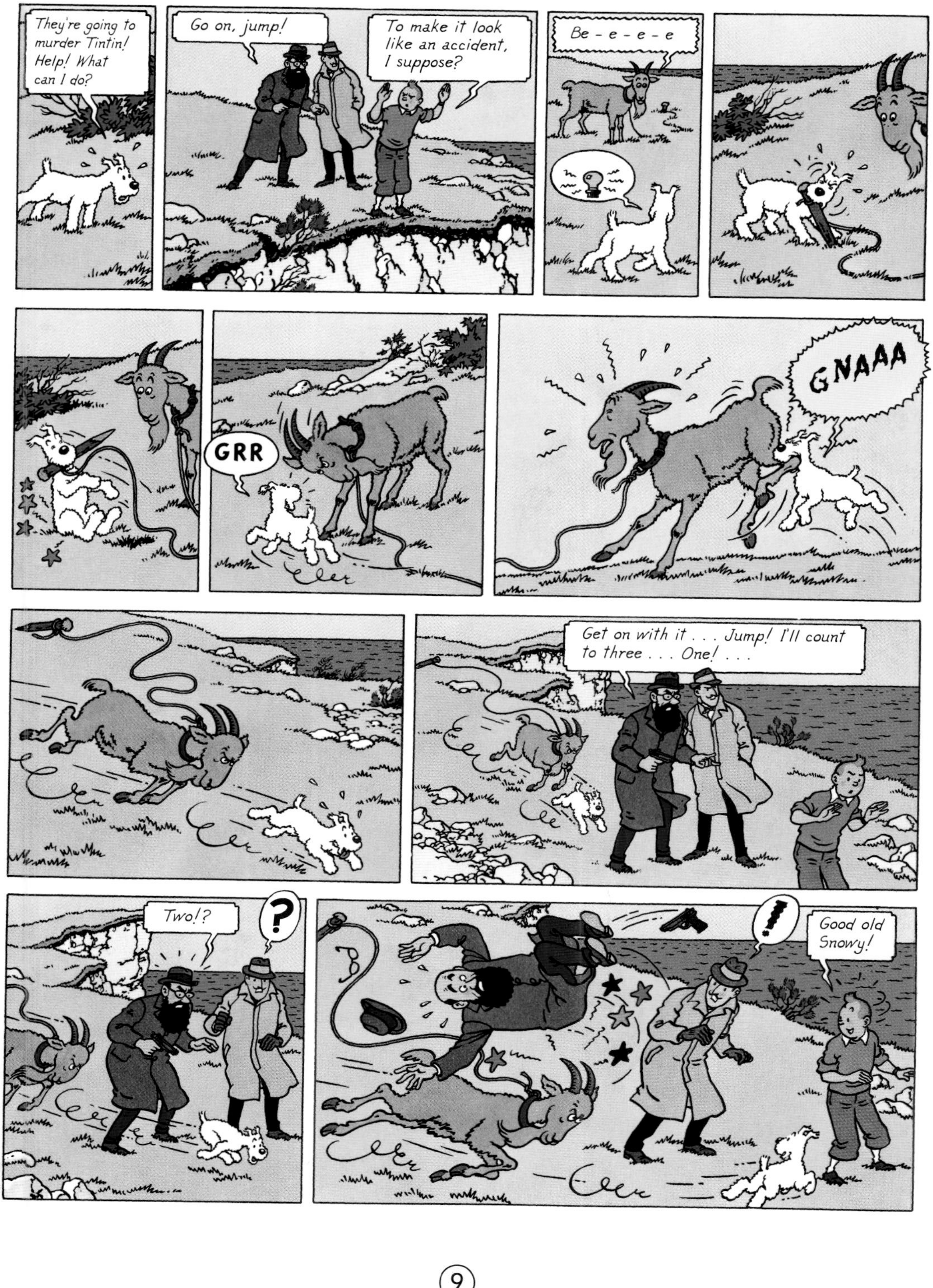

They're going to murder Tintin! Help! What can I do?
Go on, jump!
To make it look like an accident, I suppose?
Be - e - e - e
GRR
GNAAA
Get on with it . . . Jump! I'll count to three . . . One! . . .
Two!?
?
!
Good old Snowy!

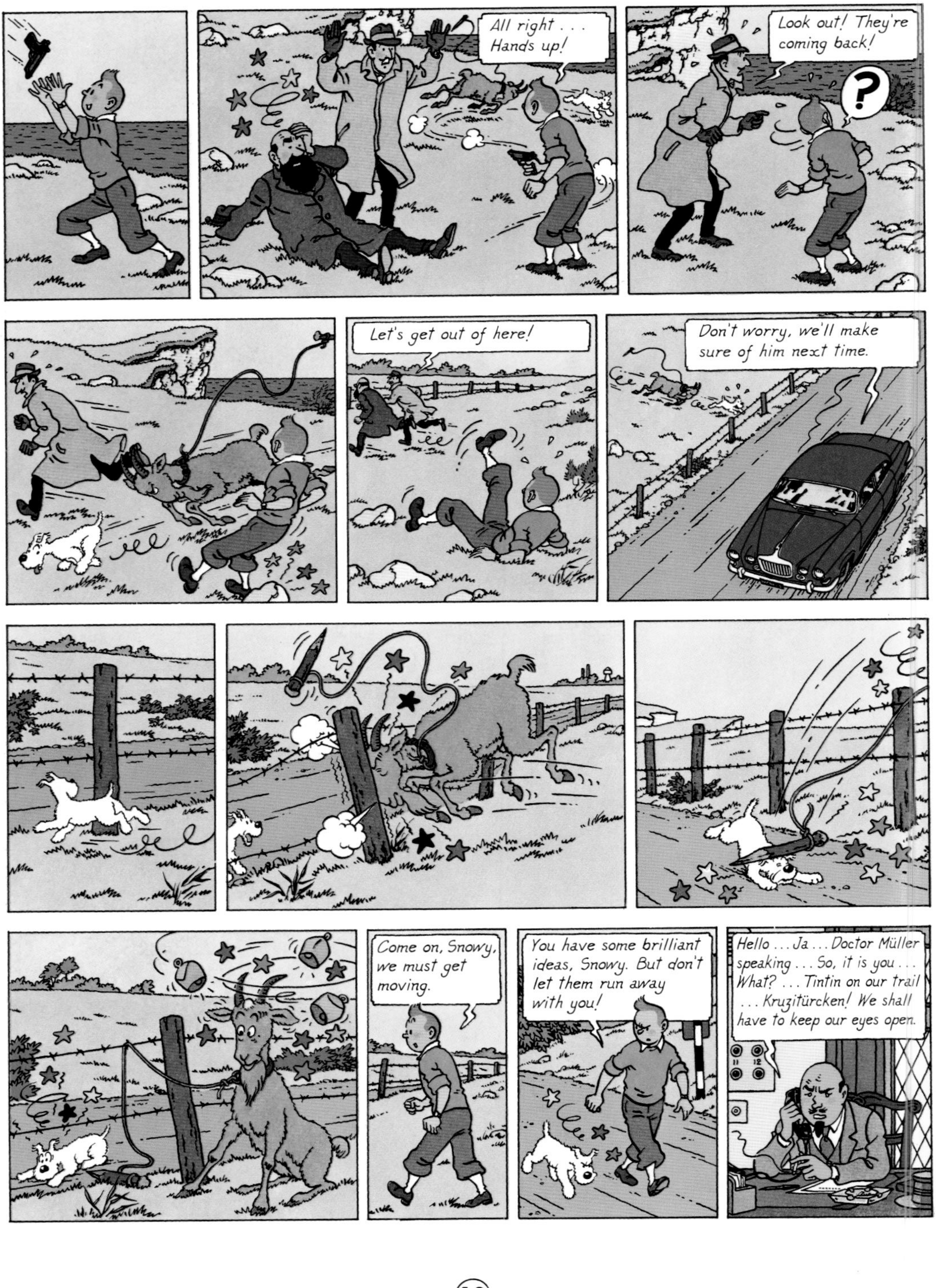
All right . . . Hands up!
Look out! They're coming back!
?
Let's get out of here!
Don't worry, we'll make sure of him next time.
Come on, Snowy, we must get moving.
You have some brilliant ideas, Snowy. But don't let them run away with you!
Hello . . . Ja . . . Doctor Müller speaking . . . So, it is you . . . What? . . . Tintin on our trail . . . Kruzitürcken! We shall have to keep our eyes open.

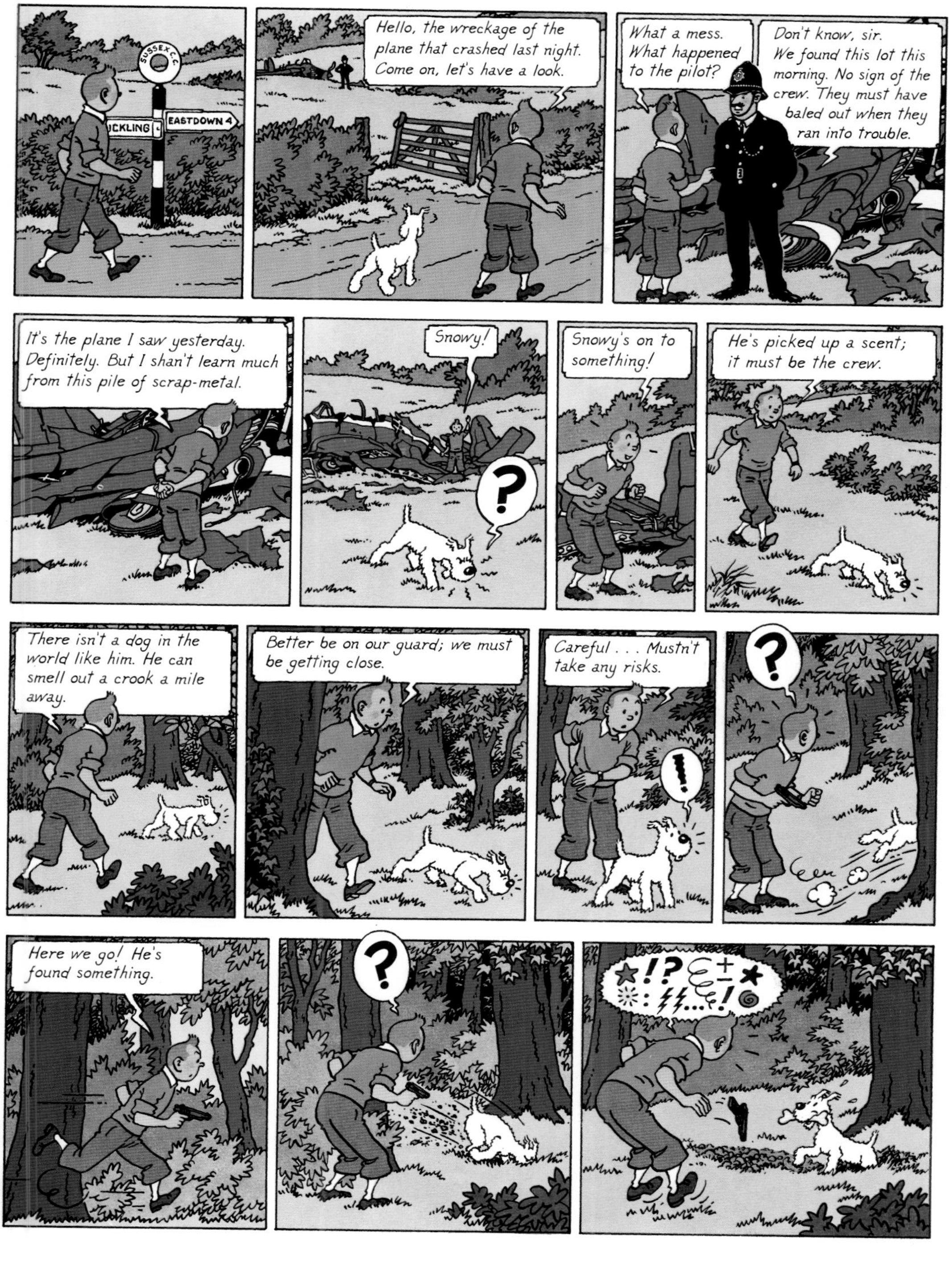
SUSSEX C.C.
...CKLING
EASTDOWN 4
Hello, the wreckage of the plane that crashed last night. Come on, let's have a look.
What a mess. What happened to the pilot?
Don't know, sir. We found this lot this morning. No sign of the crew. They must have baled out when they ran into trouble.
It's the plane I saw yesterday. Definitely. But I shan't learn much from this pile of scrap-metal.
Snowy!
?
Snowy's on to something!
He's picked up a scent; it must be the crew.
There isn't a dog in the world like him. He can smell out a crook a mile away.
Better be on our guard; we must be getting close.
Careful . . . Mustn't take any risks.
!
?
Here we go! He's found something.
?

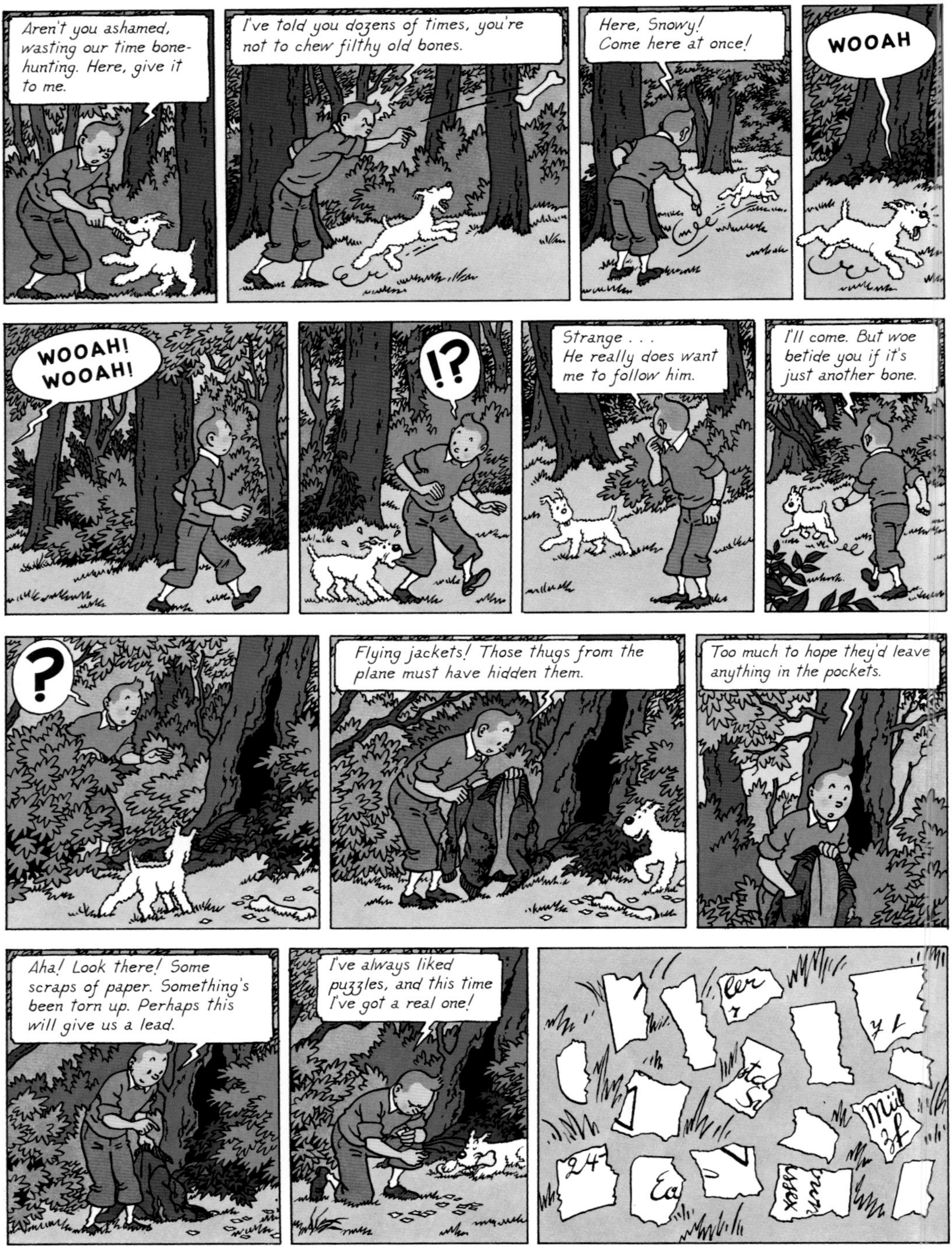

Aren't you ashamed, wasting our time bone-hunting. Here, give it to me.
I've told you dozens of times, you're not to chew filthy old bones.
Here, Snowy! Come here at once!
WOOAH
WOOAH! WOOAH!
!?
Strange . . . He really does want me to follow him.
I'll come. But woe betide you if it's just another bone.
?
Flying jackets! Those thugs from the plane must have hidden them.
Too much to hope they'd leave anything in the pockets.
Aha! Look there! Some scraps of paper. Something's been torn up. Perhaps this will give us a lead.
I've always liked puzzles, and this time I've got a real one!

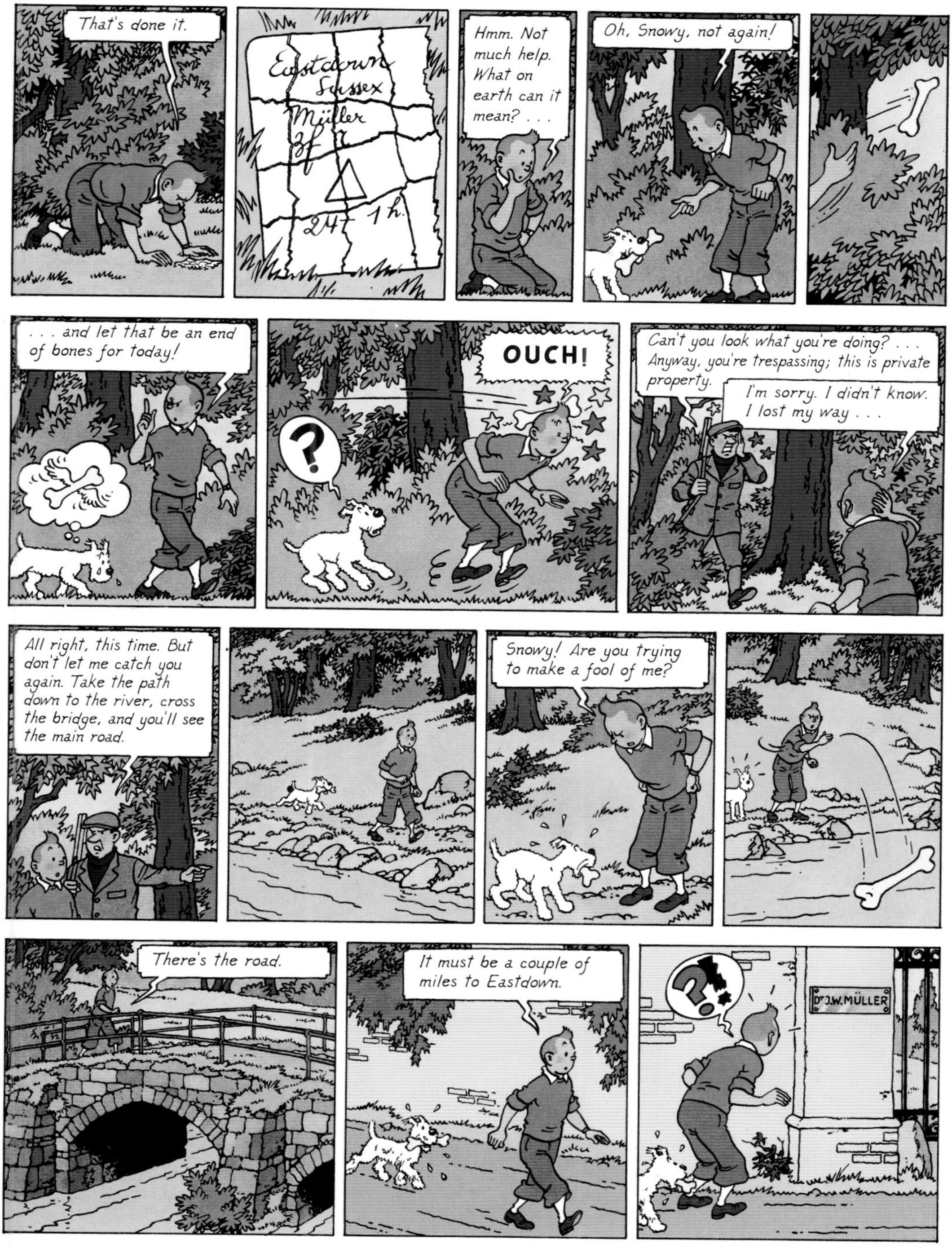
That's done it.
Eastdown
Sussex
Müller
1 h.
Hmm. Not much help. What on earth can it mean? . . .
Oh, Snowy, not again!
. . . and let that be an end of bones for today!
OUCH!
?
Can't you look what you're doing? . . . Anyway, you're trespassing; this is private property.
I'm sorry. I didn't know. I lost my way . . .
All right, this time. But don't let me catch you again. Take the path down to the river, cross the bridge, and you'll see the main road.
Snowy! Are you trying to make a fool of me?
There's the road.
It must be a couple of miles to Eastdown.
Dr J.W. MÜLLER
?

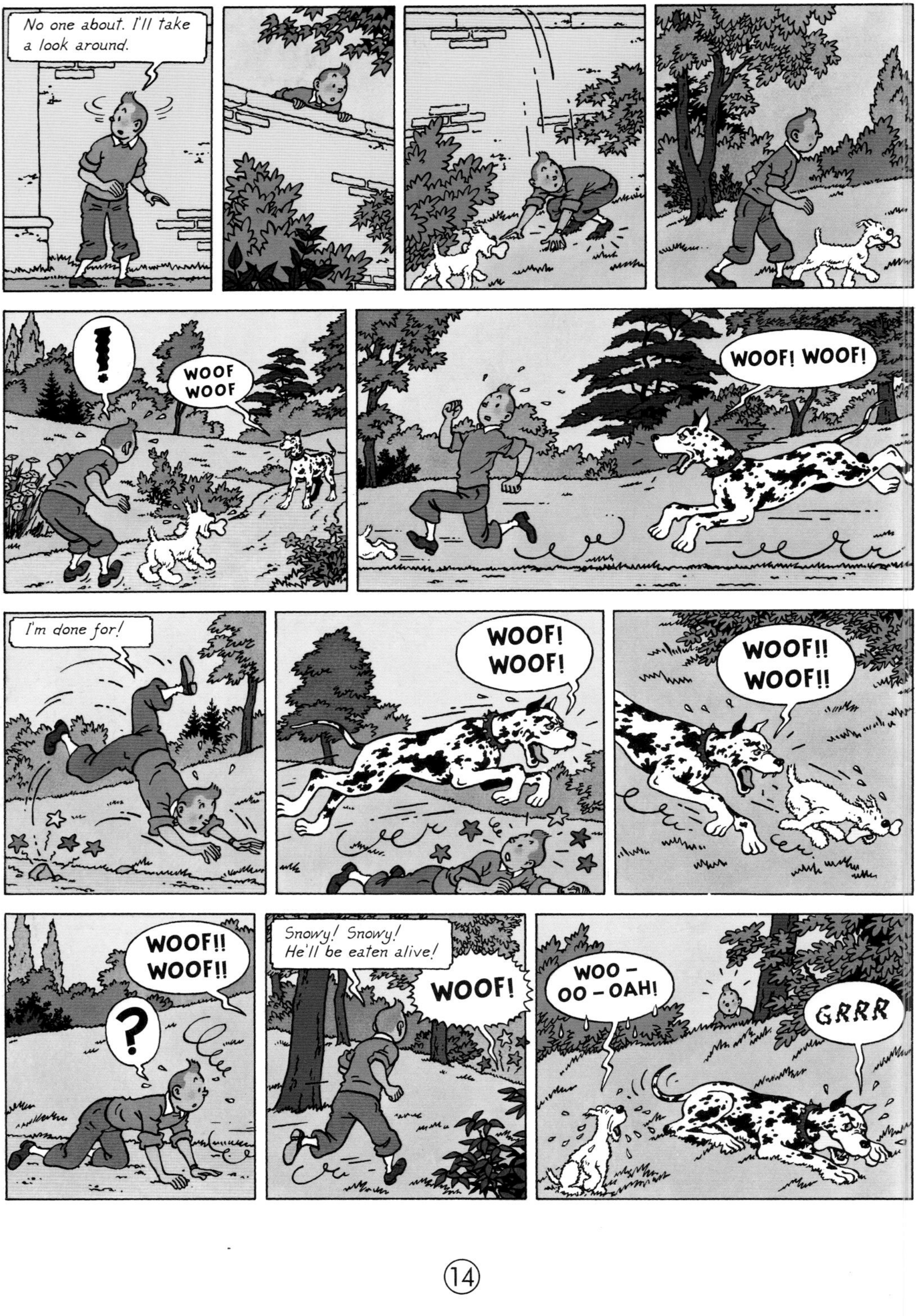
No one about. I'll take a look around.
!
WOOF WOOF
WOOF! WOOF!
I'm done for!
WOOF! WOOF!
WOOF!! WOOF!!
WOOF!! WOOF!!
?
Snowy! Snowy! He'll be eaten alive!
WOOF!
WOO – OO – OAH!
GRRR

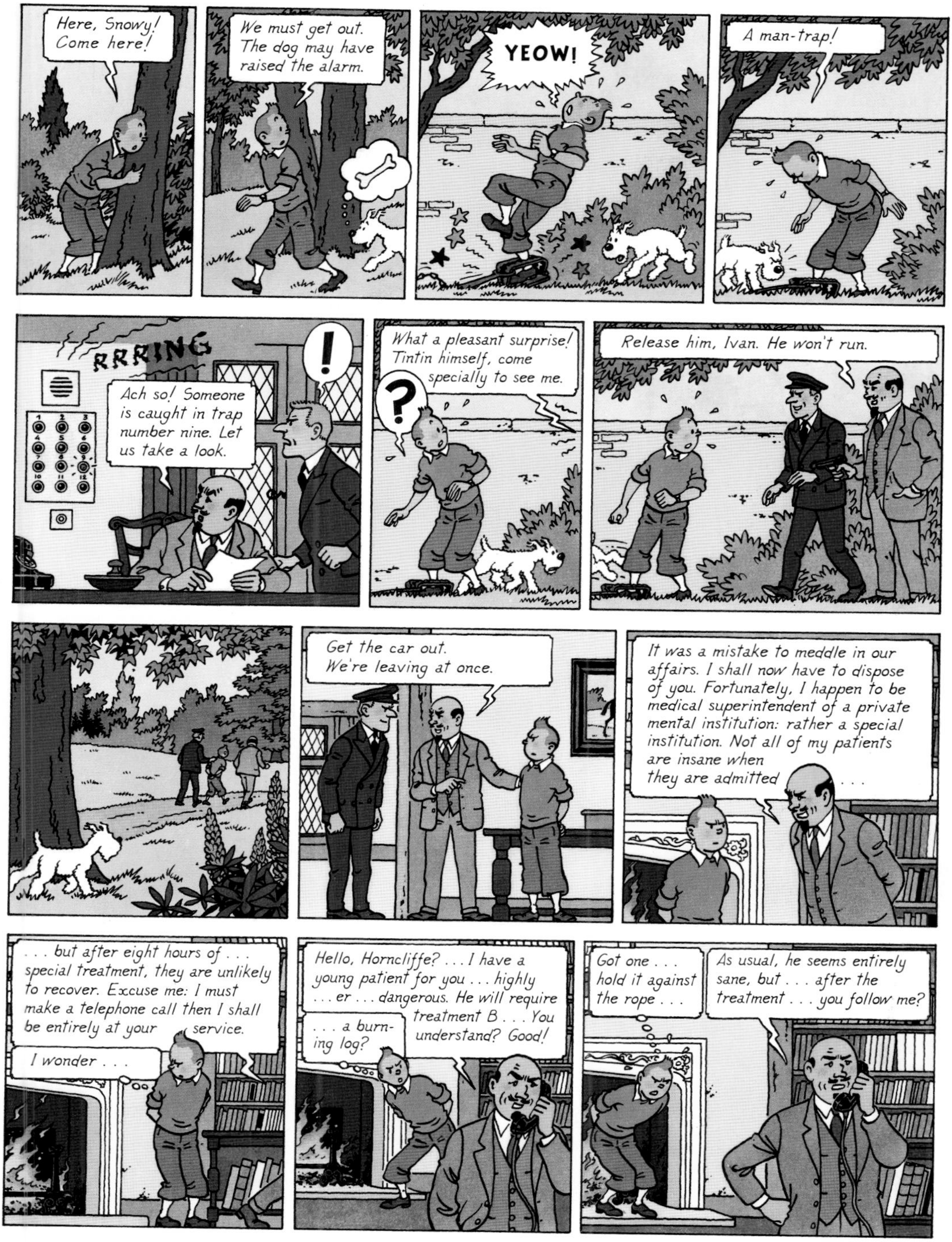

Here, Snowy! Come here!
We must get out. The dog may have raised the alarm.
YEOW!
A man-trap!
RRRING
Ach so! Someone is caught in trap number nine. Let us take a look.
!
What a pleasant surprise! Tintin himself, come specially to see me.
?
Release him, Ivan. He won't run.
Get the car out. We're leaving at once.
It was a mistake to meddle in our affairs. I shall now have to dispose of you. Fortunately, I happen to be medical superintendent of a private mental institution: rather a special institution. Not all of my patients are insane when they are admitted . . .
. . . but after eight hours of . . . special treatment, they are unlikely to recover. Excuse me: I must make a telephone call then I shall be entirely at your service.
I wonder . . .
Hello, Horncliffe? . . . I have a young patient for you . . . highly . . . er . . . dangerous. He will require treatment B . . . You understand? Good!
. . . a burning log?
Got one . . . hold it against the rope . . .
As usual, he seems entirely sane, but . . . after the treatment . . . you follow me?

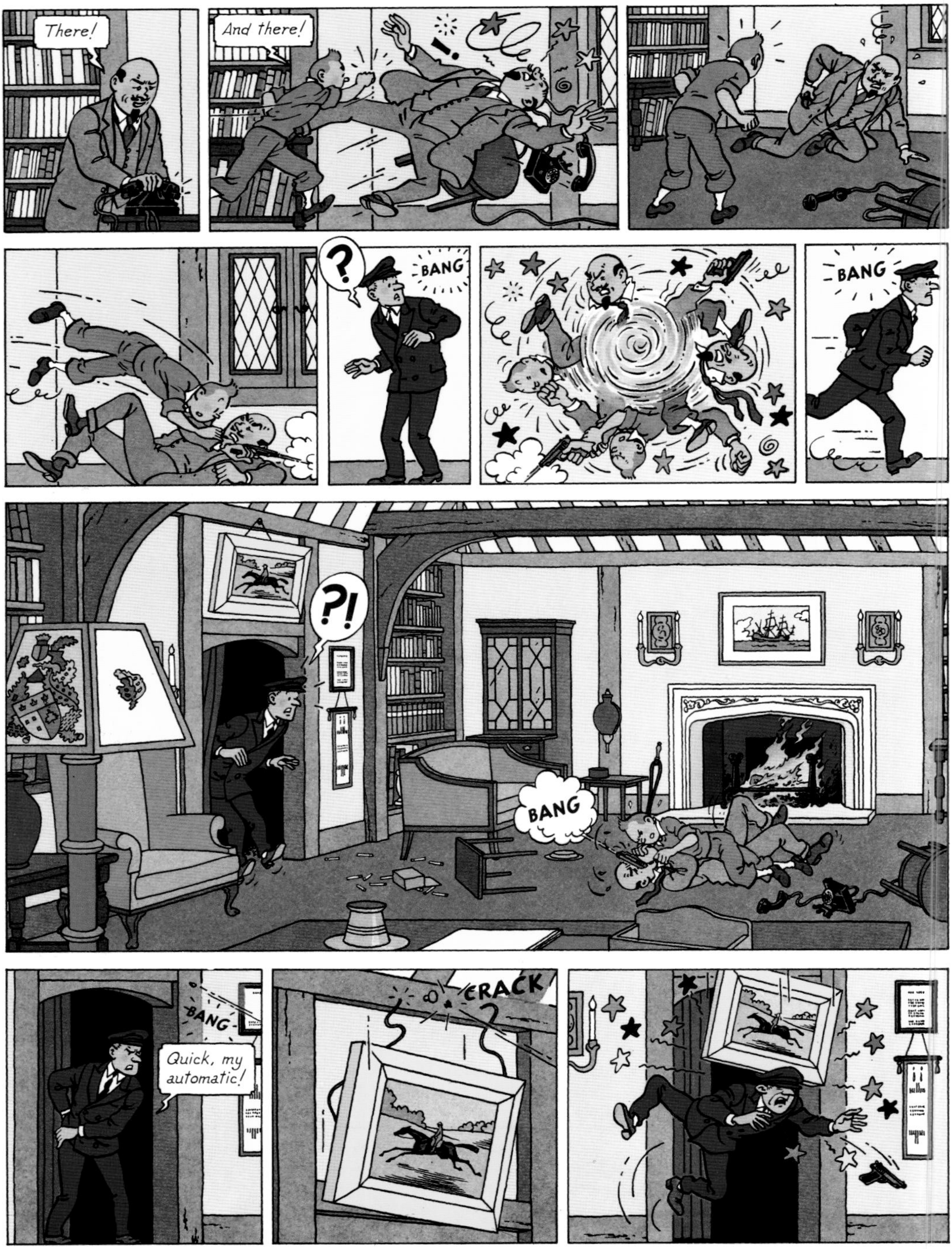

There!
And there!
?
BANG
BANG
?!
BANG
BANG
Quick, my automatic!
CRACK

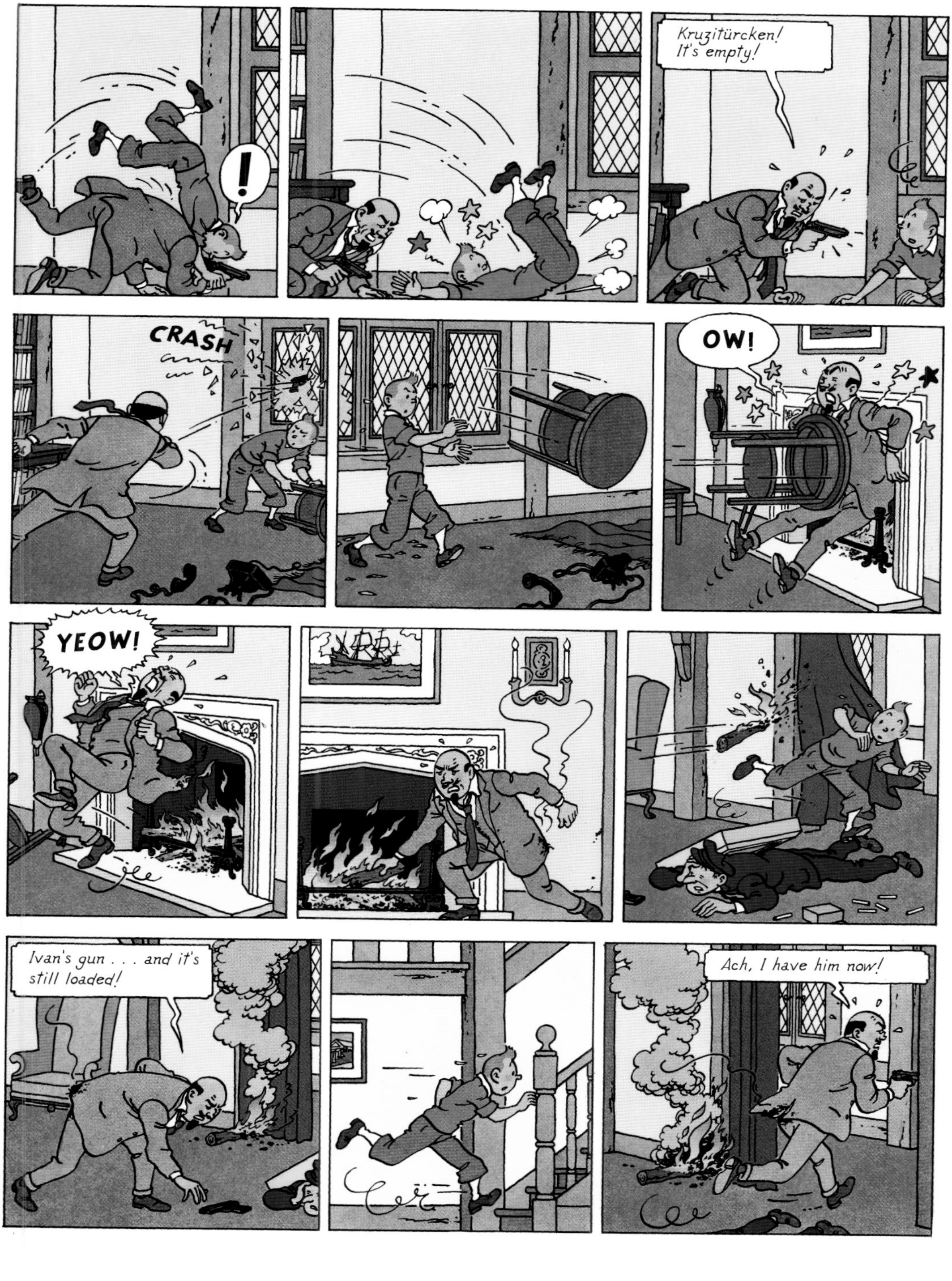
!
Kruzitürcken!
It's empty!
CRASH
OW!
YEOW!
Ivan's gun . . . and it's still loaded!
Ach, I have him now!

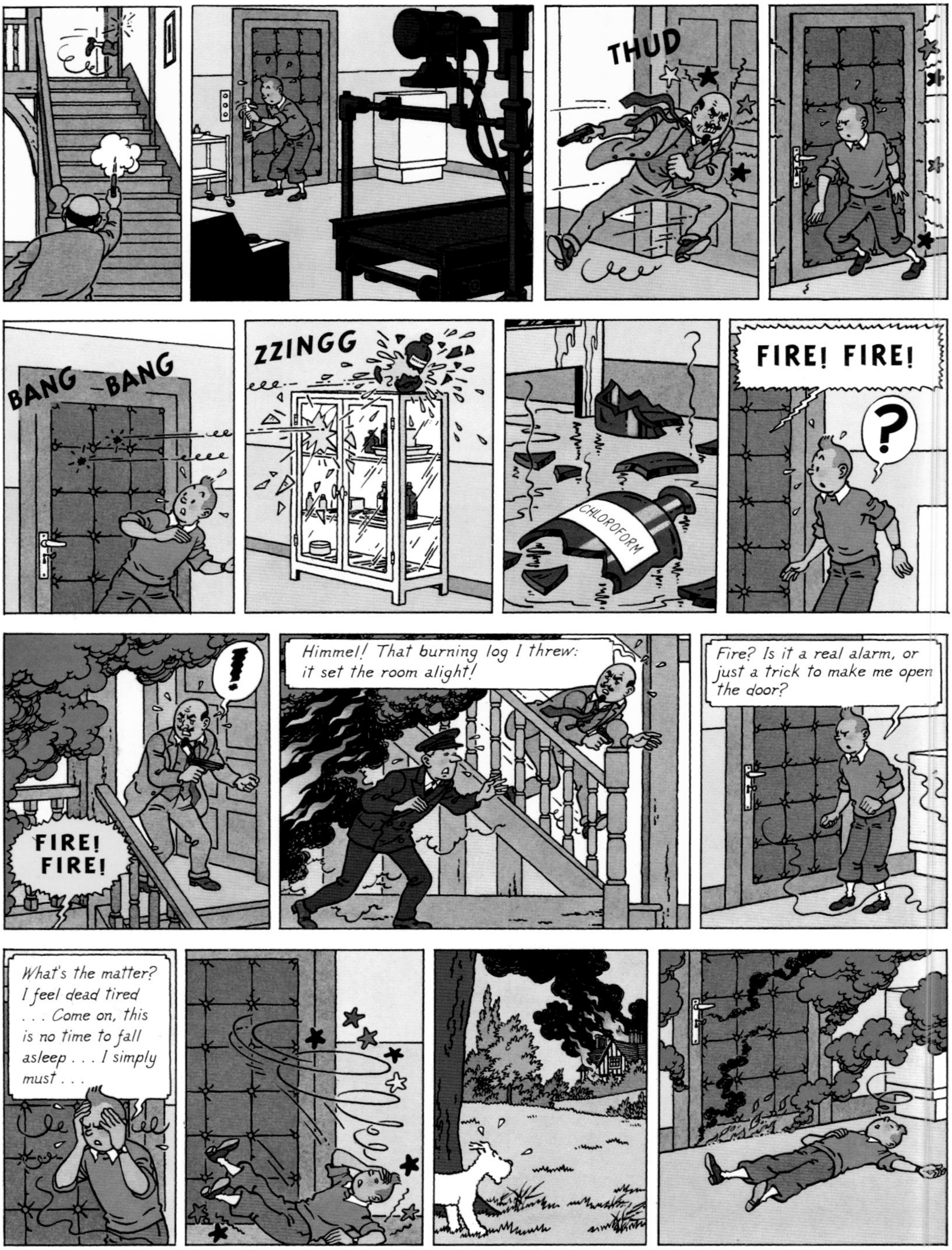

THUD
BANG
BANG
ZZINGG
CHLOROFORM
FIRE! FIRE!
?
!
FIRE! FIRE!
Himmel! That burning log I threw: it set the room alight!
Fire? Is it a real alarm, or just a trick to make me open the door?
What's the matter? I feel dead tired . . . Come on, this is no time to fall asleep . . . I simply must . . .

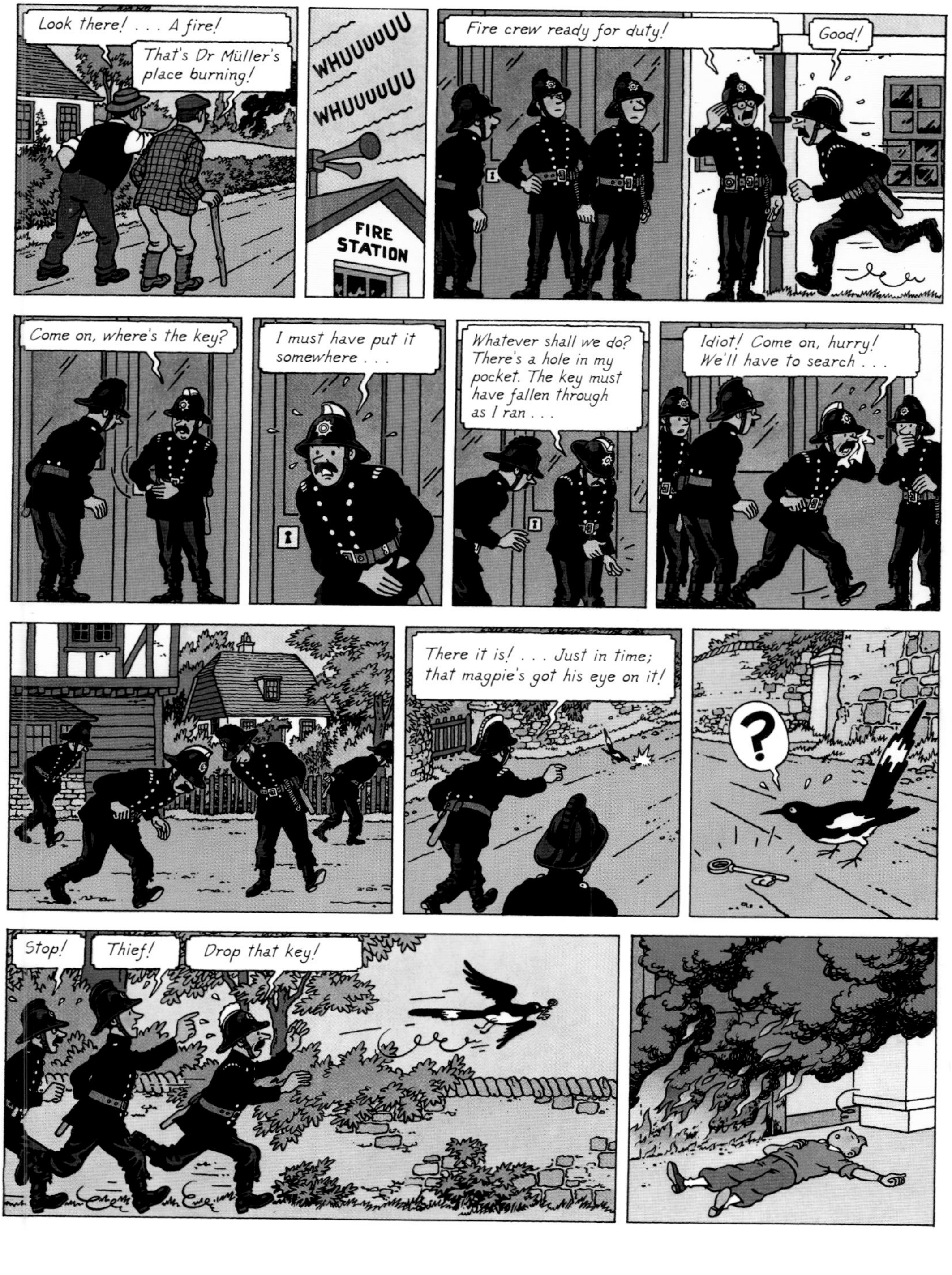
Look there! . . . A fire!
That's Dr Müller's place burning!
WHUUUUUU
WHUUUUUU
FIRE STATION
Fire crew ready for duty!
Good!
Come on, where's the key?
I must have put it somewhere . . .
Whatever shall we do? There's a hole in my pocket. The key must have fallen through as I ran . . .
Idiot! Come on, hurry! We'll have to search . . .
There it is! . . . Just in time; that magpie's got his eye on it!
?
Stop!
Thief!
Drop that key!

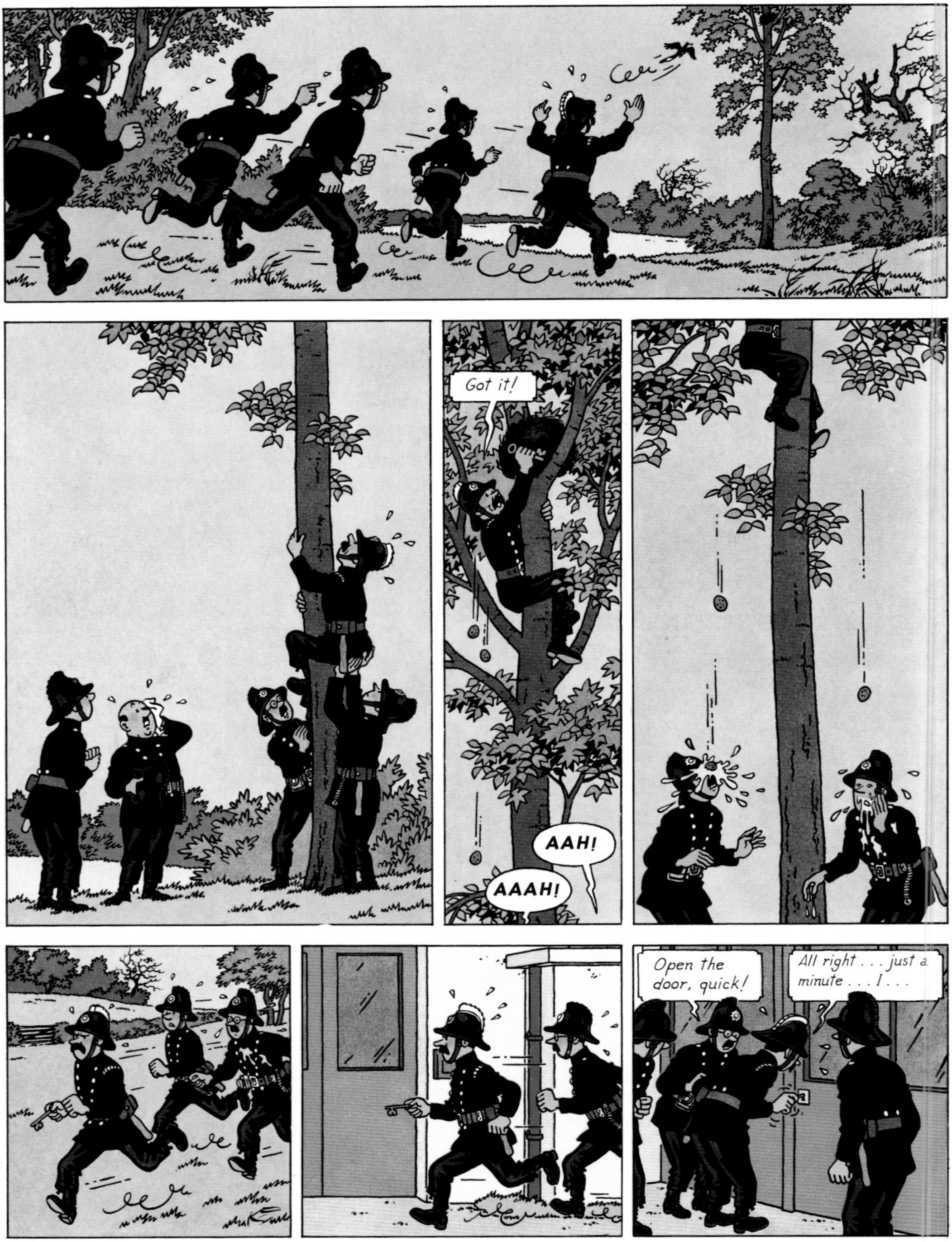
Got it!
AAH!
AAAH!
Open the door, quick!
All right . . . just a minute . . . I . . .

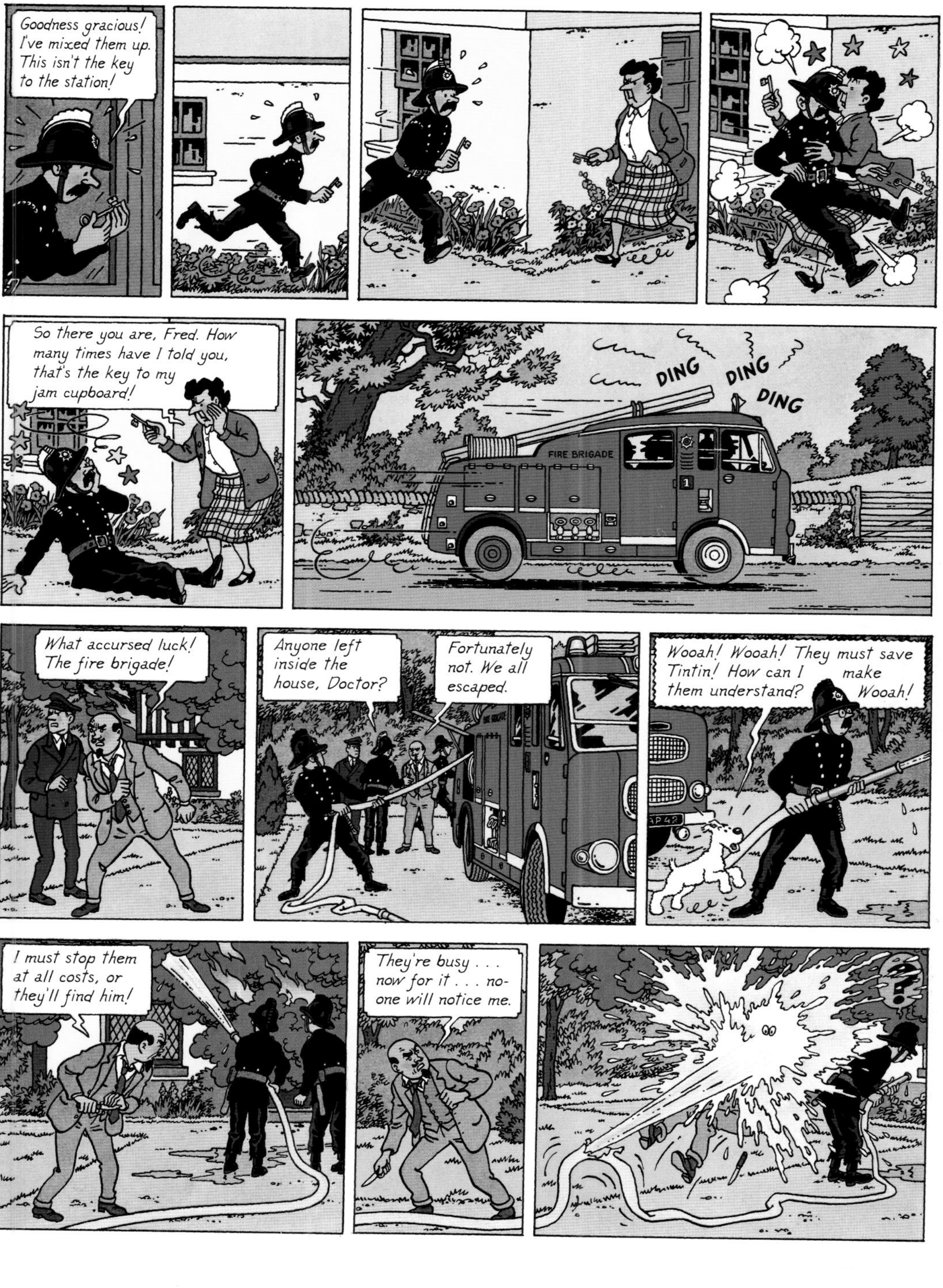
Goodness gracious! I've mixed them up. This isn't the key to the station!
So there you are, Fred. How many times have I told you, that's the key to my jam cupboard!
DING
DING
DING
FIRE BRIGADE
What accursed luck! The fire brigade!
Anyone left inside the house, Doctor?
Fortunately not. We all escaped.
Wooah! Wooah! They must save Tintin! How can I make them understand? Wooah!
I must stop them at all costs, or they'll find him!
They're busy . . . now for it . . . no-one will notice me.

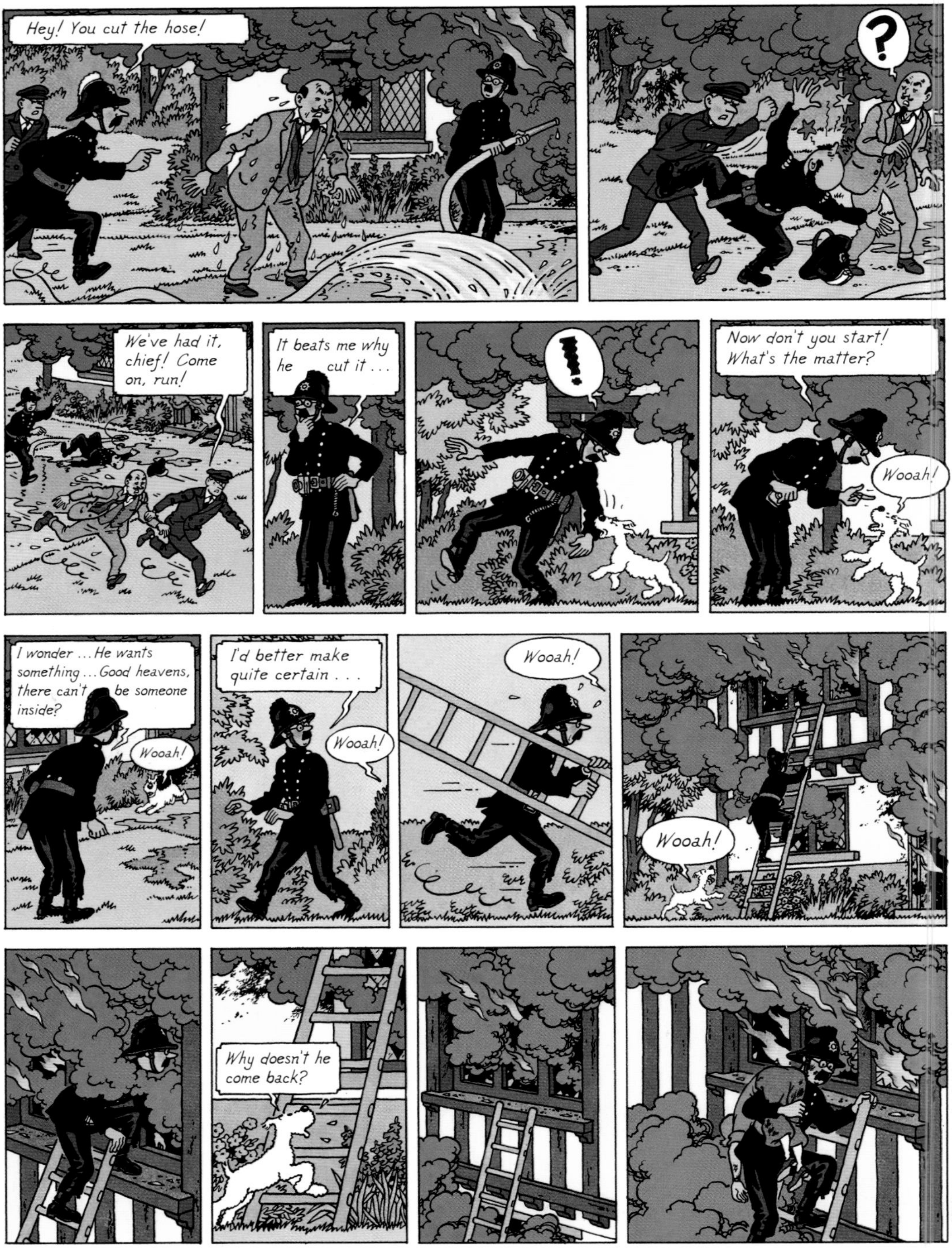
Hey! You cut the hose!
?
We've had it, chief! Come on, run!
It beats me why he cut it . . .
!
Now don't you start! What's the matter?
Wooah!
I wonder ... He wants something ... Good heavens, there can't be someone inside?
Wooah!
I'd better make quite certain . . .
Wooah!
Wooah!
Wooah!
Why doesn't he come back?

Next morning...

...And what happened to Doctor Müller?

I'm afraid my men couldn't catch him. His car was standing just by the house. He hopped in, with his driver, and they went off at top speed. We hadn't a chance.

A pity. I'd give a lot to know... why were they so anxious to get rid of me? Never mind. Perhaps I'll find a clue at the house, to put me on their track again... The fire can't have destroyed everything...

You're not getting out of bed?

Of course. I feel absolutely all right.

Heavens! There isn't much left of Dr Müller's house: it's gutted.

I shan't find anything useful here...

?

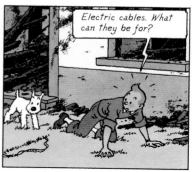

Electric cables. What can they be for?

They seem to go on...

How odd. Where on earth can they lead?

?

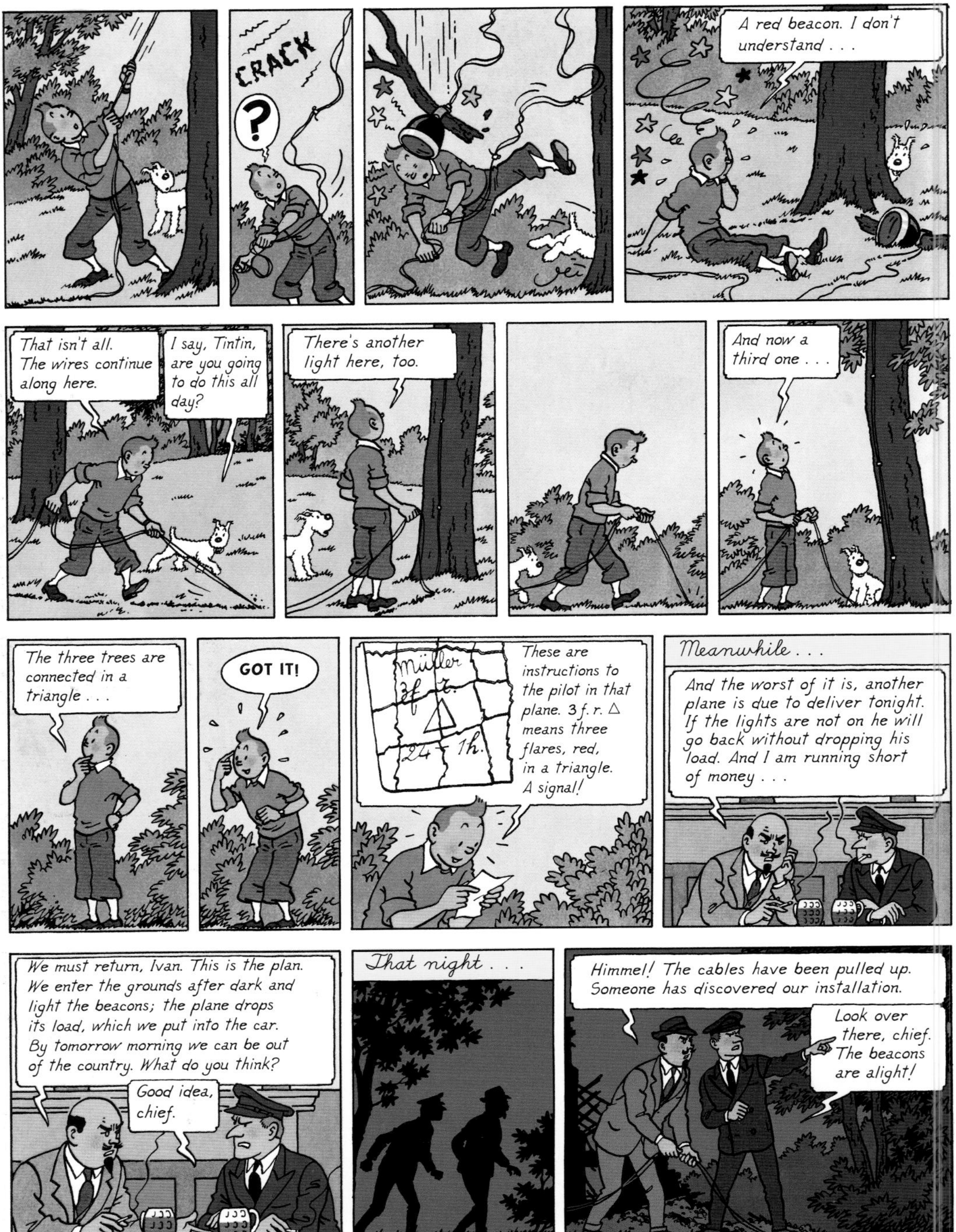
CRACK
?
A red beacon. I don't understand . . .
That isn't all. The wires continue along here.
I say, Tintin, are you going to do this all day?
There's another light here, too.
And now a third one . . .
The three trees are connected in a triangle . . .
GOT IT!
These are instructions to the pilot in that plane. 3 f. r. △ means three flares, red, in a triangle. A signal!
Meanwhile . . .
And the worst of it is, another plane is due to deliver tonight. If the lights are not on he will go back without dropping his load. And I am running short of money . . .
We must return, Ivan. This is the plan. We enter the grounds after dark and light the beacons; the plane drops its load, which we put into the car. By tomorrow morning we can be out of the country. What do you think?
Good idea, chief.
That night . . .
Himmel! The cables have been pulled up. Someone has discovered our installation.
Look over there, chief. The beacons are alight!

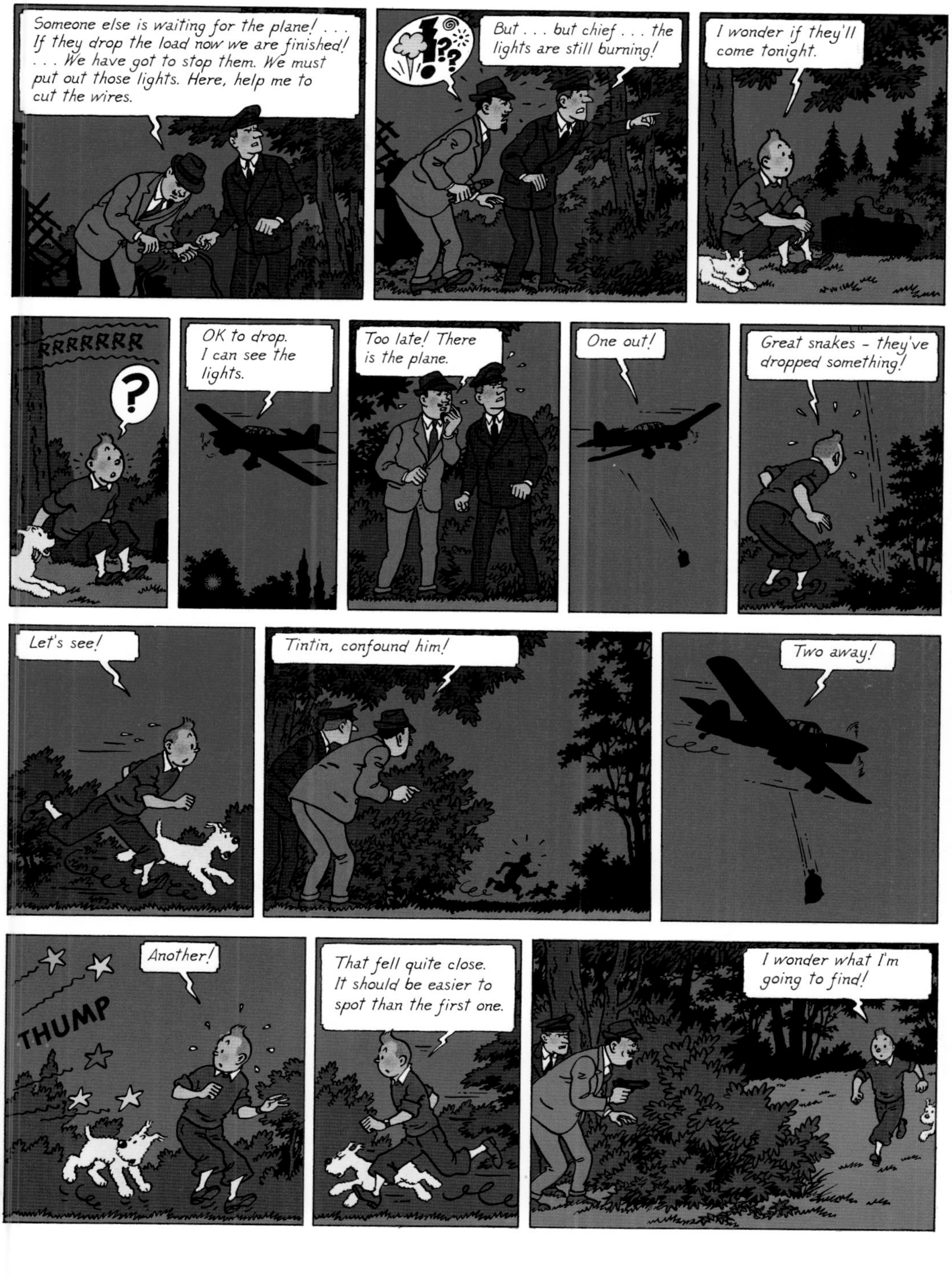
Someone else is waiting for the plane! . . . If they drop the load now we are finished! . . . We have got to stop them. We must put out those lights. Here, help me to cut the wires.
But . . . but chief . . . the lights are still burning!
I wonder if they'll come tonight.
RRRRRRR
OK to drop. I can see the lights.
Too late! There is the plane.
One out!
Great snakes - they've dropped something!
Let's see!
Tintin, confound him!
Two away!
Another!
THUMP
That fell quite close. It should be easier to spot than the first one.
I wonder what I'm going to find!

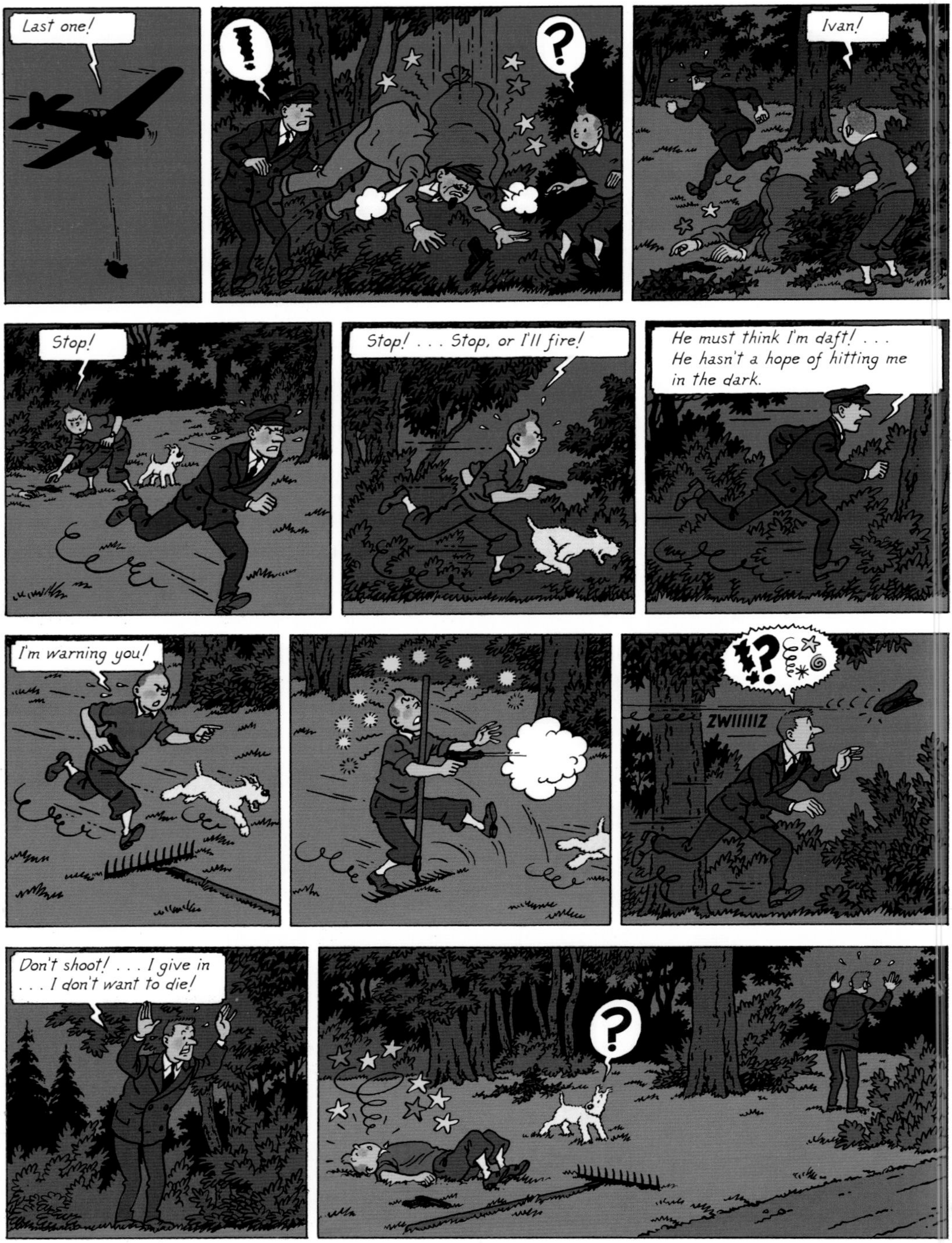
Last one!
Ivan!
Stop!
Stop! . . . Stop, or I'll fire!
He must think I'm daft! . . .
He hasn't a hope of hitting me in the dark.
I'm warning you!
ZWIIIIIZ
Don't shoot! . . . I give in . . . I don't want to die!

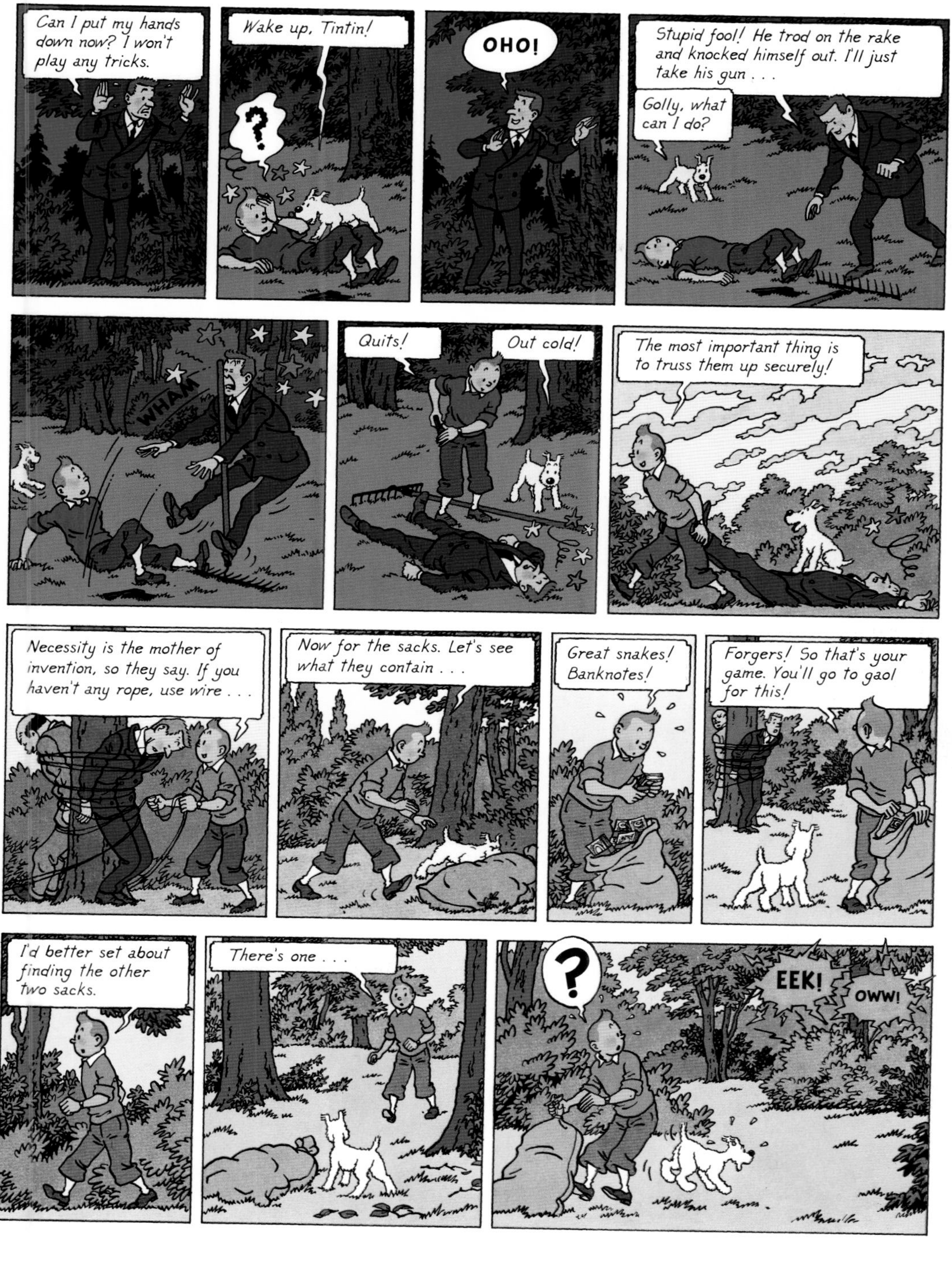
Can I put my hands down now? I won't play any tricks.
Wake up, Tintin!
OHO!
Stupid fool! He trod on the rake and knocked himself out. I'll just take his gun . . .
Golly, what can I do?
WHAM
Quits!
Out cold!
The most important thing is to truss them up securely!
Necessity is the mother of invention, so they say. If you haven't any rope, use wire . . .
Now for the sacks. Let's see what they contain . . .
Great snakes! Banknotes!
Forgers! So that's your game. You'll go to gaol for this!
I'd better set about finding the other two sacks.
There's one . . .
?
EEK!
OWW!

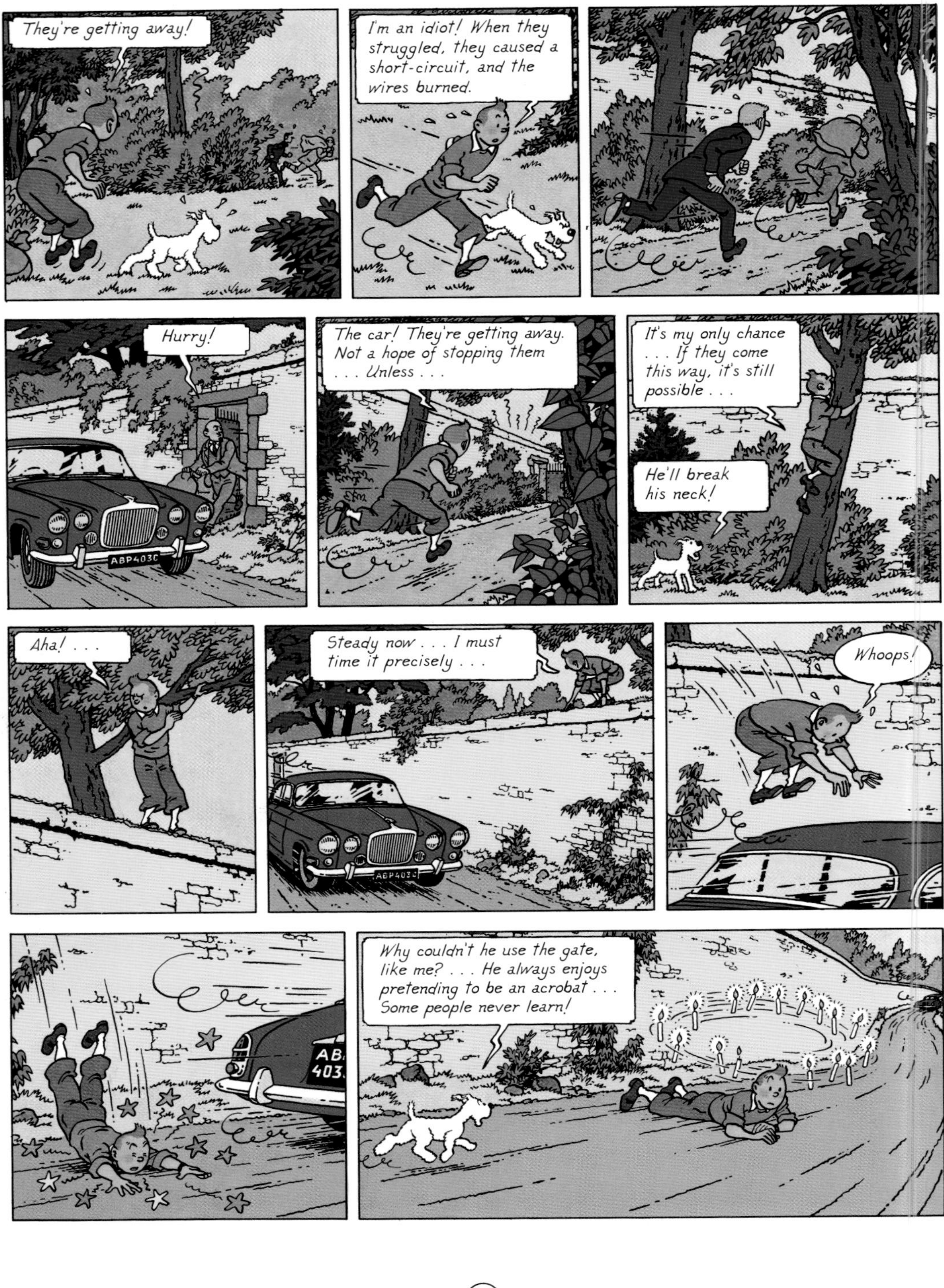
They're getting away!
I'm an idiot! When they struggled, they caused a short-circuit, and the wires burned.
Hurry!
ABP 403C
The car! They're getting away. Not a hope of stopping them . . . Unless . . .
It's my only chance . . . If they come this way, it's still possible . . .
He'll break his neck!
Aha! . . .
Steady now . . . I must time it precisely . . .
ABP 403C
Whoops!
Why couldn't he use the gate, like me? . . . He always enjoys pretending to be an acrobat . . . Some people never learn!

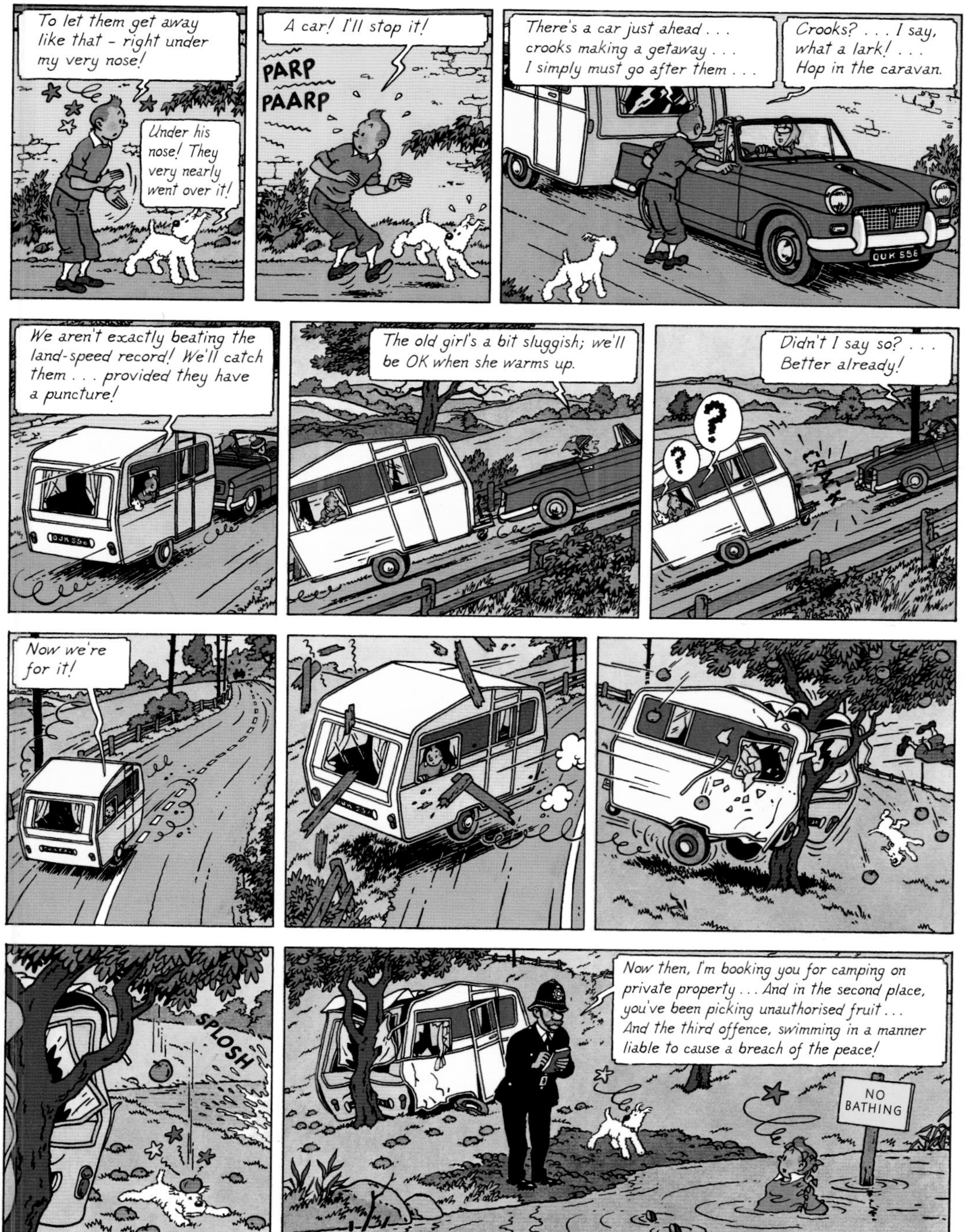

To let them get away like that - right under my very nose!
Under his nose! They very nearly went over it!
A car! I'll stop it!
PARP
PAARP
There's a car just ahead . . . crooks making a getaway . . . I simply must go after them . . .
Crooks? . . . I say, what a lark! . . . Hop in the caravan.
We aren't exactly beating the land-speed record! We'll catch them . . . provided they have a puncture!
The old girl's a bit sluggish; we'll be OK when she warms up.
Didn't I say so? . . . Better already!
CRACK
Now we're for it!
SPLOSH
Now then, I'm booking you for camping on private property . . . And in the second place, you've been picking unauthorised fruit . . . And the third offence, swimming in a manner liable to cause a breach of the peace!
NO BATHING

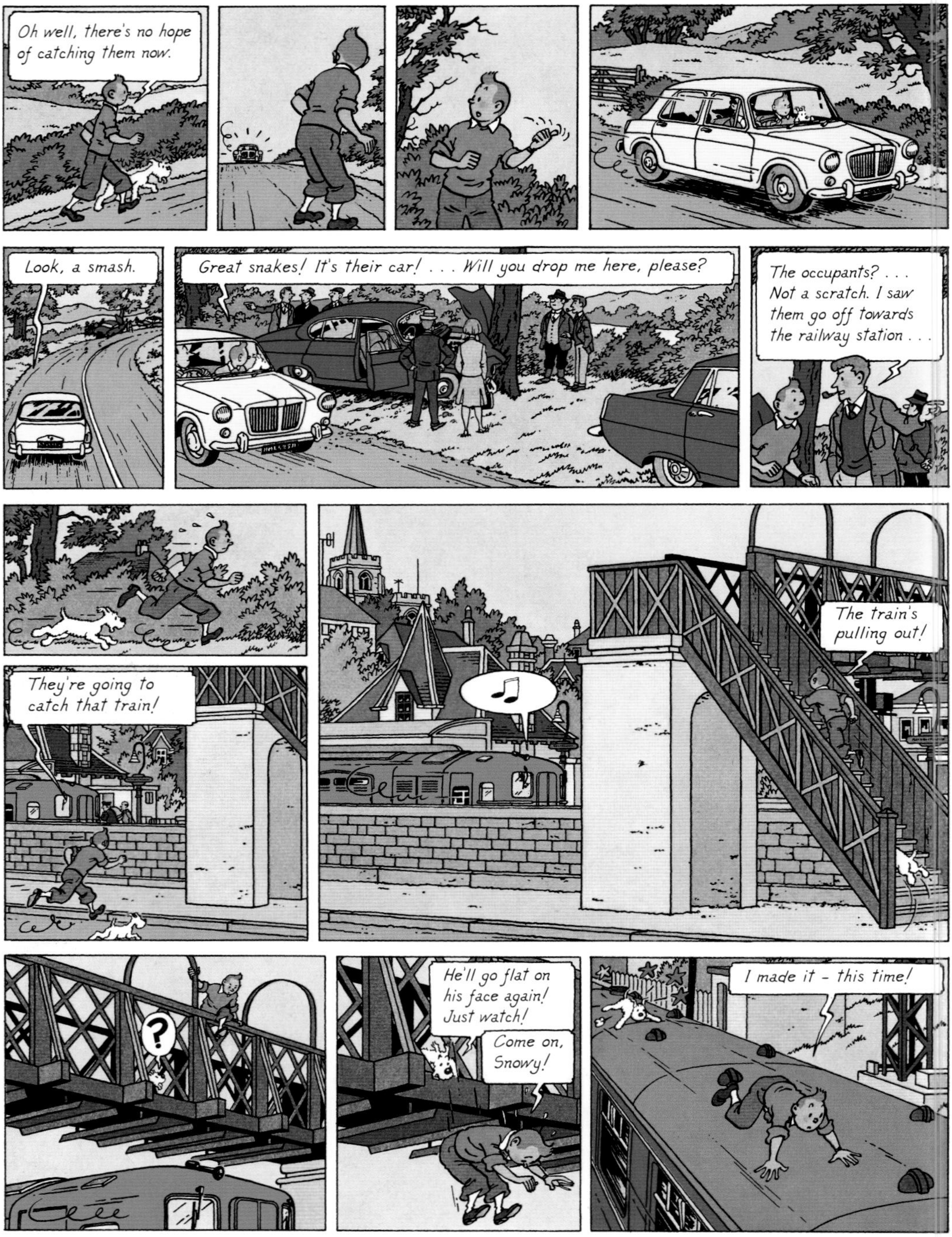

Oh well, there's no hope of catching them now.
Look, a smash.
Great snakes! It's their car! . . . Will you drop me here, please?
The occupants? . . . Not a scratch. I saw them go off towards the railway station . . .
They're going to catch that train!
The train's pulling out!
?
He'll go flat on his face again! Just watch!
Come on, Snowy!
I made it – this time!

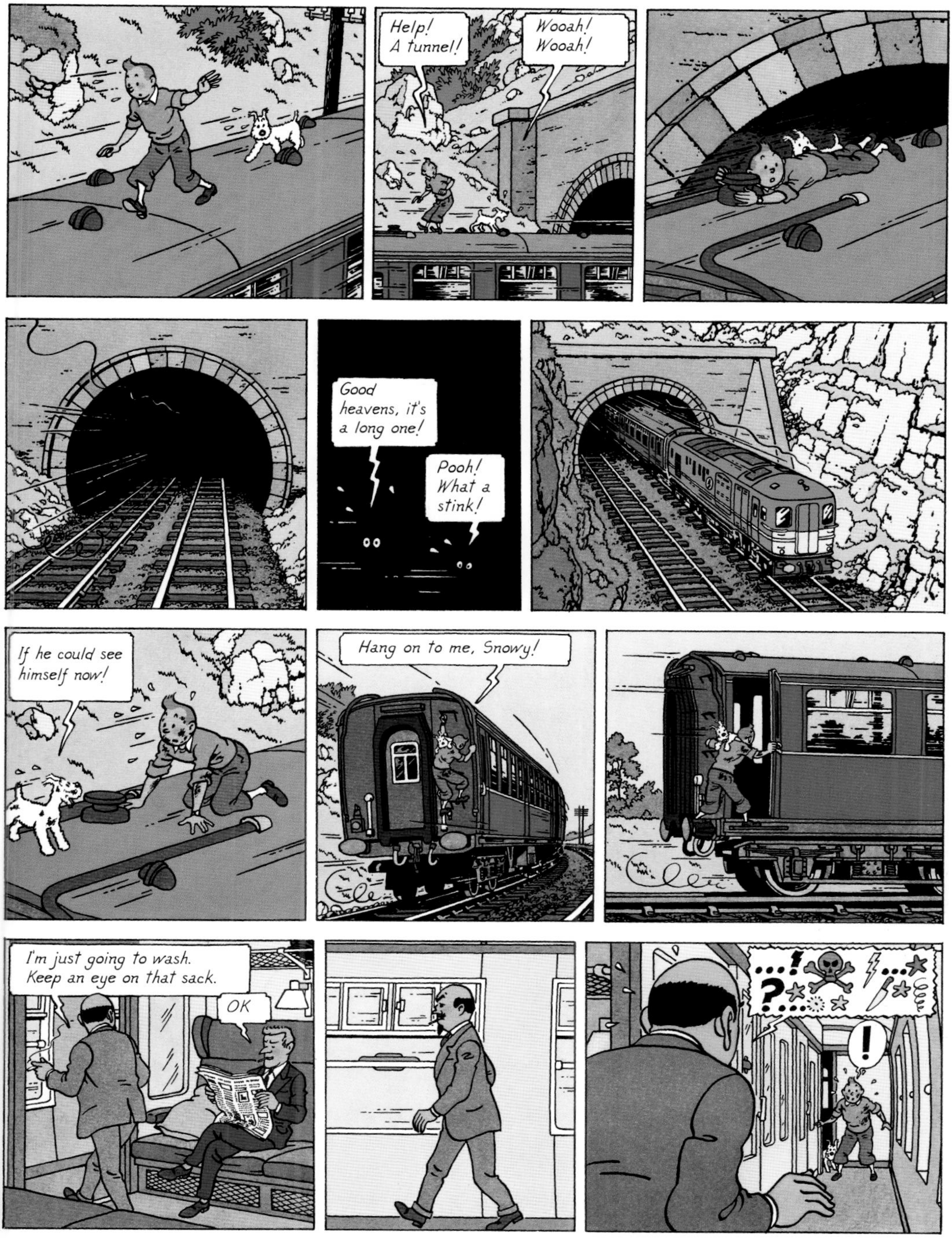
Help! A tunnel!
Wooah! Wooah!
Good heavens, it's a long one!
Pooh! What a stink!
If he could see himself now!
Hang on to me, Snowy!
I'm just going to wash. Keep an eye on that sack.
OK

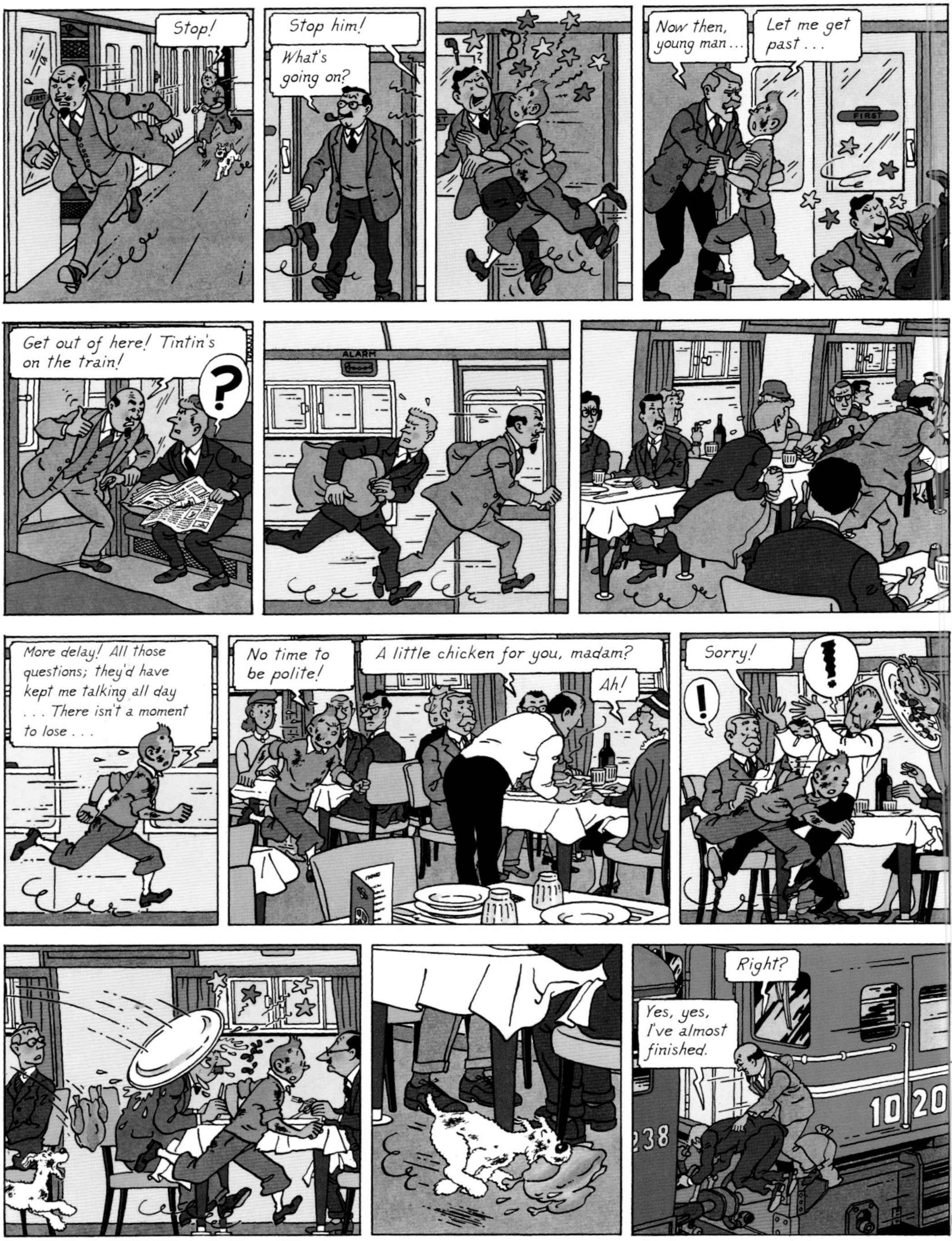
Stop!
Stop him!
What's going on?
Now then, young man...
Let me get past...
Get out of here! Tintin's on the train!
?
ALARM
More delay! All those questions; they'd have kept me talking all day . . . There isn't a moment to lose . . .
No time to be polite!
A little chicken for you, madam?
Ah!
Sorry!
!
!
Right?
Yes, yes, I've almost finished.
10 20
238

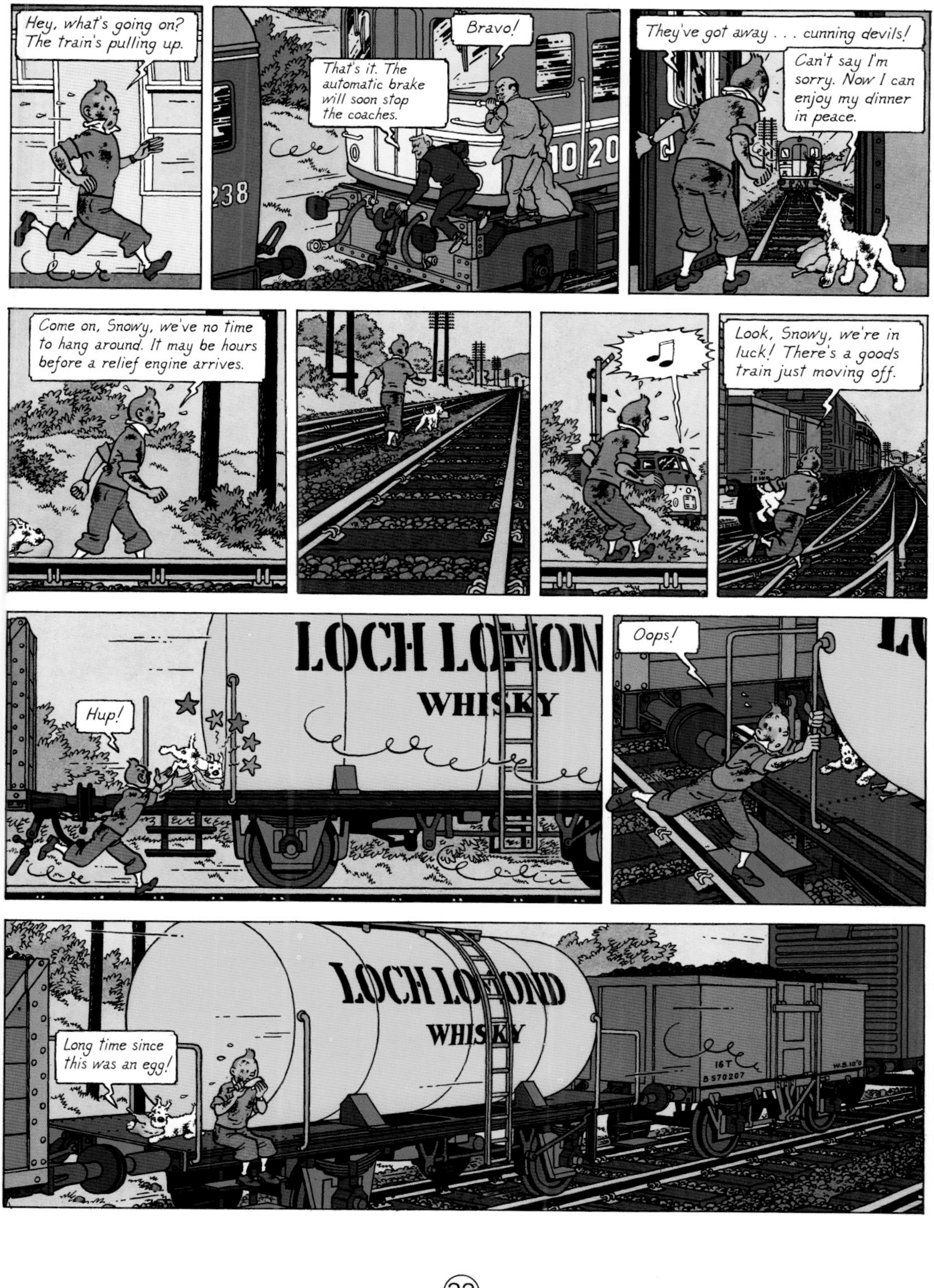
Hey, what's going on? The train's pulling up.
Bravo!
That's it. The automatic brake will soon stop the coaches.
They've got away . . . cunning devils!
Can't say I'm sorry. Now I can enjoy my dinner in peace.
Come on, Snowy, we've no time to hang around. It may be hours before a relief engine arrives.
Look, Snowy, we're in luck! There's a goods train just moving off.
LOCH LOMON
WHISKY
Hup!
Oops!
LOCH LOMOND
WHISKY
Long time since this was an egg!

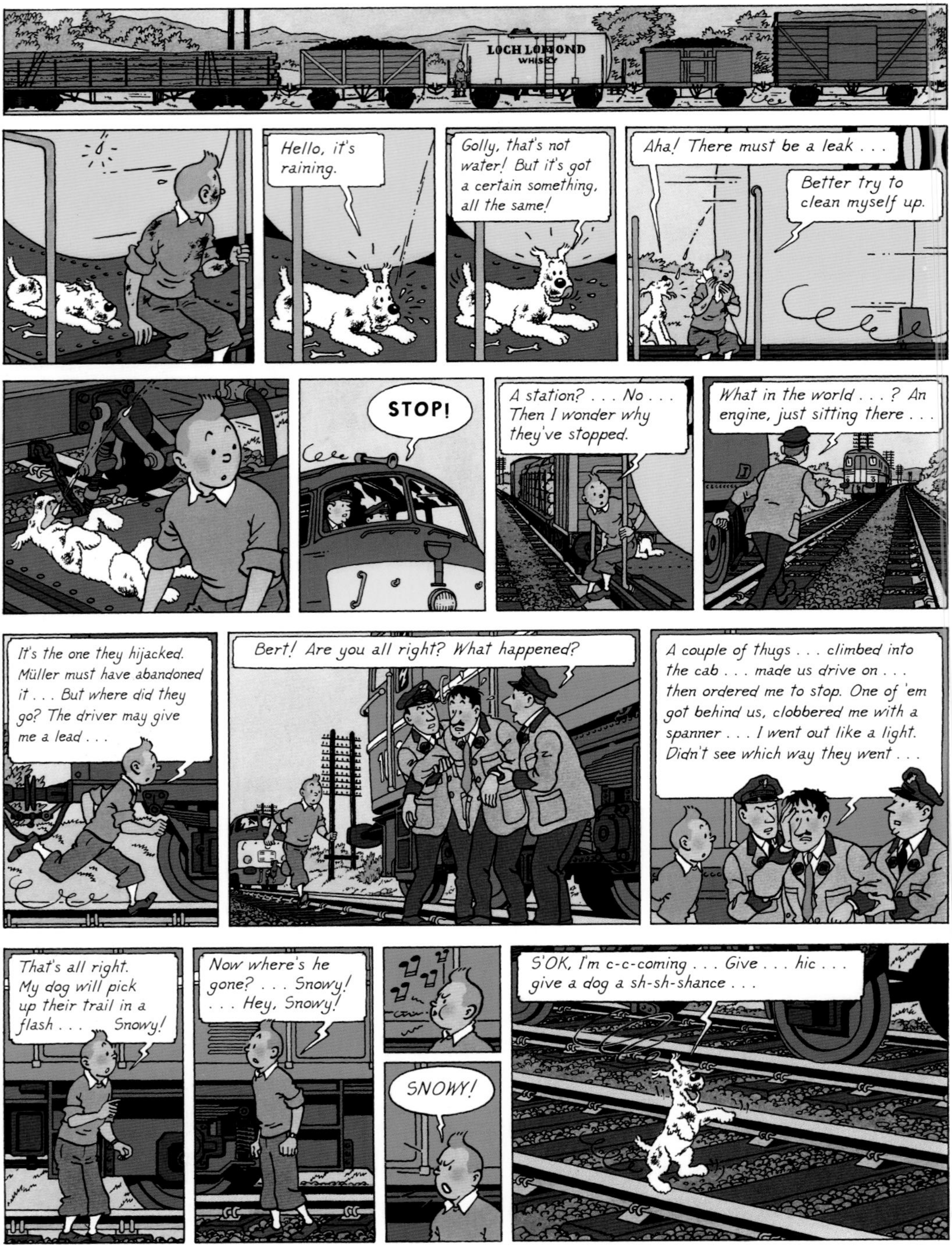
LOCH LOMOND
WHISKY
Hello, it's raining.
Golly, that's not water! But it's got a certain something, all the same!
Aha! There must be a leak . . .
Better try to clean myself up.
STOP!
A station? . . . No . . . Then I wonder why they've stopped.
What in the world . . . ? An engine, just sitting there . . .
It's the one they hijacked. Müller must have abandoned it . . . But where did they go? The driver may give me a lead . . .
Bert! Are you all right? What happened?
A couple of thugs . . . climbed into the cab . . . made us drive on . . . then ordered me to stop. One of 'em got behind us, clobbered me with a spanner . . . I went out like a light. Didn't see which way they went . . .
That's all right. My dog will pick up their trail in a flash . . . Snowy!
Now where's he gone? . . . Snowy! . . . Hey, Snowy!
SNOWY!
S'OK, I'm c-c-coming . . . Give . . . hic . . . give a dog a sh-sh-shance . . .

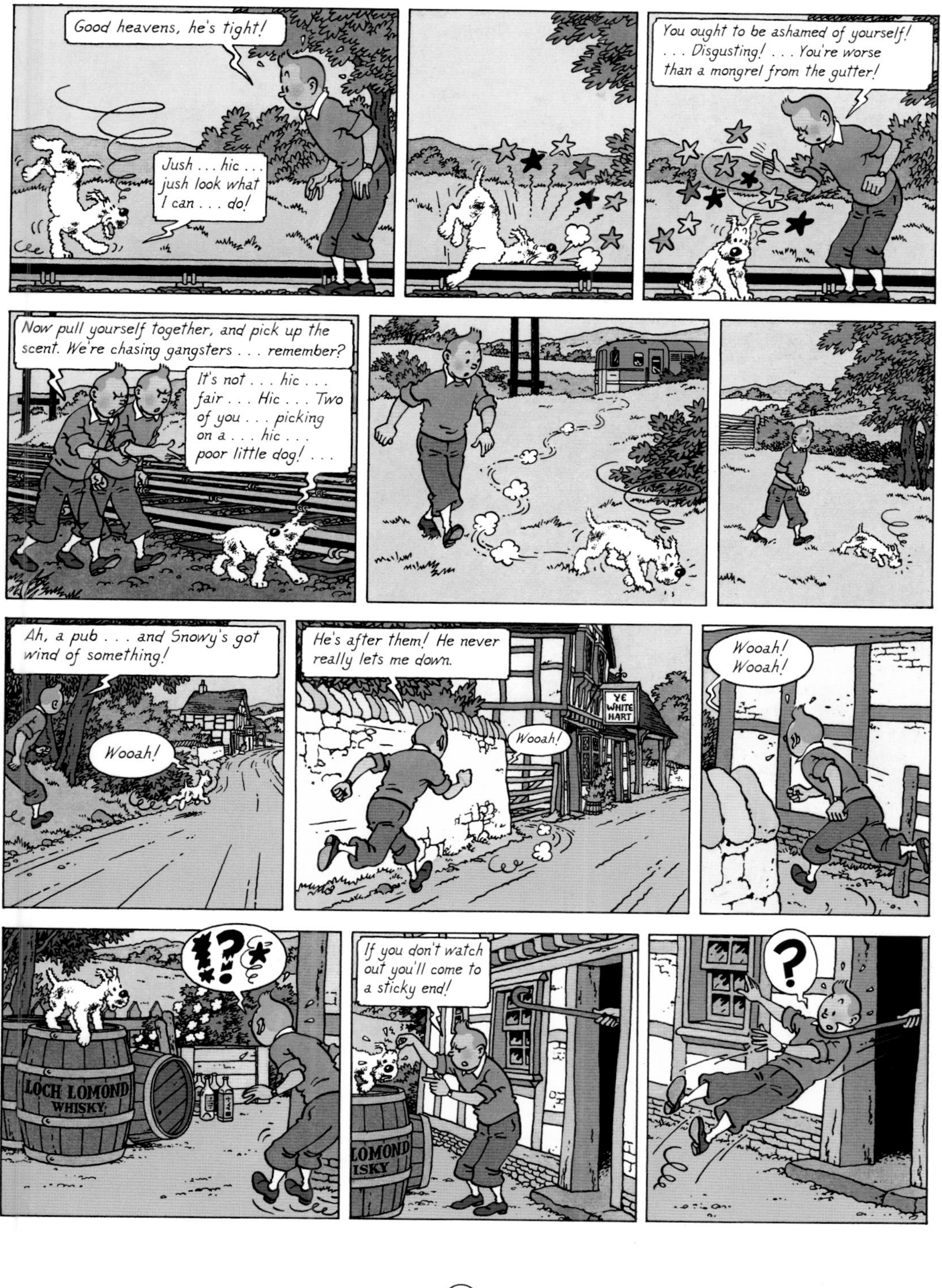
Good heavens, he's tight!
Jush . . . hic . . . jush look what I can . . . do!
You ought to be ashamed of yourself! . . . Disgusting! . . . You're worse than a mongrel from the gutter!
Now pull yourself together, and pick up the scent. We're chasing gangsters . . . remember?
It's not . . . hic . . . fair . . . Hic . . . Two of you . . . picking on a . . . hic . . . poor little dog! . . .
Ah, a pub . . . and Snowy's got wind of something!
Wooah!
He's after them! He never really lets me down.
YE WHITE HART
Wooah!
Wooah! Wooah!
LOCH LOMOND WHISKY
If you don't watch out you'll come to a sticky end!
?

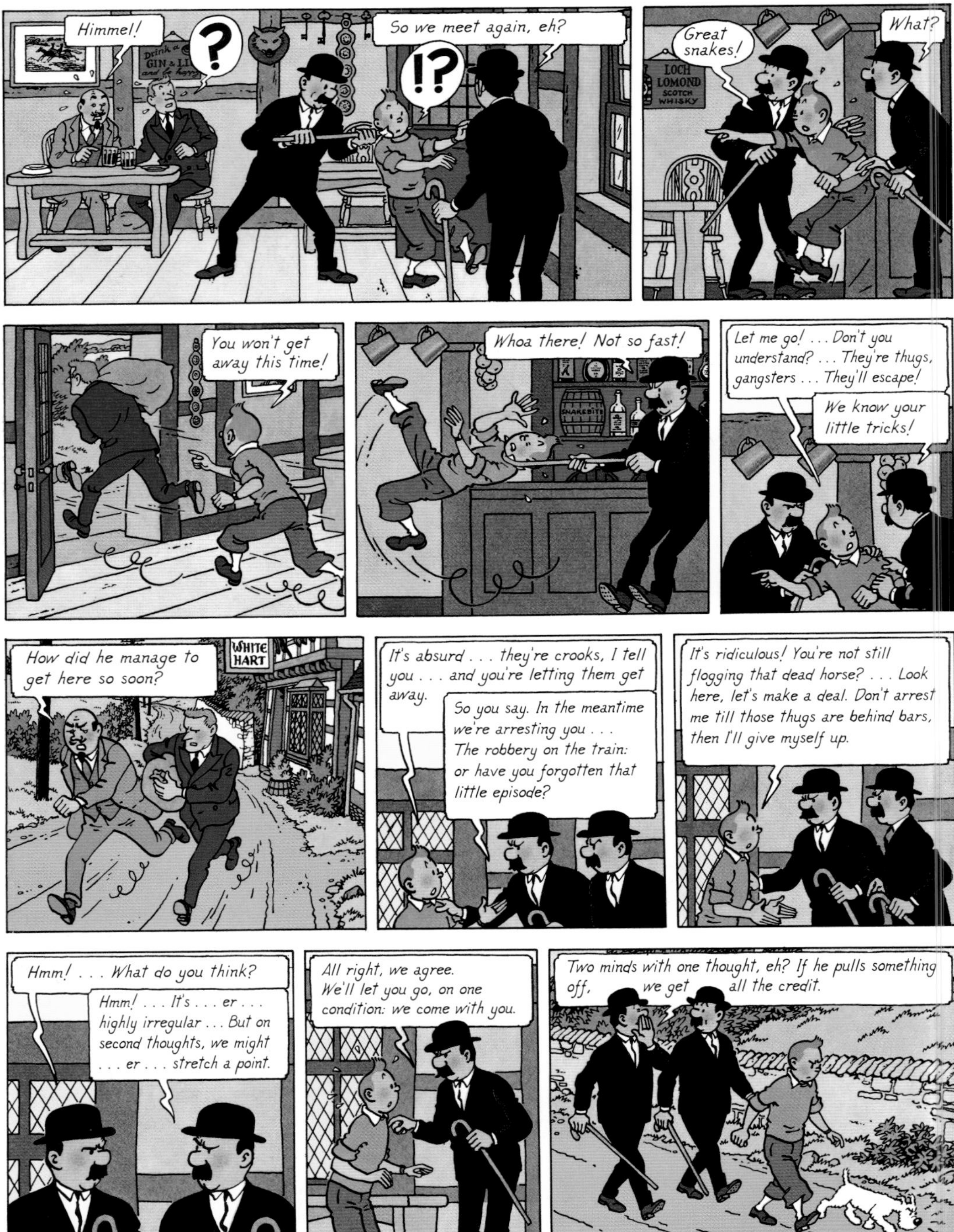
Himmel!
?
So we meet again, eh?
!?
Great snakes!
What?
You won't get away this time!
Whoa there! Not so fast!
Let me go! . . . Don't you understand? . . . They're thugs, gangsters . . . They'll escape!
We know your little tricks!
How did he manage to get here so soon?
WHITE HART
It's absurd . . . they're crooks, I tell you . . . and you're letting them get away.
So you say. In the meantime we're arresting you . . . The robbery on the train: or have you forgotten that little episode?
It's ridiculous! You're not still flogging that dead horse? . . . Look here, let's make a deal. Don't arrest me till those thugs are behind bars, then I'll give myself up.
Hmm! . . . What do you think?
Hmm! . . . It's . . . er . . . highly irregular . . . But on second thoughts, we might . . . er . . . stretch a point.
All right, we agree. We'll let you go, on one condition: we come with you.
Two minds with one thought, eh? If he pulls something off, we get all the credit.

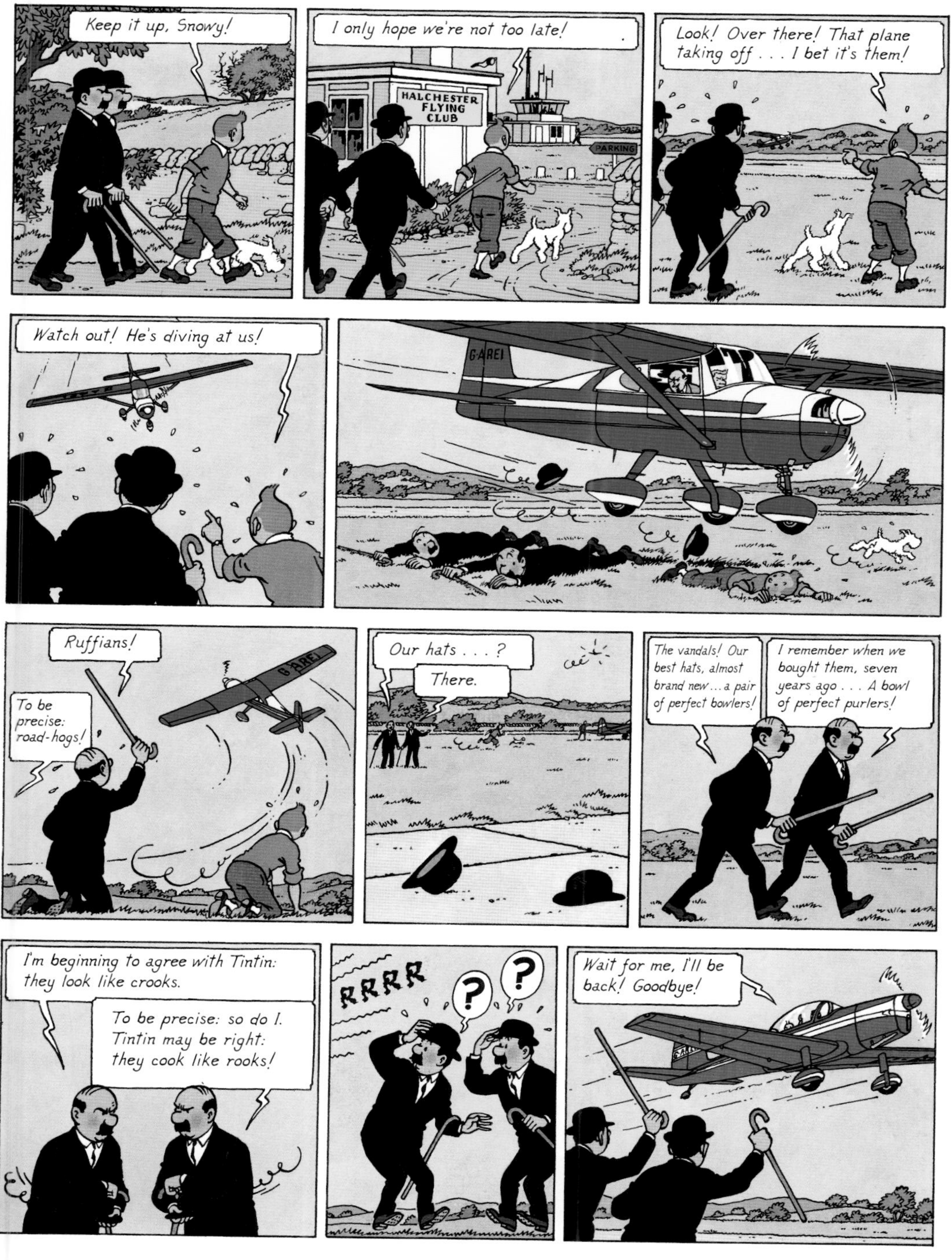

Keep it up, Snowy!
I only hope we're not too late!
HALCHESTER FLYING CLUB
PARKING
Look! Over there! That plane taking off . . . I bet it's them!
Watch out! He's diving at us!
G-AREI
Ruffians!
To be precise: road-hogs!
Our hats . . . ?
There.
The vandals! Our best hats, almost brand new... a pair of perfect bowlers!
I remember when we bought them, seven years ago . . . A bowl of perfect purlers!
I'm beginning to agree with Tintin: they look like crooks.
To be precise: so do I. Tintin may be right: they cook like rooks!
RRRR
?
?
Wait for me, I'll be back! Goodbye!

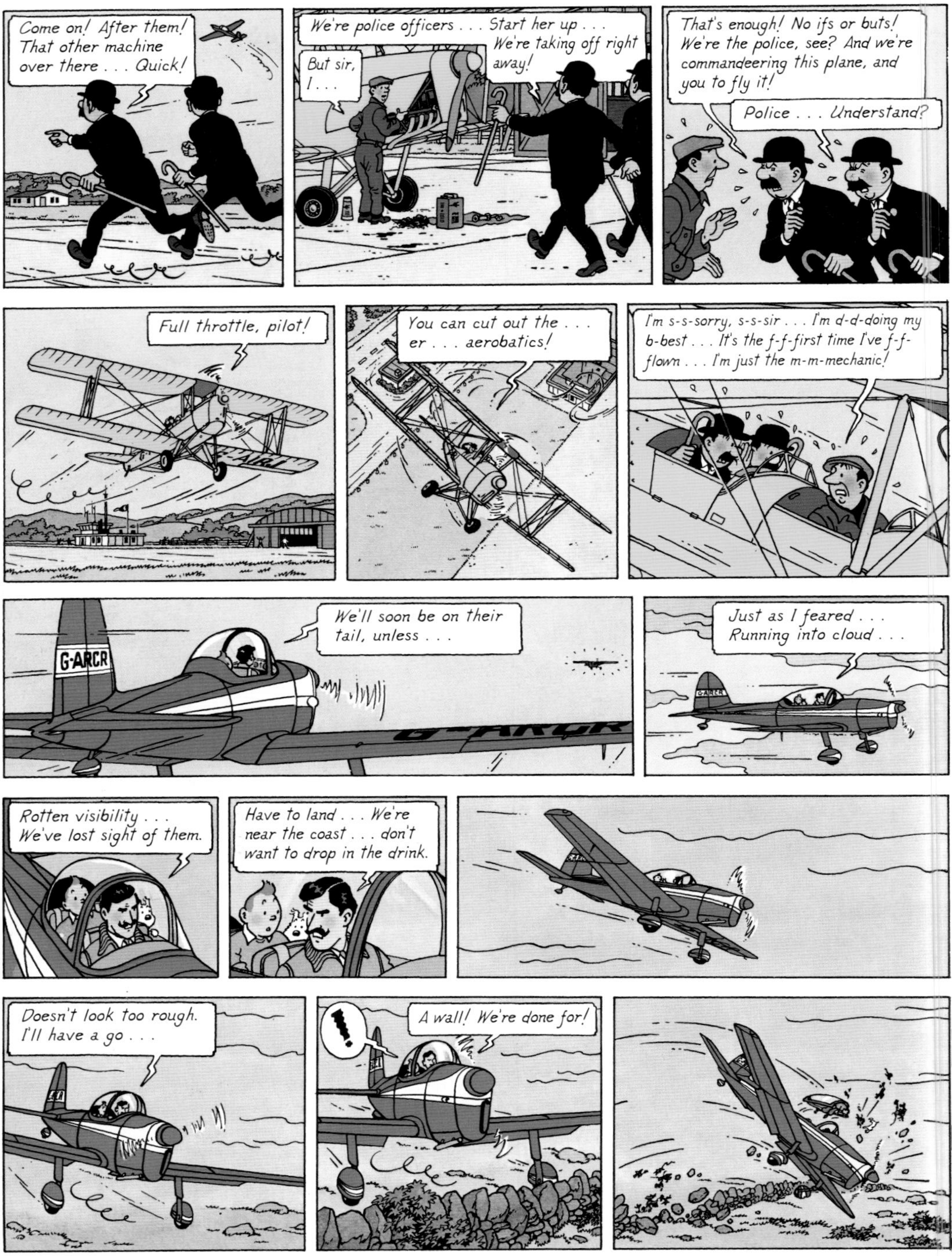
Come on! After them! That other machine over there . . . Quick!
We're police officers . . . Start her up . . .
But sir, I . . .
We're taking off right away!
That's enough! No ifs or buts! We're the police, see? And we're commandeering this plane, and you to fly it!
Police . . . Understand?
Full throttle, pilot!
You can cut out the . . . er . . . aerobatics!
I'm s-s-sorry, s-s-sir . . . I'm d-d-doing my b-best . . . It's the f-f-first time I've f-f-flown . . . I'm just the m-m-mechanic!
G-ARCR
We'll soon be on their tail, unless . . .
Just as I feared . . . Running into cloud . . .
Rotten visibility . . . We've lost sight of them.
Have to land . . . We're near the coast . . . don't want to drop in the drink.
Doesn't look too rough. I'll have a go . . .
A wall! We're done for!

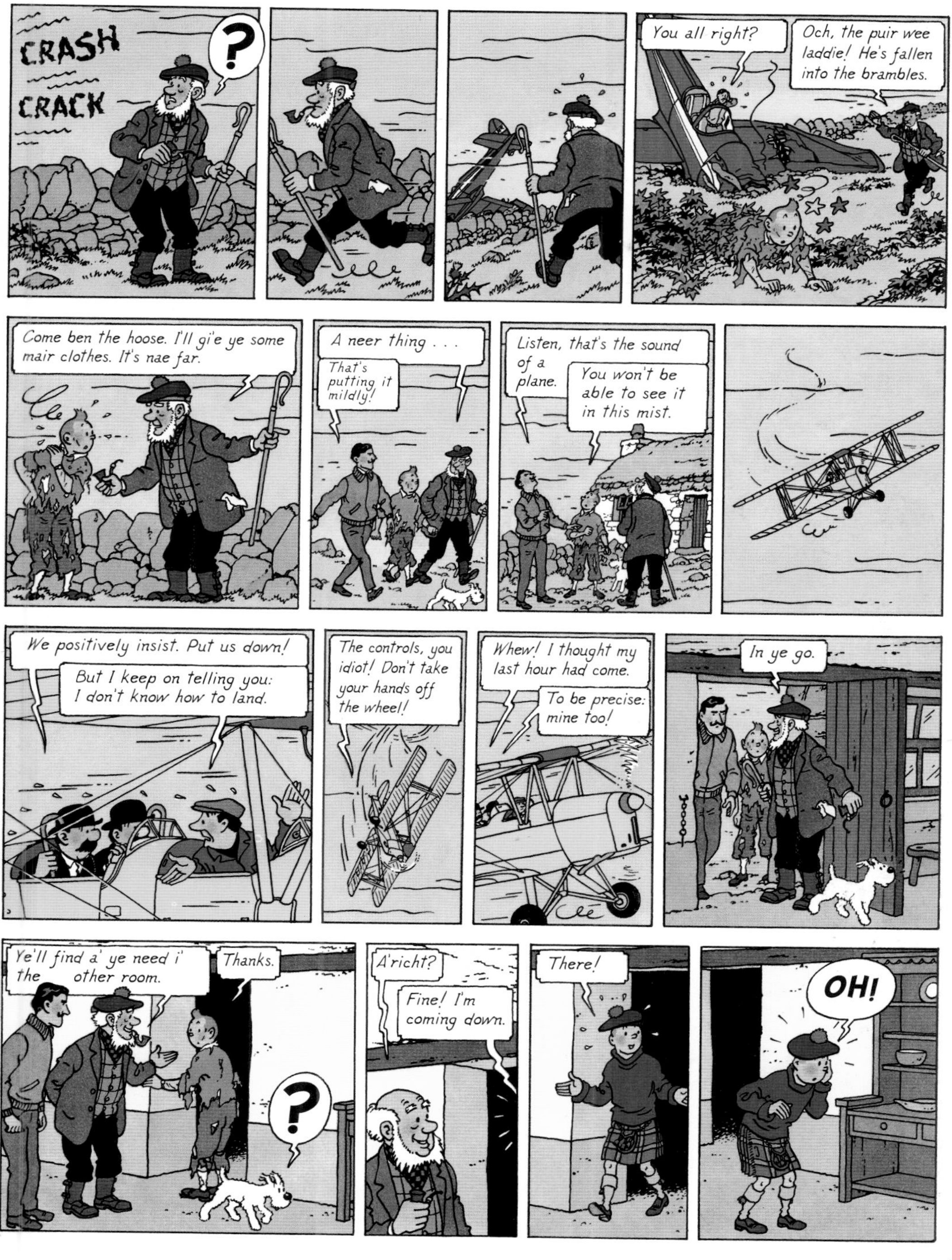
CRASH
CRACK
?
You all right?
Och, the puir wee laddie! He's fallen into the brambles.
Come ben the hoose. I'll gi'e ye some mair clothes. It's nae far.
A neer thing . . .
That's putting it mildly!
Listen, that's the sound of a plane.
You won't be able to see it in this mist.
We positively insist. Put us down!
But I keep on telling you: I don't know how to land.
The controls, you idiot! Don't take your hands off the wheel!
Whew! I thought my last hour had come.
To be precise: mine too!
In ye go.
Ye'll find a' ye need i' the other room.
Thanks.
?
A'richt?
Fine! I'm coming down.
There!
OH!

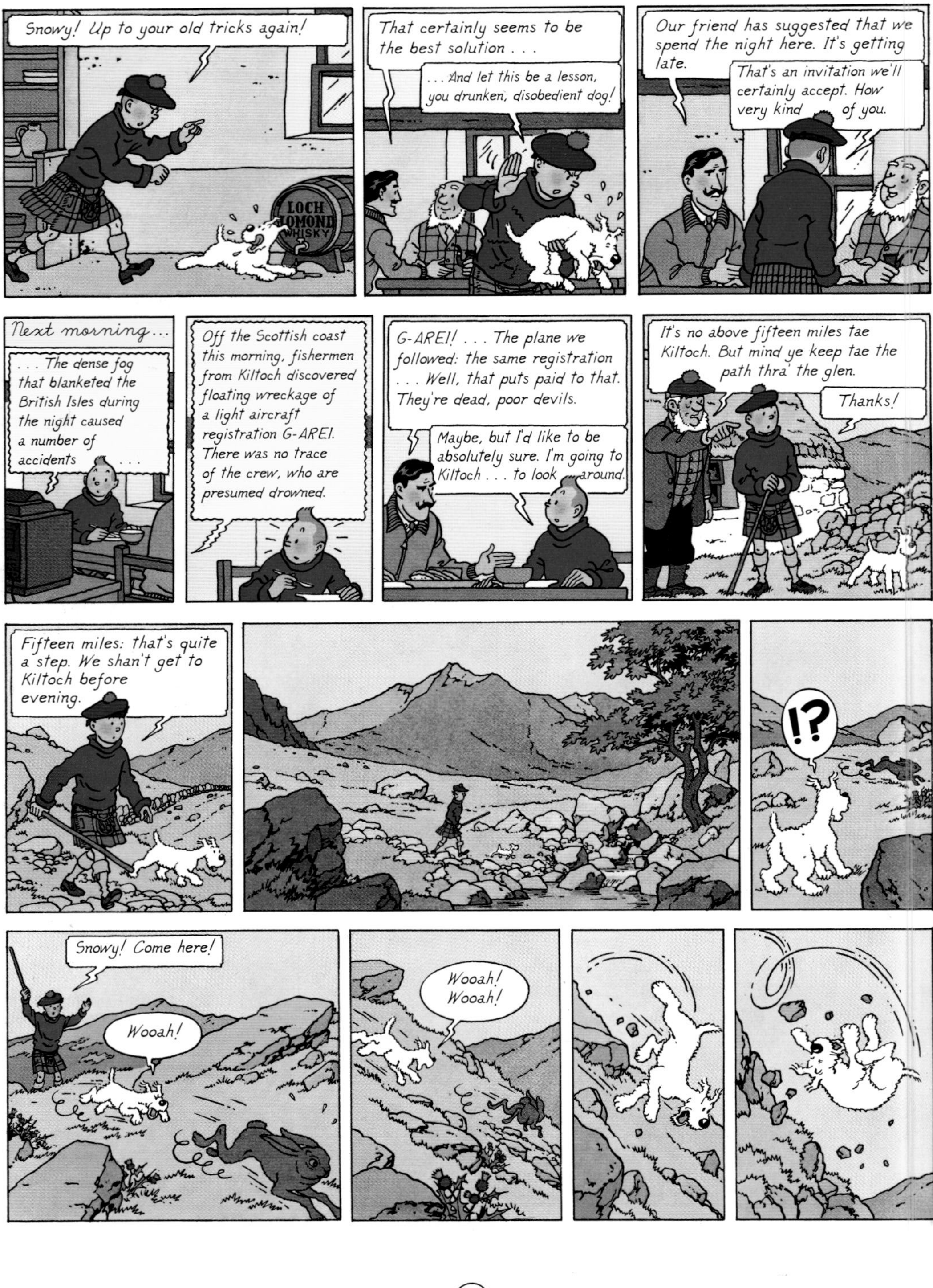

Snowy! Up to your old tricks again!
LOCH LOMOND WHISKY
That certainly seems to be the best solution . . .
. . . And let this be a lesson, you drunken, disobedient dog!
Our friend has suggested that we spend the night here. It's getting late.
That's an invitation we'll certainly accept. How very kind of you.
Next morning . . .
. . . The dense fog that blanketed the British Isles during the night caused a number of accidents . . .
Off the Scottish coast this morning, fishermen from Kiltoch discovered floating wreckage of a light aircraft registration G-AREI. There was no trace of the crew, who are presumed drowned.
G-AREI! . . . The plane we followed: the same registration . . . Well, that puts paid to that. They're dead, poor devils.
Maybe, but I'd like to be absolutely sure. I'm going to Kiltoch . . . to look around.
It's no above fifteen miles tae Kiltoch. But mind ye keep tae the path thra' the glen.
Thanks!
Fifteen miles: that's quite a step. We shan't get to Kiltoch before evening.
!?
Snowy! Come here!
Wooah!
Wooah! Wooah!

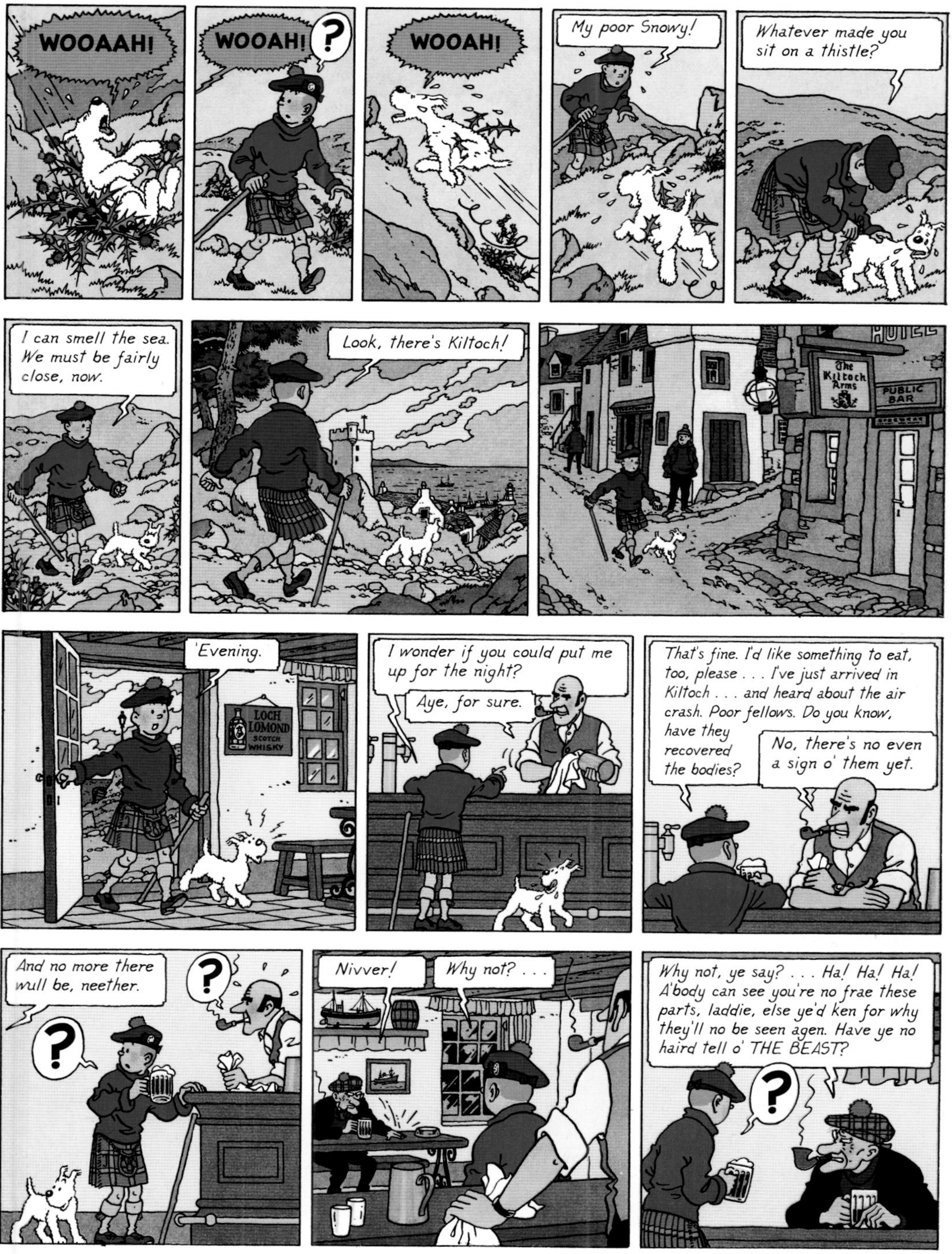

WOOAAH!
WOOAH!
?
WOOAH!
My poor Snowy!
Whatever made you sit on a thistle?
I can smell the sea. We must be fairly close, now.
Look, there's Kiltoch!
HOTEL
The Kiltoch Arms
PUBLIC BAR
'Evening.
LOCH LOMOND SCOTCH WHISKY
I wonder if you could put me up for the night?
Aye, for sure.
That's fine. I'd like something to eat, too, please . . . I've just arrived in Kiltoch . . . and heard about the air crash. Poor fellows. Do you know, have they recovered the bodies?
No, there's no even a sign o' them yet.
And no more there wull be, neether.
?
?
Nivver!
Why not? . . .
Why not, ye say? . . . Ha! Ha! Ha! A'body can see you're no frae these parts, laddie, else ye'd ken for why they'll no be seen agen. Have ye no haird tell o' THE BEAST?
?

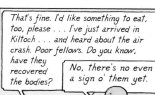

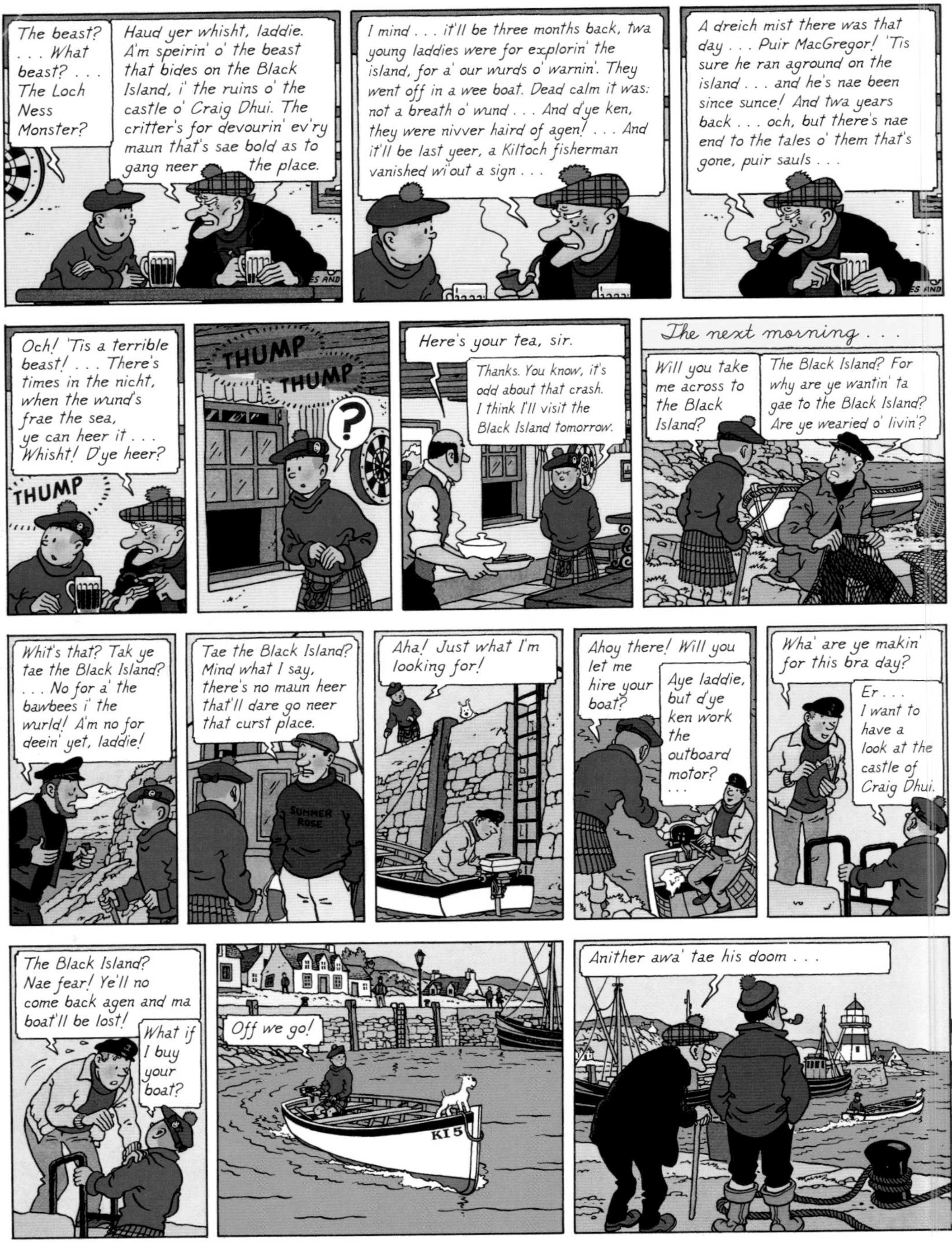
The beast? . . . What beast? . . . The Loch Ness Monster?
Haud yer whisht, laddie. A'm speirin' o' the beast that bides on the Black Island, i' the ruins o' the castle o' Craig Dhui. The critter's for devourin' ev'ry maun that's sae bold as to gang neer the place.
I mind . . . it'll be three months back, twa young laddies were for explorin' the island, for a' our wurds o' warnin'. They went off in a wee boat. Dead calm it was: not a breath o' wund . . . And d'ye ken, they were nivver haird of agen! . . . And it'll be last yeer, a Kiltoch fisherman vanished wi'out a sign . . .
A dreich mist there was that day . . . Puir MacGregor! 'Tis sure he ran aground on the island . . . and he's nae been since sunce! And twa years back . . . och, but there's nae end to the tales o' them that's gone, puir sauls . . .
Och! 'Tis a terrible beast! . . . There's times in the nicht, when the wund's frae the sea, ye can heer it . . . Whisht! D'ye heer?
THUMP
THUMP
THUMP
?
Here's your tea, sir.
Thanks. You know, it's odd about that crash. I think I'll visit the Black Island tomorrow.
The next morning . . .
Will you take me across to the Black Island?
The Black Island? For why are ye wantin' ta gae to the Black Island? Are ye wearied o' livin'?
Whit's that? Tak ye tae the Black Island? . . . No for a' the bawbees i' the wurld! A'm no for deein' yet, laddie!
Tae the Black Island? Mind what I say, there's no maun heer that'll dare go neer that curst place.
SUMMER ROSE
Aha! Just what I'm looking for!
Ahoy there! Will you let me hire your boat?
Aye laddie, but d'ye ken work the outboard motor? . . .
Wha' are ye makin' for this bra day?
Er . . . I want to have a look at the castle of Craig Dhui.
The Black Island? Nae fear! Ye'll no come back agen and ma boat'll be lost!
What if I buy your boat?
Off we go!
KI 5
Anither awa' tae his doom . . .

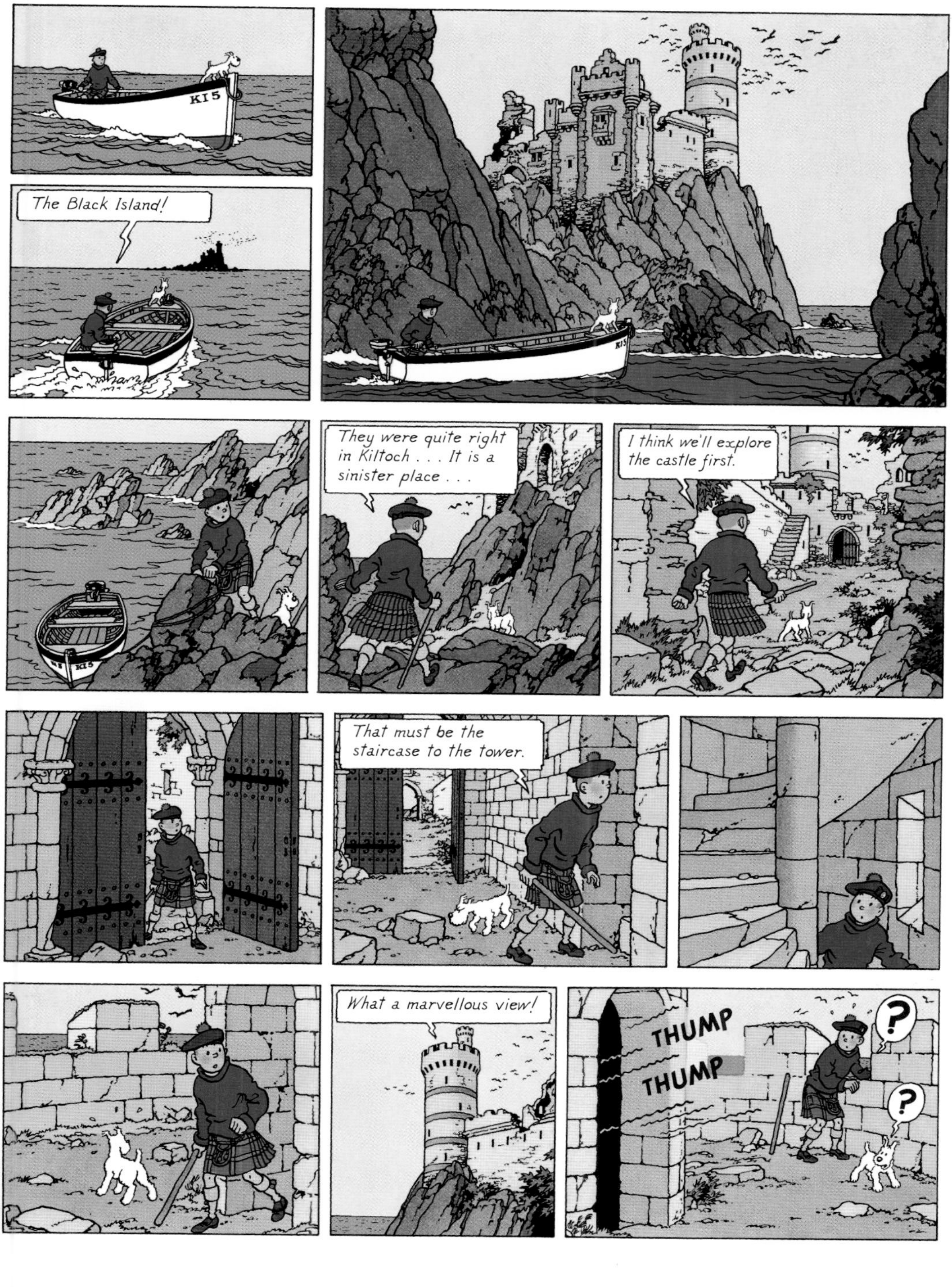
KI 5
The Black Island!
KI 5
They were quite right in Kiltoch . . . It is a sinister place . . .
I think we'll explore the castle first.
That must be the staircase to the tower.
What a marvellous view!
THUMP
THUMP
?
?

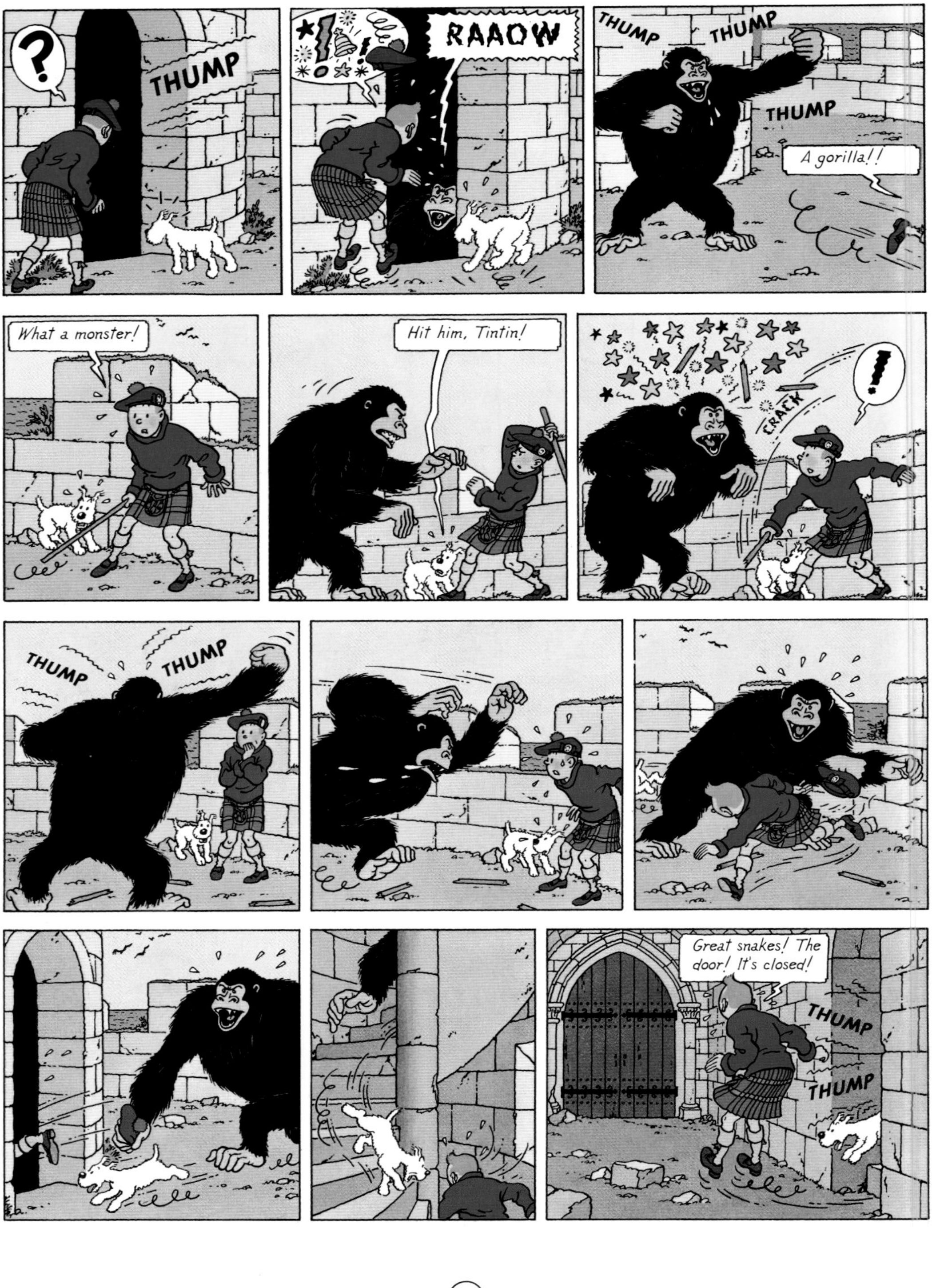
?
THUMP
RAAOW
THUMP
THUMP
THUMP
A gorilla!!
What a monster!
Hit him, Tintin!
!
CRACK
THUMP
THUMP
Great snakes! The door! It's closed!
THUMP
THUMP

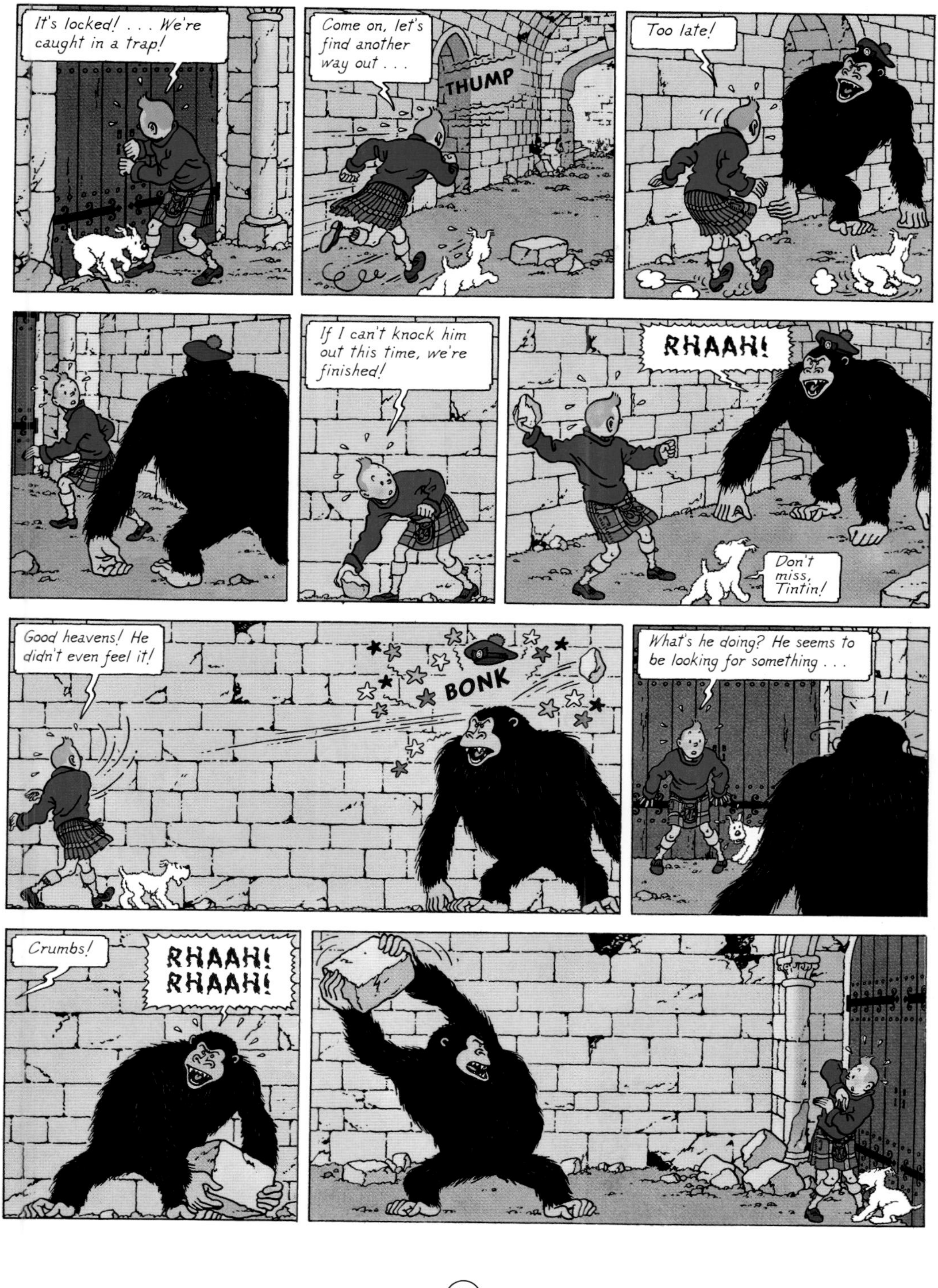
It's locked! . . . We're caught in a trap!
Come on, let's find another way out . . .
THUMP
Too late!
If I can't knock him out this time, we're finished!
RHAAH!
Don't miss, Tintin!
Good heavens! He didn't even feel it!
BONK
What's he doing? He seems to be looking for something . . .
Crumbs!
RHAAH! RHAAH!

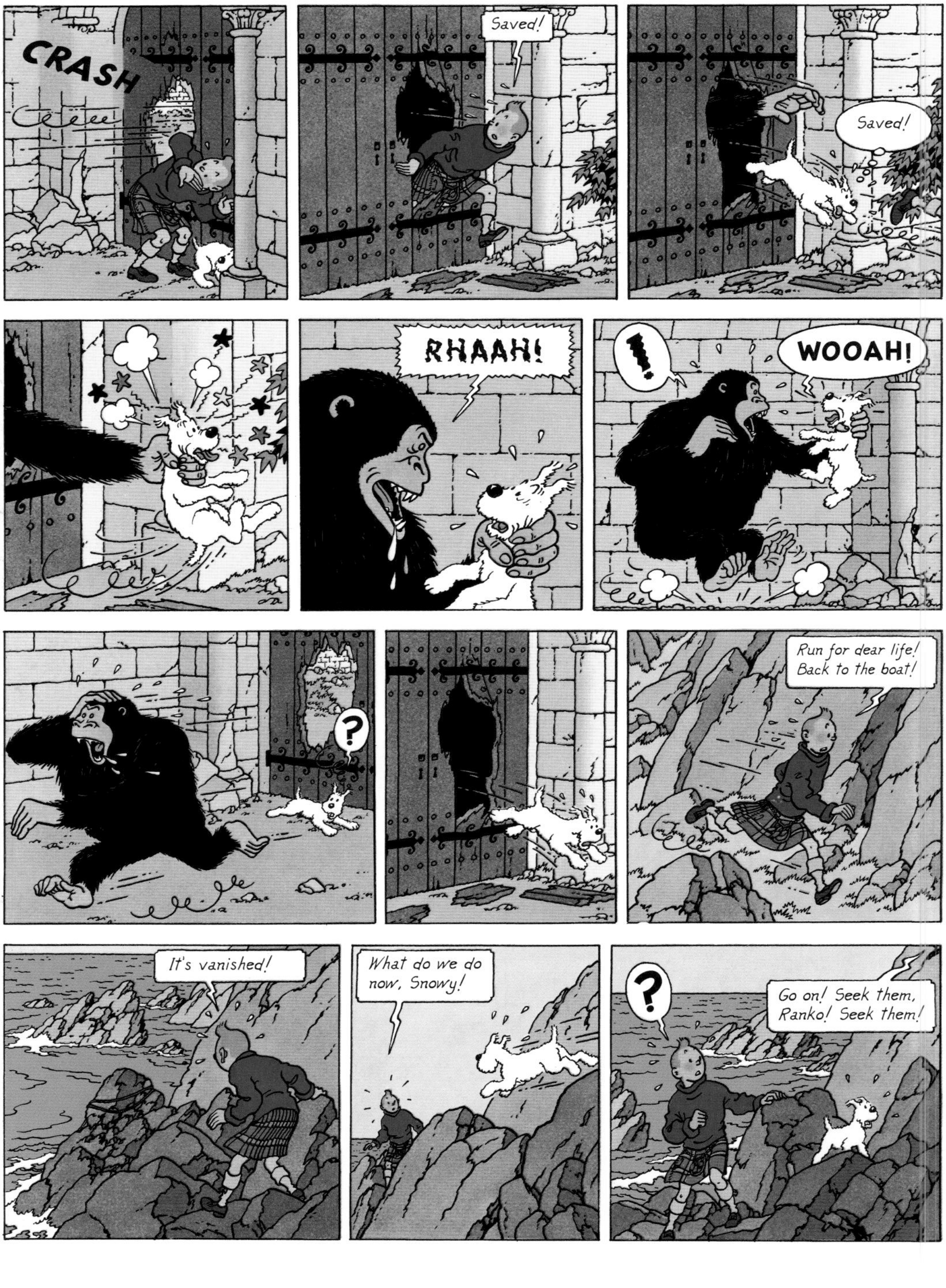
CRASH
Saved!
Saved!
RHAAH!
!
WOOAH!
?
Run for dear life! Back to the boat!
It's vanished!
What do we do now, Snowy!
?
Go on! Seek them, Ranko! Seek them!

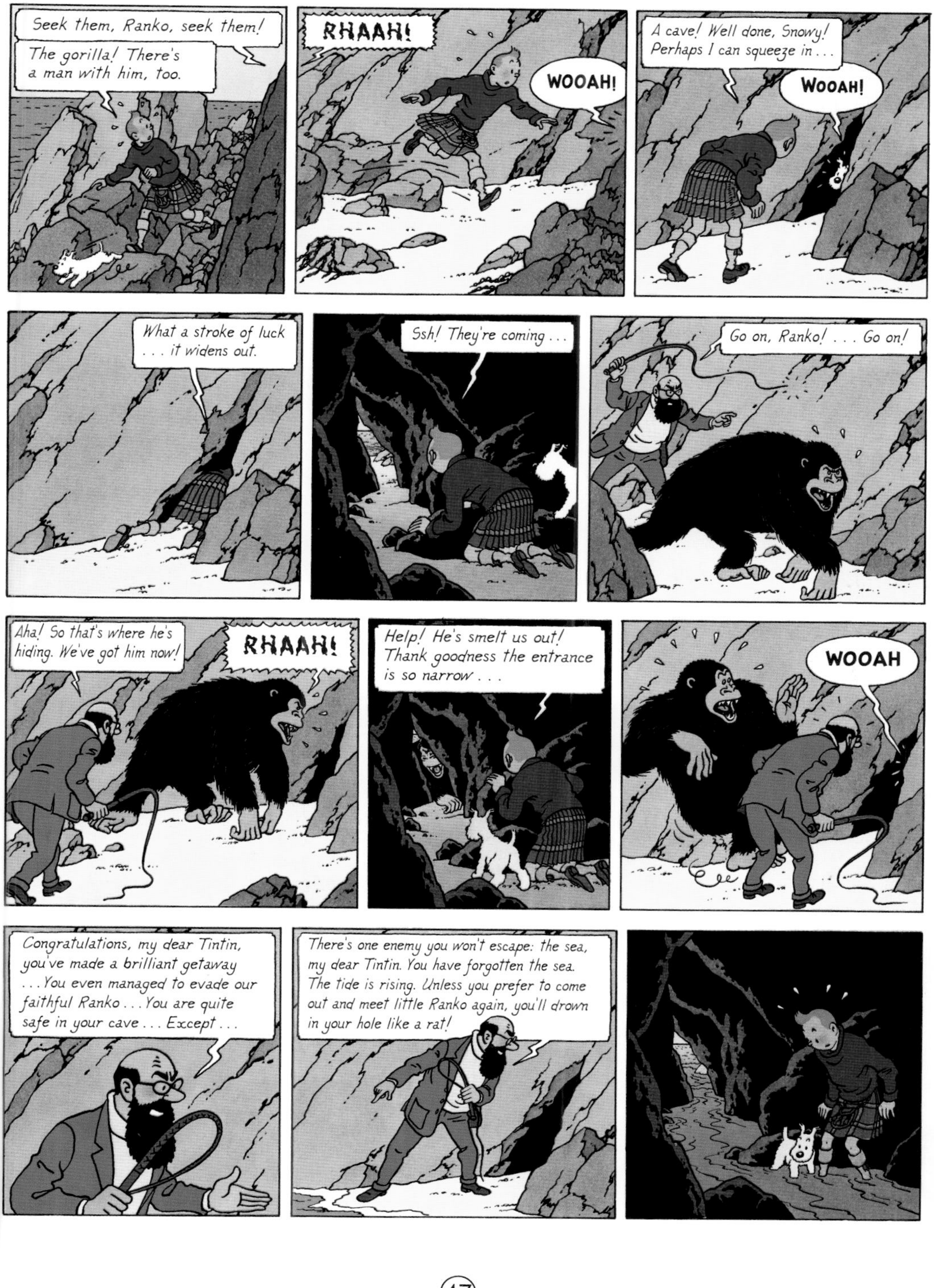

Seek them, Ranko, seek them!
The gorilla! There's a man with him, too.
RHAAH!
WOOAH!
A cave! Well done, Snowy! Perhaps I can squeeze in . . .
WOOAH!
What a stroke of luck . . . it widens out.
Ssh! They're coming . . .
Go on, Ranko! . . . Go on!
Aha! So that's where he's hiding. We've got him now!
RHAAH!
Help! He's smelt us out! Thank goodness the entrance is so narrow . . .
WOOAH
Congratulations, my dear Tintin, you've made a brilliant getaway . . . You even managed to evade our faithful Ranko . . . You are quite safe in your cave . . . Except . . .
There's one enemy you won't escape: the sea, my dear Tintin. You have forgotten the sea. The tide is rising. Unless you prefer to come out and meet little Ranko again, you'll drown in your hole like a rat!

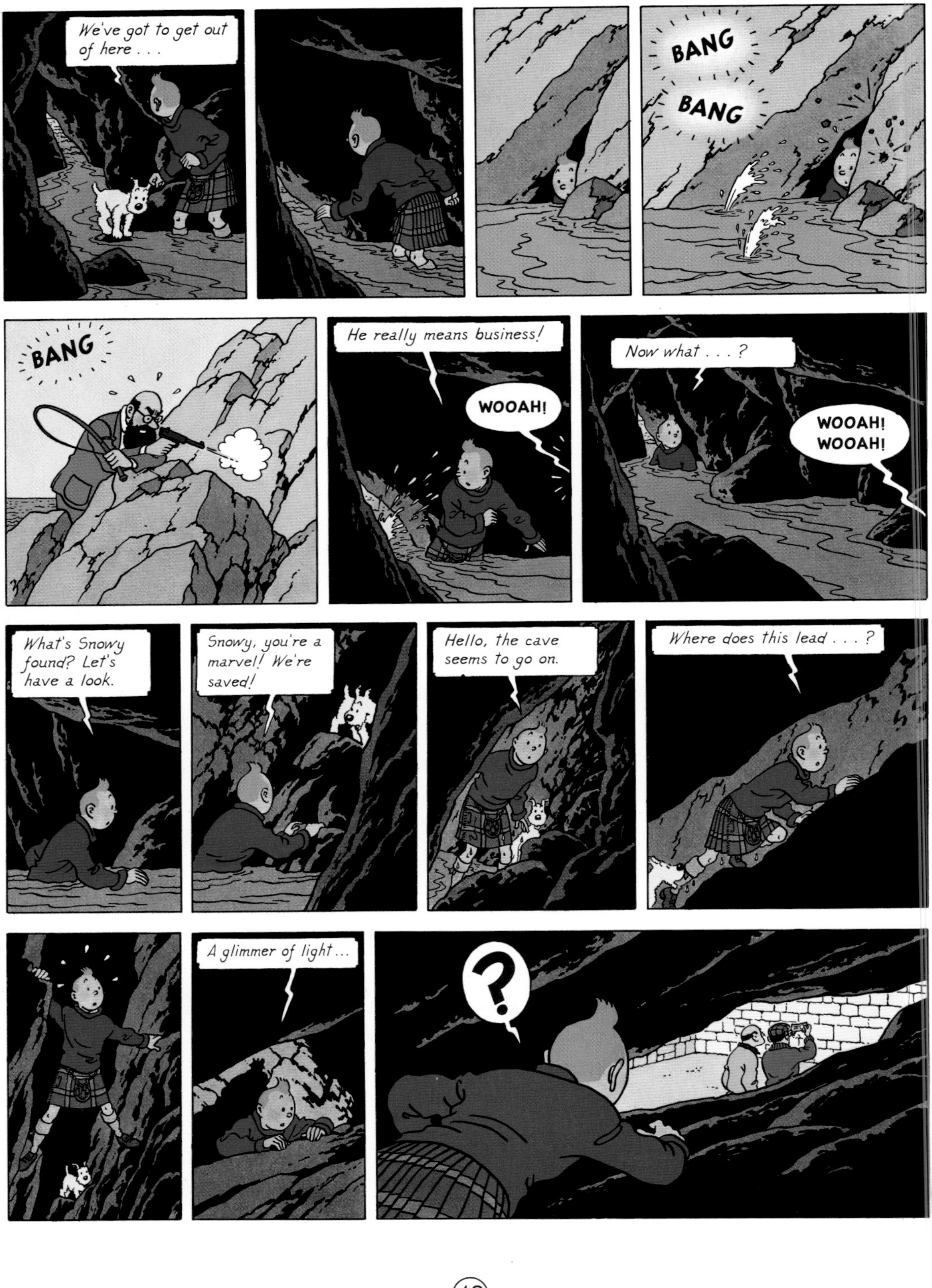
We've got to get out of here . . .
BANG
BANG
BANG
He really means business!
WOOAH!
Now what . . . ?
WOOAH! WOOAH!
What's Snowy found? Let's have a look.
Snowy, you're a marvel! We're saved!
Hello, the cave seems to go on.
Where does this lead . . . ?
A glimmer of light . . .
?

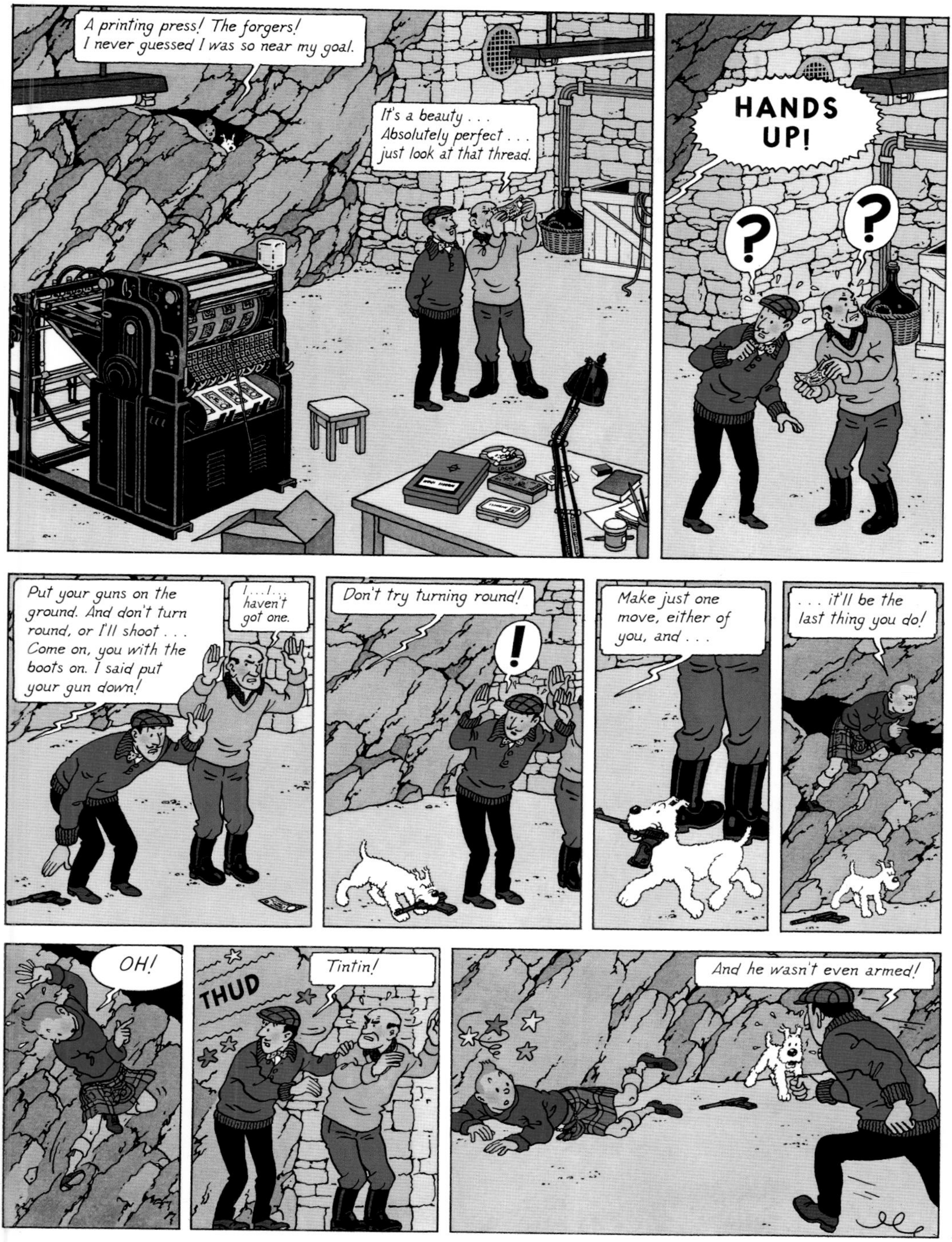
A printing press! The forgers! I never guessed I was so near my goal.
It's a beauty . . . Absolutely perfect . . . just look at that thread.
HANDS UP!
?
?
Put your guns on the ground. And don't turn round, or I'll shoot . . . Come on, you with the boots on. I said put your gun down!
I . . . I . . . haven't got one.
Don't try turning round!
!
Make just one move, either of you, and . . .
. . . it'll be the last thing you do!
OH!
THUD
Tintin!
And he wasn't even armed!

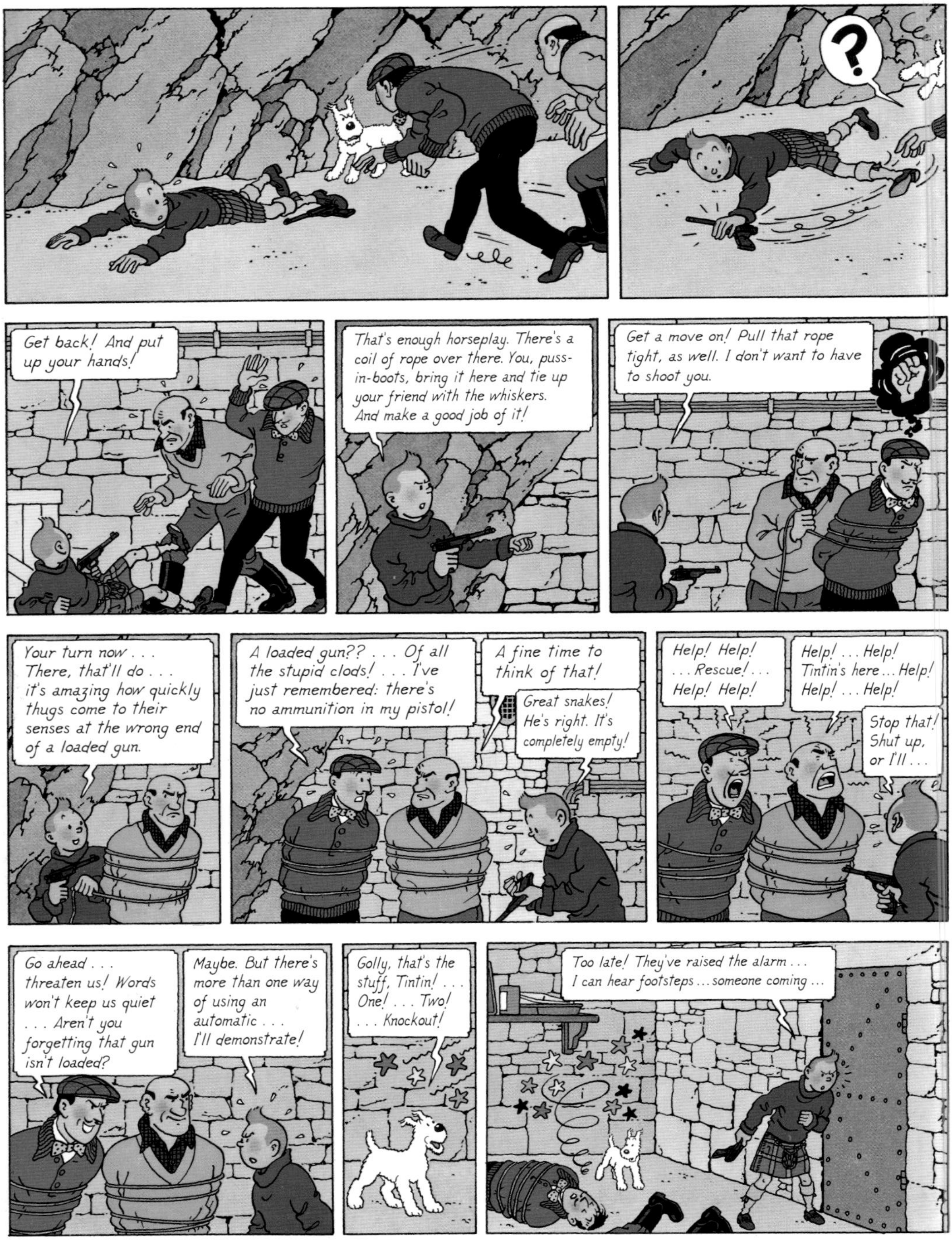
?
Get back! And put up your hands!
That's enough horseplay. There's a coil of rope over there. You, puss-in-boots, bring it here and tie up your friend with the whiskers. And make a good job of it!
Get a move on! Pull that rope tight, as well. I don't want to have to shoot you.
Your turn now . . . There, that'll do . . . it's amazing how quickly thugs come to their senses at the wrong end of a loaded gun.
A loaded gun?? . . . Of all the stupid clods! . . . I've just remembered: there's no ammunition in my pistol!
A fine time to think of that!
Great snakes! He's right. It's completely empty!
Help! Help! . . . Rescue! . . . Help! Help!
Help! . . . Help! Tintin's here . . . Help! Help! . . . Help!
Stop that! Shut up, or I'll . . .
Go ahead . . . threaten us! Words won't keep us quiet . . . Aren't you forgetting that gun isn't loaded?
Maybe. But there's more than one way of using an automatic . . . I'll demonstrate!
Golly, that's the stuff, Tintin! . . . One! . . . Two! . . . Knockout!
Too late! They've raised the alarm . . . I can hear footsteps . . . someone coming . . .

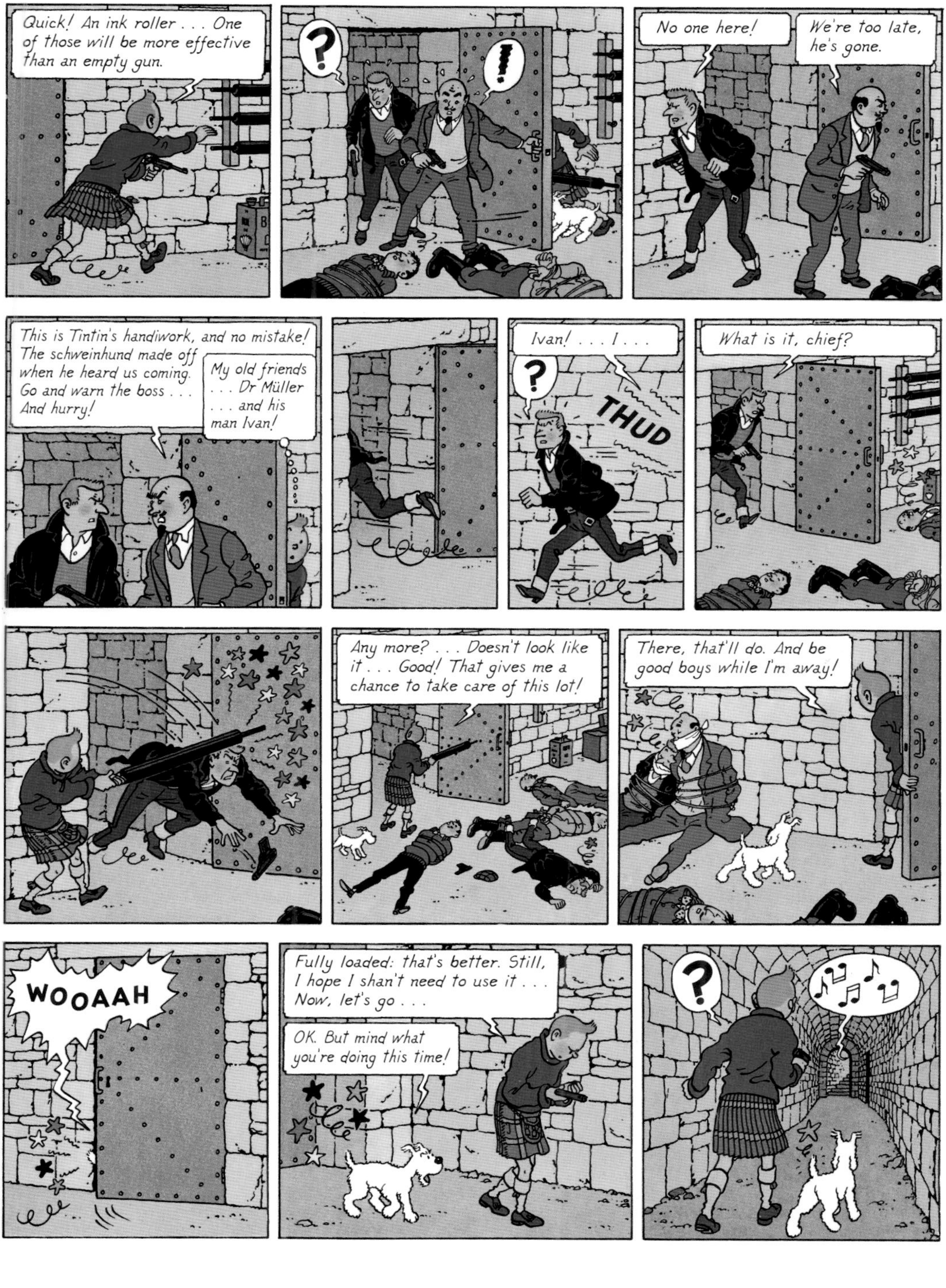

Quick! An ink roller . . . One of those will be more effective than an empty gun.
?
!
No one here!
We're too late, he's gone.
This is Tintin's handiwork, and no mistake! The schweinhund made off when he heard us coming. Go and warn the boss . . . And hurry!
My old friends . . . Dr Müller . . . and his man Ivan!
Ivan! . . . I . . .
?
THUD
What is it, chief?
Any more? . . . Doesn't look like it . . . Good! That gives me a chance to take care of this lot!
There, that'll do. And be good boys while I'm away!
WOOAAH
Fully loaded: that's better. Still, I hope I shan't need to use it . . . Now, let's go . . .
OK. But mind what you're doing this time!
?

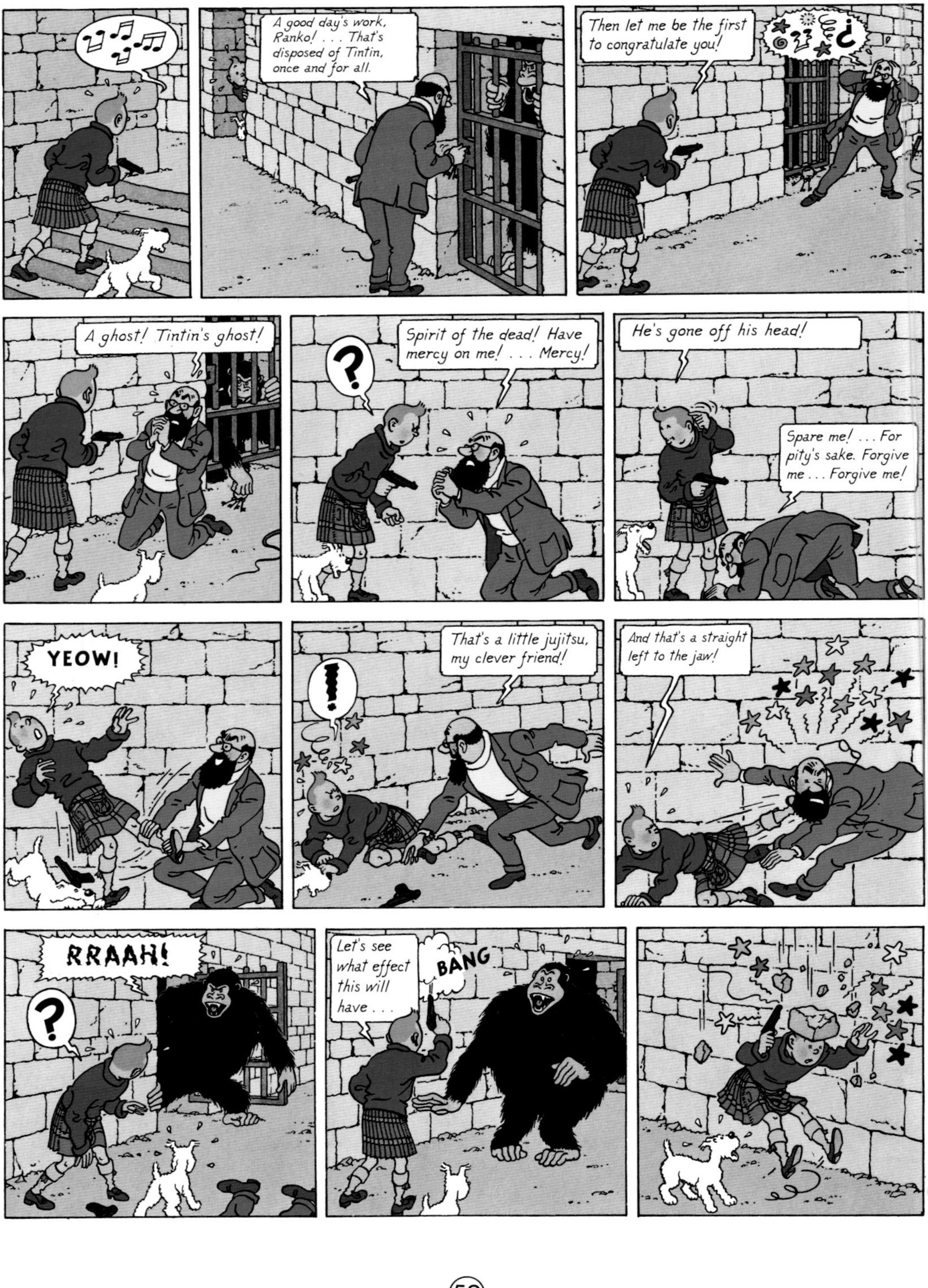

A good day's work, Ranko! . . . That's disposed of Tintin, once and for all.
Then let me be the first to congratulate you!
A ghost! Tintin's ghost!
Spirit of the dead! Have mercy on me! . . . Mercy!
He's gone off his head!
Spare me! . . . For pity's sake. Forgive me . . . Forgive me!
YEOW!
That's a little jujitsu, my clever friend!
And that's a straight left to the jaw!
RRAAH!
Let's see what effect this will have . . .
BANG

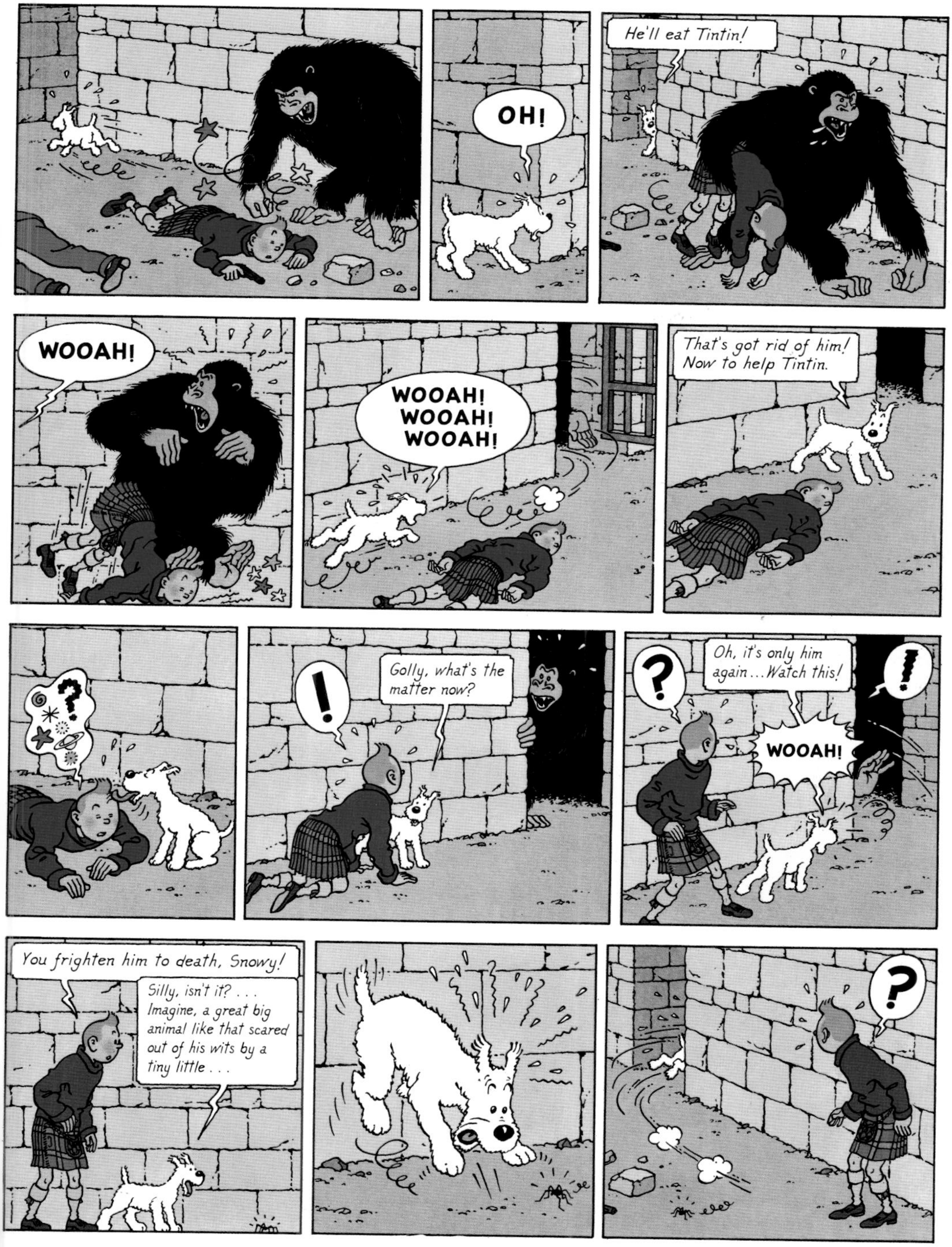
OH!
He'll eat Tintin!
WOOAH!
WOOAH! WOOAH! WOOAH!
That's got rid of him! Now to help Tintin.
Golly, what's the matter now?
Oh, it's only him again... Watch this!
WOOAH!
You frighten him to death, Snowy!
Silly, isn't it? . . . Imagine, a great big animal like that scared out of his wits by a tiny little . . .

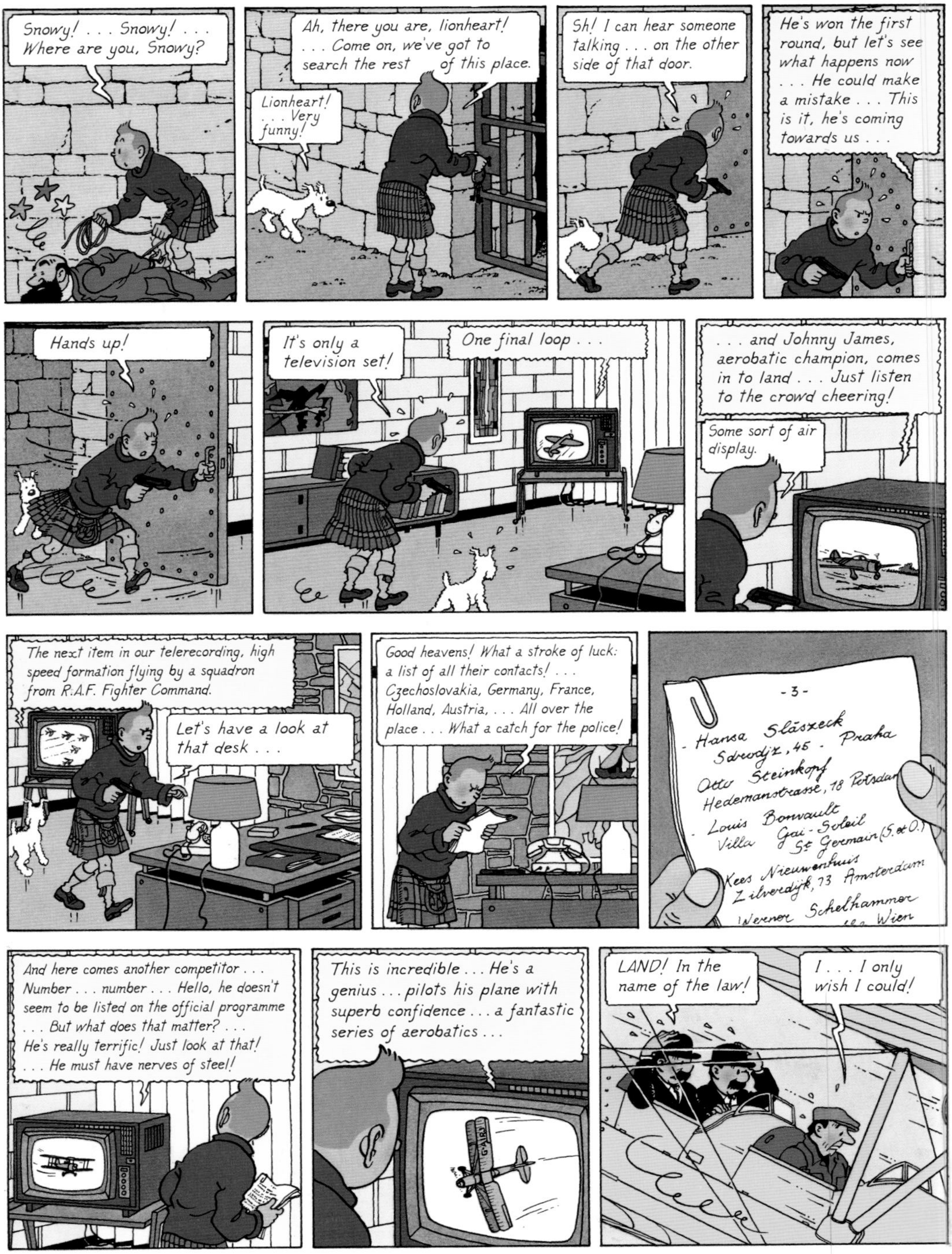
Snowy! . . . Snowy! . . . Where are you, Snowy?
Ah, there you are, lionheart! . . . Come on, we've got to search the rest of this place.
Lionheart! . . . Very funny!
Sh! I can hear someone talking . . . on the other side of that door.
He's won the first round, but let's see what happens now . . . He could make a mistake . . . This is it, he's coming towards us . . .
Hands up!
It's only a television set!
One final loop . . .
. . . and Johnny James, aerobatic champion, comes in to land . . . Just listen to the crowd cheering!
Some sort of air display.
The next item in our telerecording, high speed formation flying by a squadron from R.A.F. Fighter Command.
Let's have a look at that desk . . .
Good heavens! What a stroke of luck: a list of all their contacts! . . . Czechoslovakia, Germany, France, Holland, Austria, . . . All over the place . . . What a catch for the police!
-3-
Hansa Slászeck
Sdrodjz, 45 - Praha
Otto Steinkopf
Hedemanstrasse, 18 Potsdam
Louis Bonvault
Villa Gai-Soleil
St Germain (S. et O.)
Kees Nieuwenhuis
Zilverdijk, 73 Amsterdam
Werner Schelhammer
Wien
And here comes another competitor . . . Number . . . number . . . Hello, he doesn't seem to be listed on the official programme . . . But what does that matter? . . . He's really terrific! Just look at that! . . . He must have nerves of steel!
This is incredible . . . He's a genius . . . pilots his plane with superb confidence . . . a fantastic series of aerobatics . . .
LAND! In the name of the law!
I . . . I only wish I could!

Now the plane comes roaring down, skims over the field and shoots up like a rocket . . .

Stop! We want to get down, d'you hear?

Now he's heading for the ground again . . . and into another flawless loop he goes, then . . . Good heavens! One of the passengers has slipped out of his seat . . . This is terrible!

Whew! What a stunt! That really had us fooled!

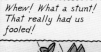

And this time he really is coming down . . . He's going to land . . . He's cut the motor . . .

He touches down . . . the plane bounces . . .

. . . and does one last, hair-raising somersault before it comes to rest in the centre of the field.

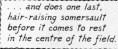

A clear victory! The judges are unanimous . . . the aerobatic championship is yours!

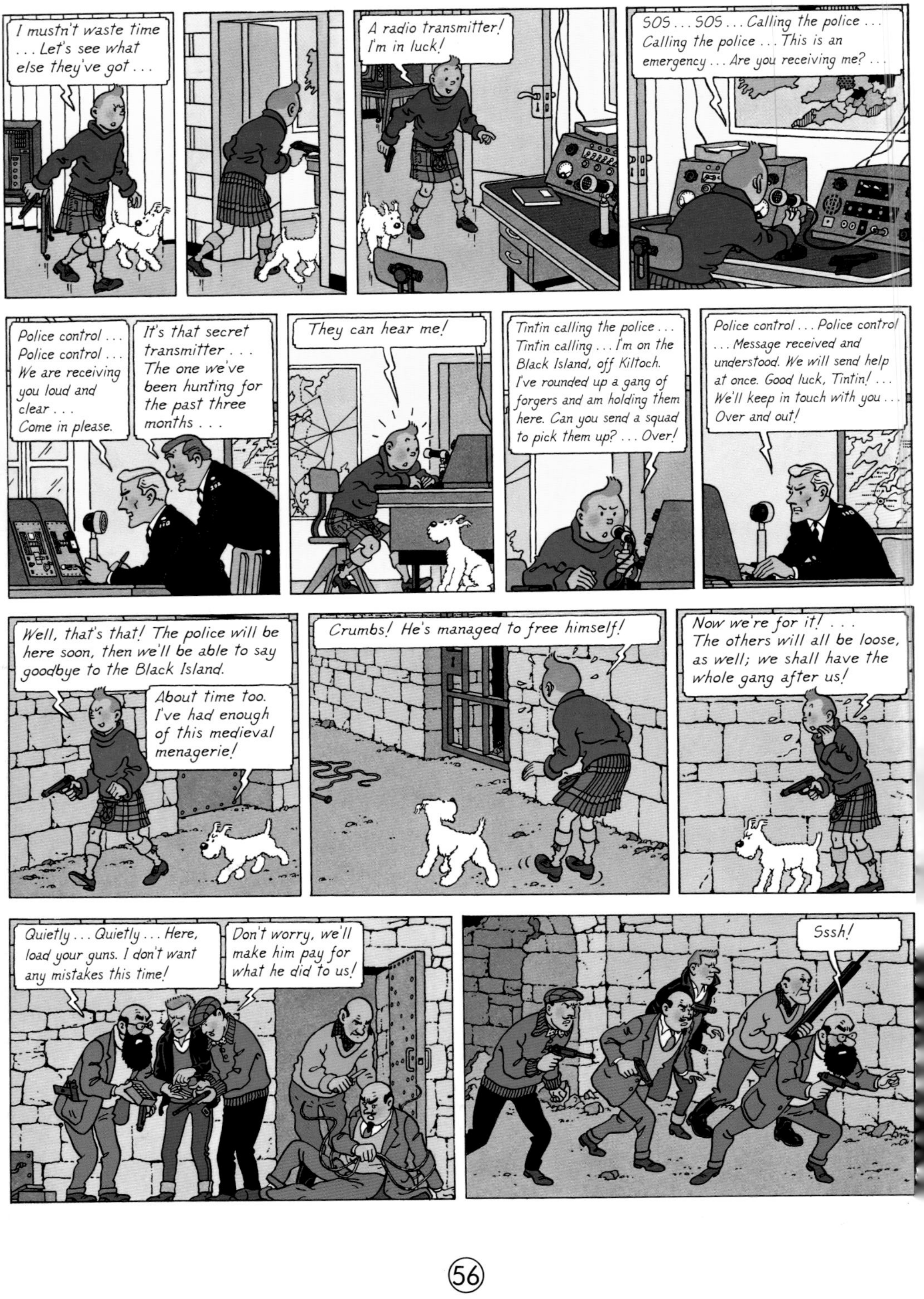
I mustn't waste time . . . Let's see what else they've got . . .
A radio transmitter! I'm in luck!
SOS . . . SOS . . . Calling the police . . . Calling the police . . . This is an emergency . . . Are you receiving me? . . .
Police control . . . Police control . . . We are receiving you loud and clear . . . Come in please.
It's that secret transmitter . . . The one we've been hunting for the past three months . . .
They can hear me!
Tintin calling the police . . . Tintin calling . . . I'm on the Black Island, off Kiltoch. I've rounded up a gang of forgers and am holding them here. Can you send a squad to pick them up? . . . Over!
Police control . . . Police control . . . Message received and understood. We will send help at once. Good luck, Tintin! . . . We'll keep in touch with you . . . Over and out!
Well, that's that! The police will be here soon, then we'll be able to say goodbye to the Black Island.
About time too. I've had enough of this medieval menagerie!
Crumbs! He's managed to free himself!
Now we're for it! . . . The others will all be loose, as well; we shall have the whole gang after us!
Quietly . . . Quietly . . . Here, load your guns. I don't want any mistakes this time!
Don't worry, we'll make him pay for what he did to us!
Sssh!

There!

You go round outside and cut off his retreat.

ZZZING

Got you!

Trapped!

BANG

BANG

He's taken refuge in the tower.

Excellent! We've got him cornered!

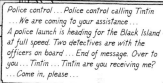

Police control...Police control calling Tintin...We are coming to your assistance...A police launch is heading for the Black Island at full speed. Two detectives are with the officers on board...End of message. Over to you...Tintin...Tintin are you receiving me? ...Come in, please...

Crumbs! No more ammunition! ...I'm done for!

Come on! His gun's empty. Bring him down!

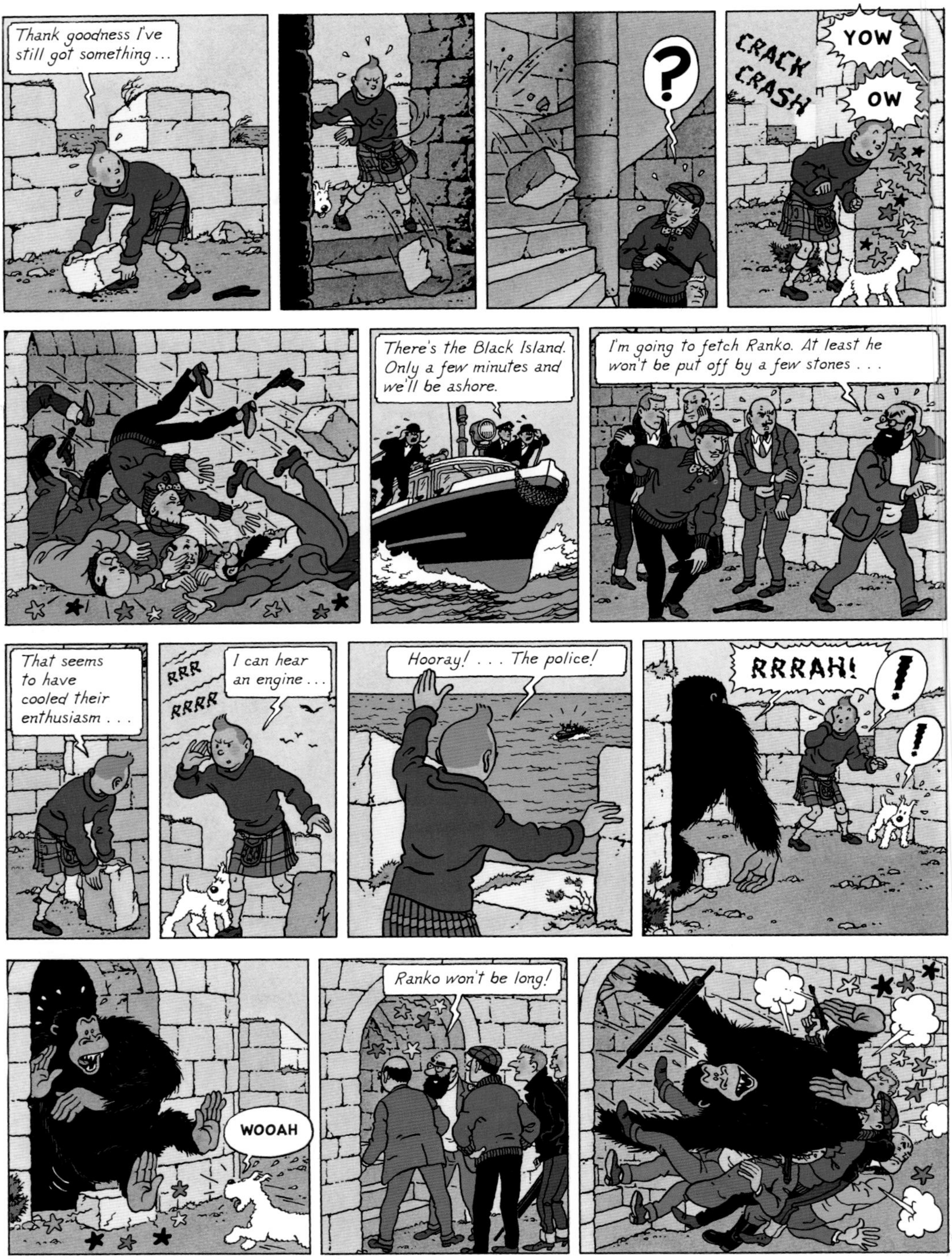
Thank goodness I've still got something ...
?
CRACK
CRASH
YOW
OW
There's the Black Island. Only a few minutes and we'll be ashore.
I'm going to fetch Ranko. At least he won't be put off by a few stones . . .
That seems to have cooled their enthusiasm . . .
RRR
RRRR
I can hear an engine . . .
Hooray! . . . The police!
RRRAH!
!
!
WOOAH
Ranko won't be long!

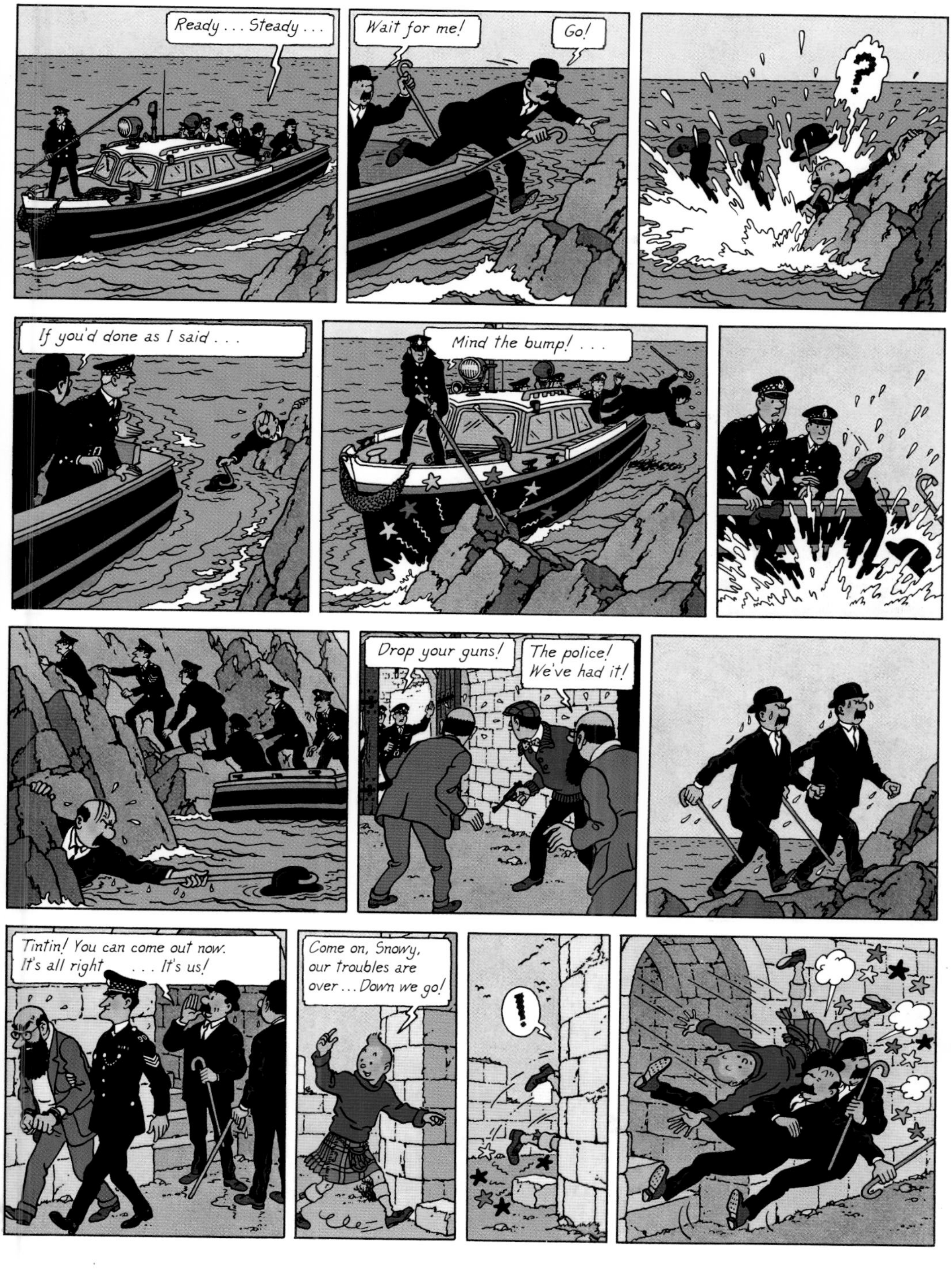

Ready . . . Steady . . .
Wait for me!
Go!
?
If you'd done as I said . . .
Mind the bump! . . .
Drop your guns!
The police! We've had it!
Tintin! You can come out now. It's all right . . . It's us!
Come on, Snowy, our troubles are over . . . Down we go!
!

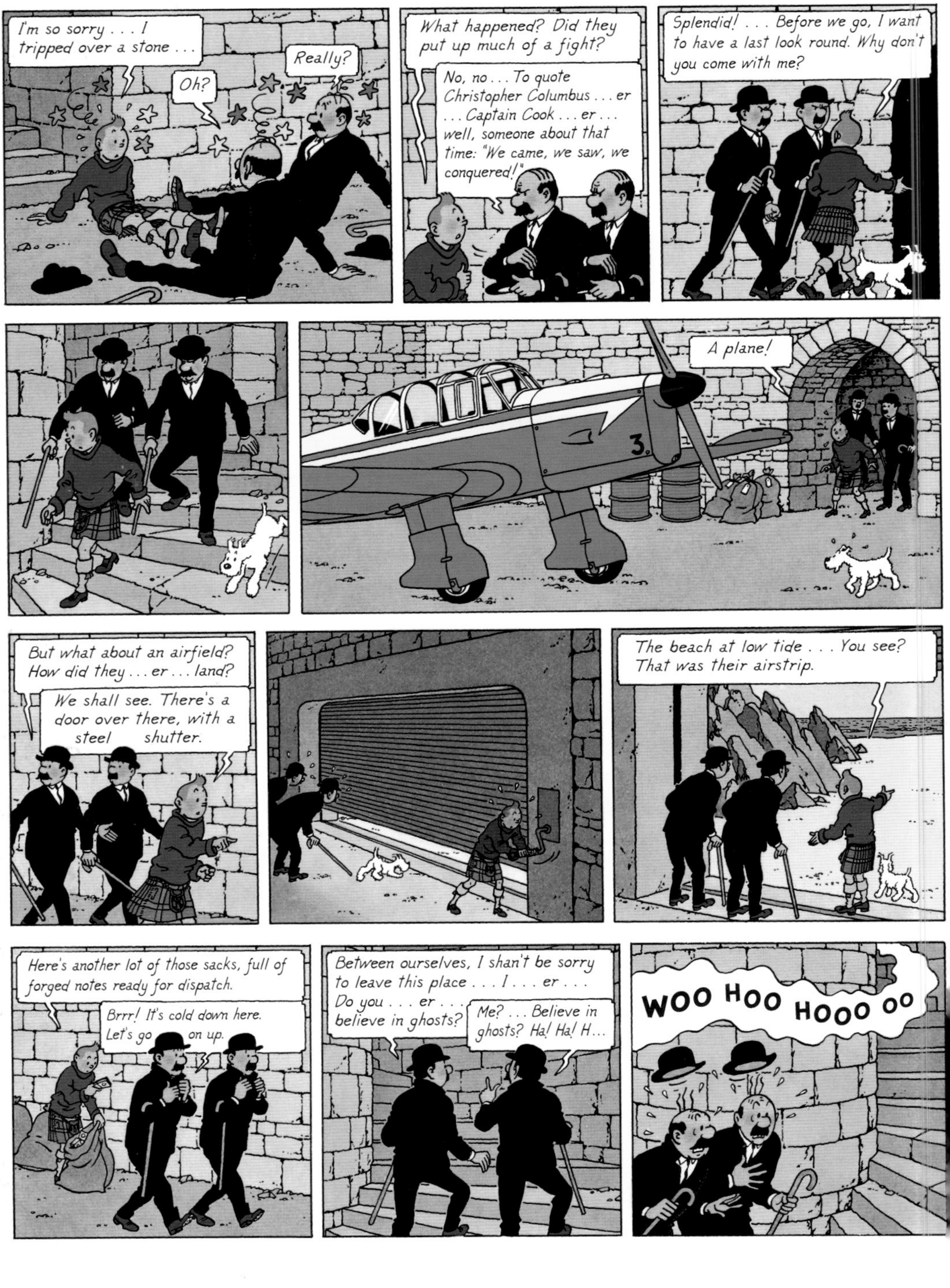

I'm so sorry . . . I tripped over a stone . . .
Oh?
Really?
What happened? Did they put up much of a fight?
No, no . . . To quote Christopher Columbus . . . er . . . Captain Cook . . . er . . . well, someone about that time: "We came, we saw, we conquered!"
Splendid! . . . Before we go, I want to have a last look round. Why don't you come with me?
A plane!
But what about an airfield? How did they . . . er . . . land?
We shall see. There's a door over there, with a steel shutter.
The beach at low tide . . . You see? That was their airstrip.
Here's another lot of those sacks, full of forged notes ready for dispatch.
Brrr! It's cold down here. Let's go on up.
Between ourselves, I shan't be sorry to leave this place . . . I . . . er . . . Do you . . . er . . . believe in ghosts?
Me? . . . Believe in ghosts? Ha! Ha! H . . .
WOO HOO HOOO OO

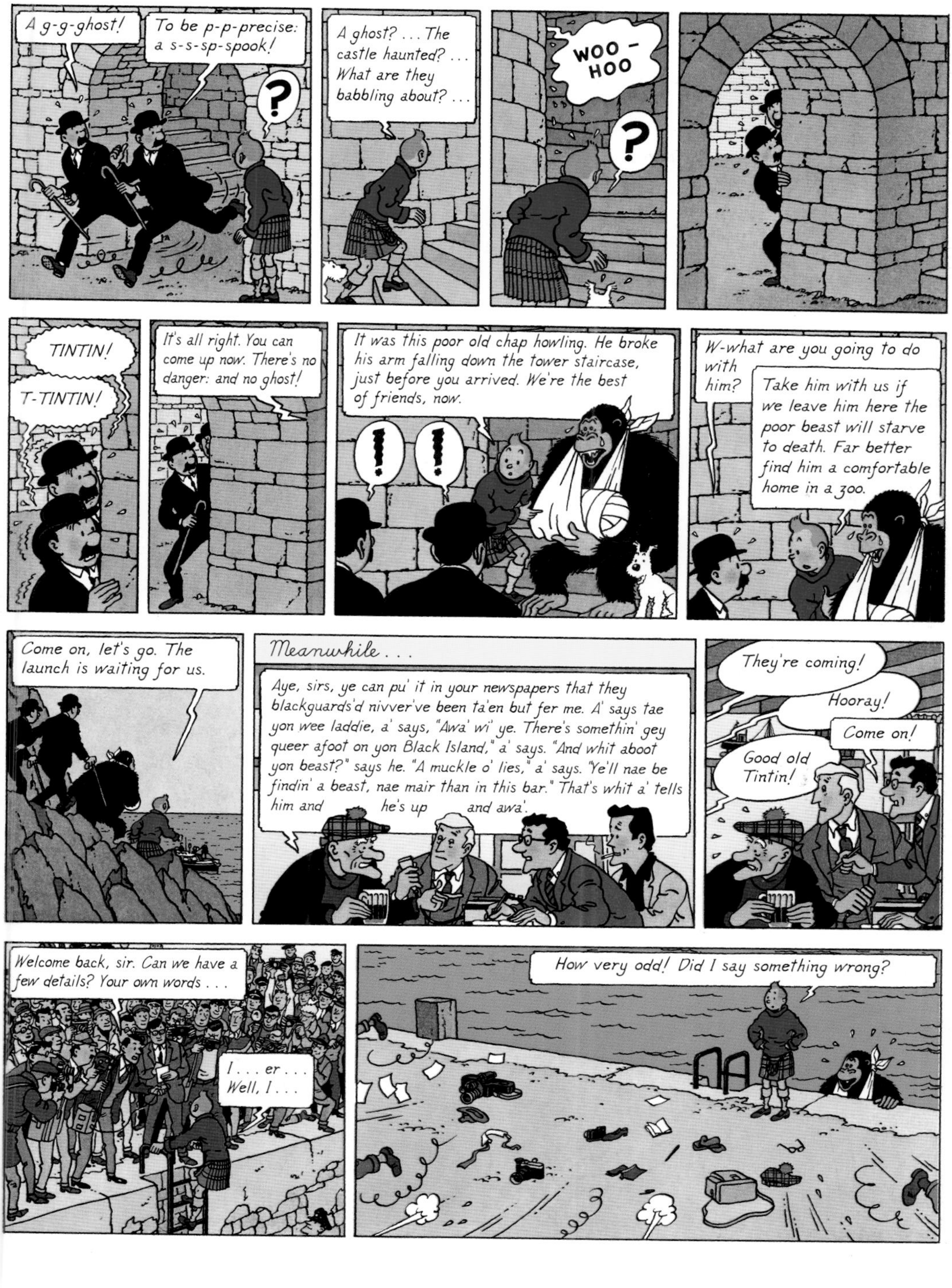
A g-g-ghost!
To be p-p-precise: a s-s-sp-spook!
?
A ghost? . . . The castle haunted? . . . What are they babbling about? . . .
WOO – HOO
?
TINTIN!
T-TINTIN!
It's all right. You can come up now. There's no danger: and no ghost!
It was this poor old chap howling. He broke his arm falling down the tower staircase, just before you arrived. We're the best of friends, now.
!
!
W-what are you going to do with him?
Take him with us if we leave him here the poor beast will starve to death. Far better find him a comfortable home in a zoo.
Come on, let's go. The launch is waiting for us.
Meanwhile . . .
Aye, sirs, ye can pu' it in your newspapers that they blackguards'd nivver've been ta'en but fer me. A' says tae yon wee laddie, a' says, "Awa' wi' ye. There's somethin' gey queer afoot on yon Black Island," a' says. "And whit aboot yon beast?" says he. "A muckle o' lies," a' says. "Ye'll nae be findin' a beast, nae mair than in this bar." That's whit a' tells him and he's up and awa'.
They're coming!
Hooray!
Come on!
Good old Tintin!
Welcome back, sir. Can we have a few details? Your own words . . .
I . . . er . . . Well, I . . .
How very odd! Did I say something wrong?

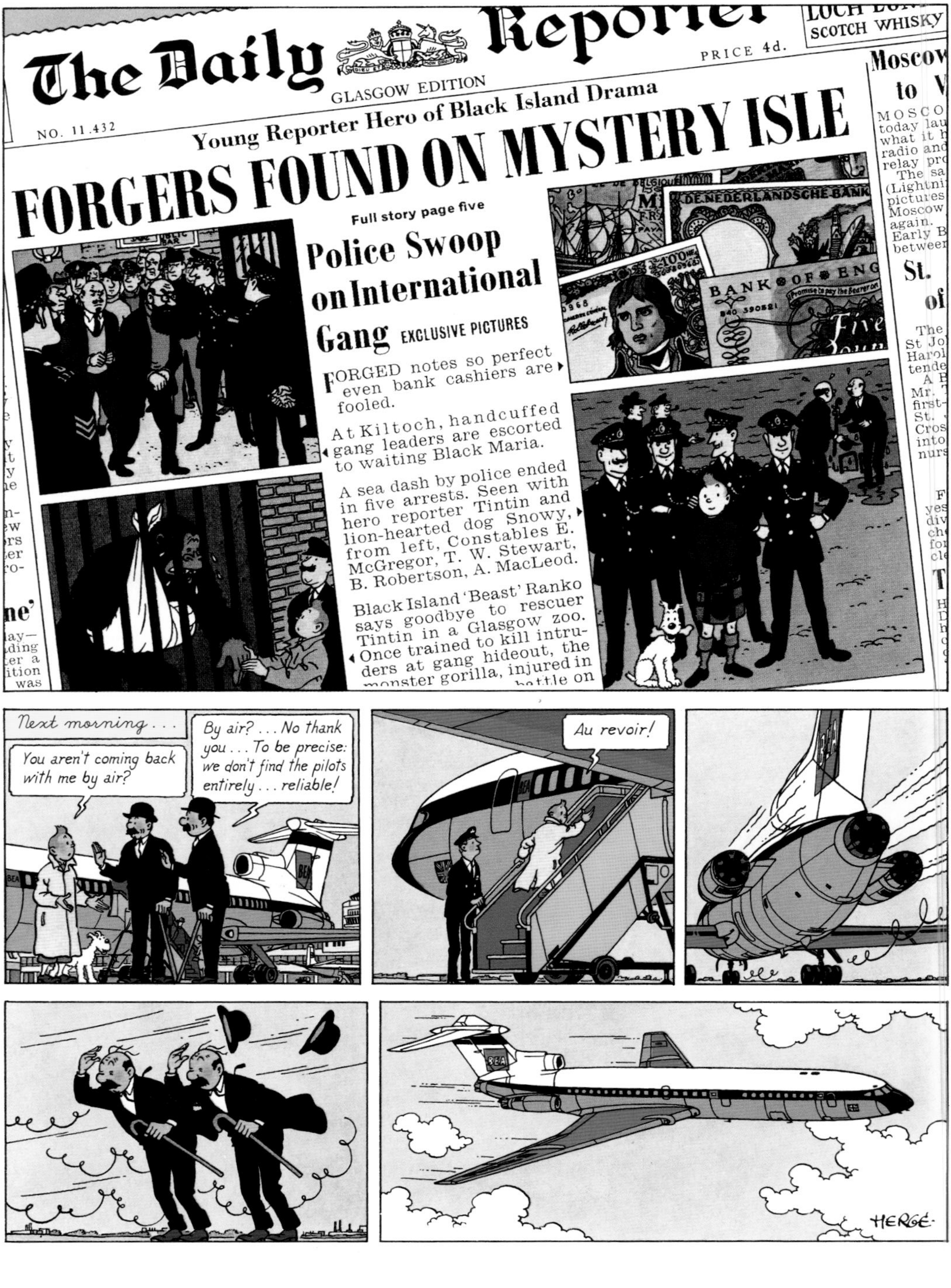
The Daily Reporter
PRICE 4d.
LOCH LOMOND
SCOTCH WHISKY
GLASGOW EDITION
NO. 11.432
Young Reporter Hero of Black Island Drama
FORGERS FOUND ON MYSTERY ISLE
Full story page five
Police Swoop on International Gang
EXCLUSIVE PICTURES
FORGED notes so perfect even bank cashiers are fooled.
At Kiltoch, handcuffed gang leaders are escorted to waiting Black Maria.
A sea dash by police ended in five arrests. Seen with hero reporter Tintin and lion-hearted dog Snowy, from left, Constables E. McGregor, T. W. Stewart, B. Robertson, A. MacLeod.
Black Island 'Beast' Ranko says goodbye to rescuer Tintin in a Glasgow zoo. Once trained to kill intruders at gang hideout, the monster gorilla, injured in battle on
Moscow
St.
BANK OF ENG
DE NEDERLANDSCHE BANK
Next morning . . .
You aren't coming back with me by air?
By air? . . . No thank you . . . To be precise: we don't find the pilots entirely . . . reliable!
Au revoir!
BEA
HERGÉ

THE REAL-LIFE INSPIRATION
BEHIND
TINTIN'S ADVENTURES

Written by Stuart Tett
with the collaboration of Studio Moulinsart.

GEORGES REMI BORN IN BELGIUM	CHOOSES PEN-NAME "HERGÉ"—HIS INITIALS "G.R." REVERSED	HERGÉ LEAVES SCHOOL	HERGÉ HELPS TO CREATE CHILDREN'S MAGAZINE *LE PETIT VINGTIÈME*	TINTIN'S FIRST ADVENTURE, *TINTIN IN THE LAND OF THE SOVIETS*, APPEARS IN *LE PETIT VINGTIÈME*
1907	**1924**	**1925**	**1928**	**1929**

HERGÉ

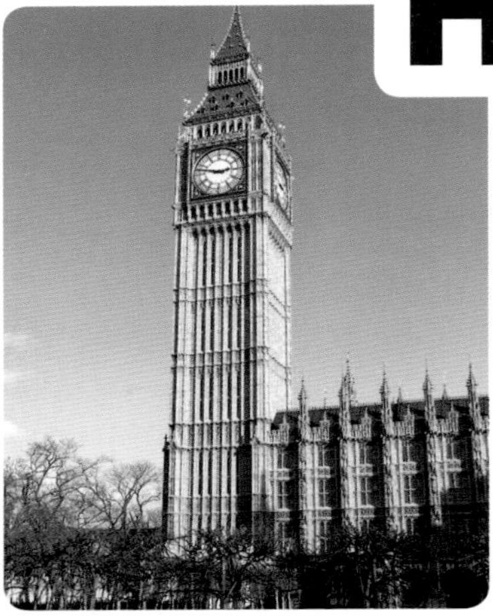

In England

Hergé loved England and said that when visiting London, he felt more at home than he did when visiting Paris.

The photo below shows Hergé with Michael Turner and Leslie Lonsdale-Cooper, the two British translators who began translating Tintin into English for the British publisher Methuen in 1956 (the first Methuen Tintin books were published in 1958). In an interview in 2009, when asked why they chose to work on the English versions of Tintin, Leslie Lonsdale-Cooper said, "We did it because it was fun!"

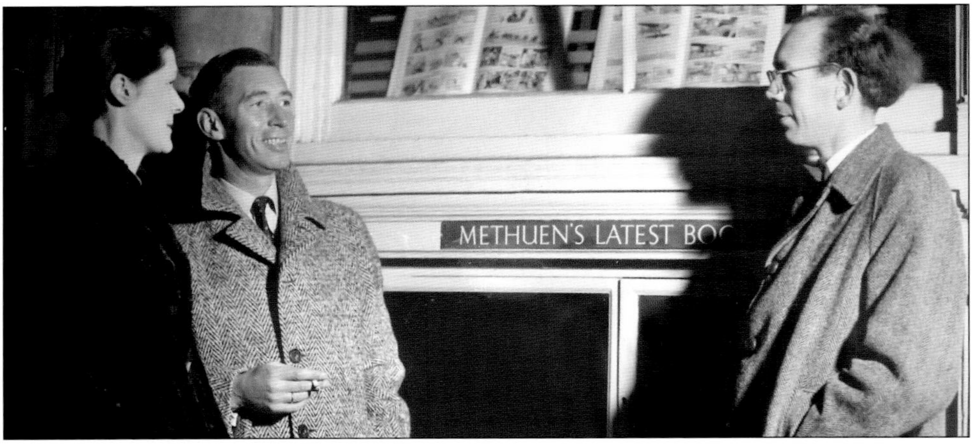
METHUEN'S LATEST BO

1938	1946	1971	1976	1983
PUBLICATION OF *THE BLACK ISLAND*	LAUNCH OF *TINTIN* MAGAZINE	HERGÉ VISITS AMERICA	PUBLICATION OF TINTIN'S LAST ADVENTURE, *TINTIN AND THE PICAROS*	HERGÉ DIES AGED 75

about Tintin and his creator Hergé!

TINTIN

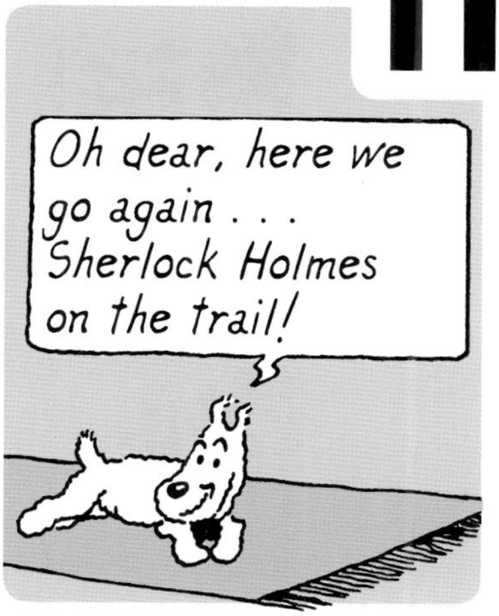
Oh dear, here we go again . . . Sherlock Holmes on the trail!

Detective

As he goes from adventure to adventure, Tintin's job seems to change. He goes from being a reporter to an explorer and, in the case of *The Black Island*, a detective.

Tintin has all the right qualities for detective work: an inquisitive nature, a sharp mind and plenty of determination. In some of the Tintin stories, Snowy even refers to his master as "Sherlock Holmes"!

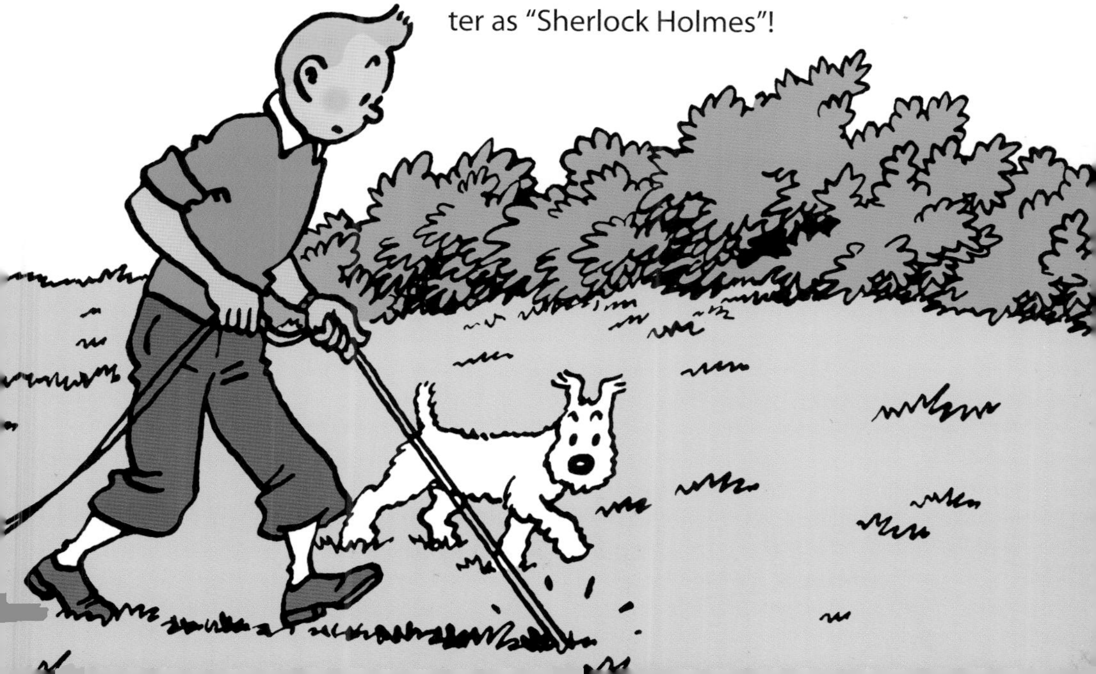

THE TRUE STORY
...behind *The Black Island*

The Black Island is an unusual Tintin adventure because it is the only story for which three different versions were published. The original 124-page black-and-white edition was published in 1938, and the second version was published in 1943 when Hergé was revising the first Tintin books by adding color and reformatting them to fit into 62 pages.

When Methuen began publishing the Tintin books in English, they were worried that the depiction of Britain in *The Black Island* was out of date. So in 1961 the publisher sent Hergé a list of 131 necessary modifications. This led to the creation of the third version (which you have just read), published in 1966. How was this third version created?

les aventures de
TINTIN
reporter
L'ÎLE NOIRE
CASTERMAN - PARIS - TOURNAI

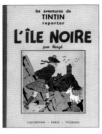

The original front cover, 1938

HERGÉ
LES AVENTURES DE TINTIN
L'ÎLE NOIRE

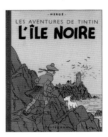

Cover for the second version, 1943

HERGÉ
LES AVENTURES DE TINTIN
L'ILE NOIRE

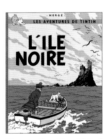

Cover for the third version, 1966

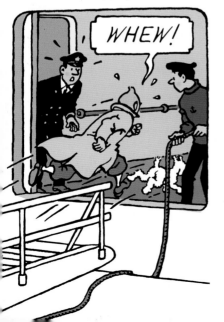

WHEW!

Once upon a time...

Tintin leaps on board the ferry to England, off on a new adventure! In 1961, Hergé thought hard about how to redraw the story to show a modern Britain that British readers would recognize. He decided to send his assistant—a cartoonist named Bob De Moor—on his own adventure to Great Britain. De Moor's mission was to sketch and photograph all kinds of British scenery. On October 22, 1961, Bob De Moor caught the ferry to England, just like Tintin!

Bob De Moor

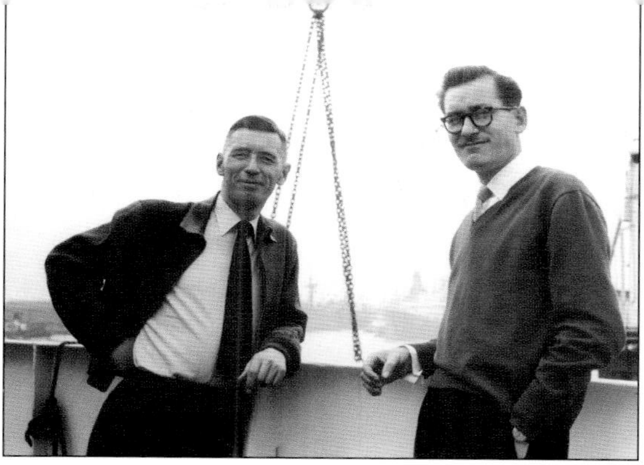

Robert Frans Marie De Moor (pen name Bob De Moor) was a Belgian comic strip artist who lived from 1925 to 1992. Bob De Moor was born in the Belgian port of Antwerp, and when he was growing up he liked to draw ships. In 1950, when Hergé set up a team of assistants called Studios Hergé, Bob De Moor joined the team and quickly became Hergé's right-hand man. De Moor was able to draw fast and imitate his boss's style so well that he was given the job of drawing furniture, vehicles, and all kinds of scenery in the Tintin stories.

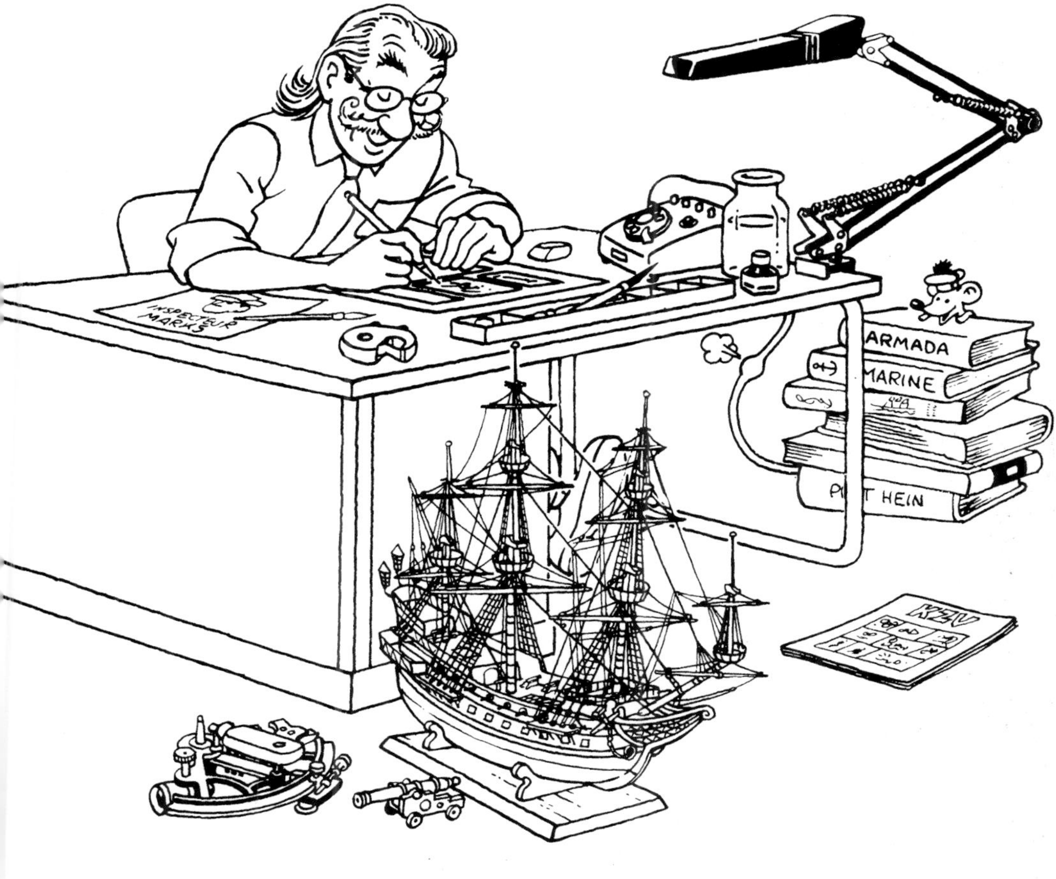
INSPECTEUR MARKS
ARMADA
MARINE
HEIN
BOB DE MOOR.

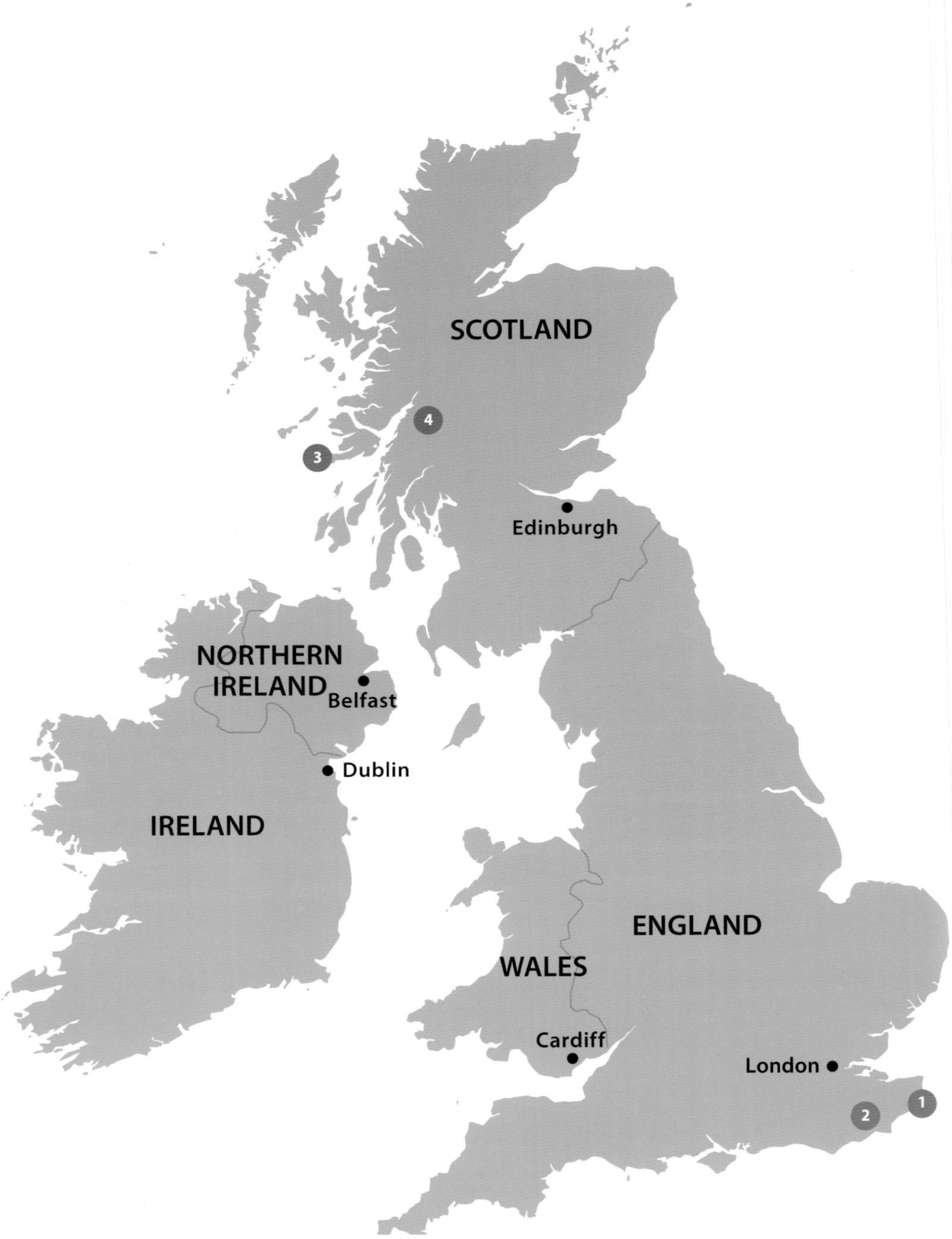
SCOTLAND
4
3
Edinburgh
NORTHERN
IRELAND
Belfast
Dublin
IRELAND
ENGLAND
WALES
Cardiff
London
1
2

Following in Tintin's footsteps

Bob De Moor traveled Great Britain for a week, looking for scenery from the regions Tintin visits in *The Black Island*. The map on the left indicates (in blue) the locations of the places in some of the photographs (shown on this page) that De Moor brought home to Belgium. Check out the postcard that he sent back when he first arrived!

1

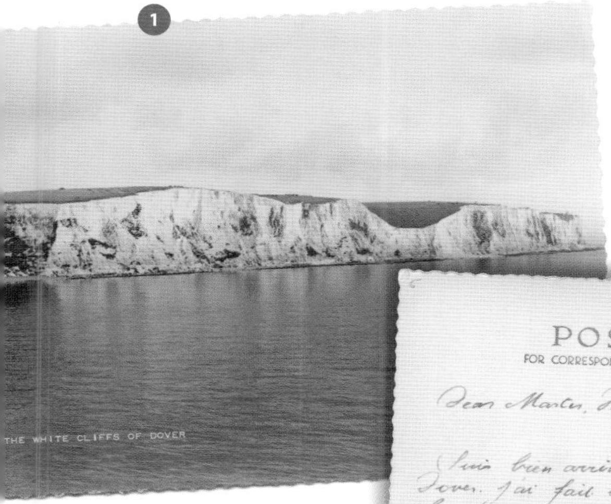

THE WHITE CLIFFS OF DOVER

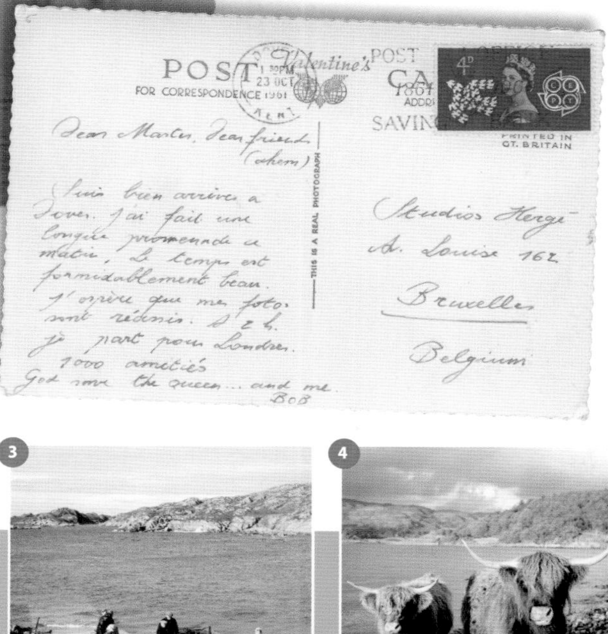

POST CARD
FOR CORRESPONDENCE
Valentine's
THIS IS A REAL PHOTOGRAPH
PRINTED IN GT. BRITAIN
Dear Master, Dear friend (ahem)
Suis bien arrivé à Dover. J'ai fait une longue promenade ce matin. Le temps est formidablement beau. J'espère que mes fotos sont réussis. À 2 h. je part pour Londres.
1000 amitiés
God save the queen... and me.
BOB
Studios Hergé
Av. Louise 162
Bruxelles
Belgium

Postcard sent to Brussels showing the white cliffs of Dover, England, where De Moor arrived from Belgium.

2

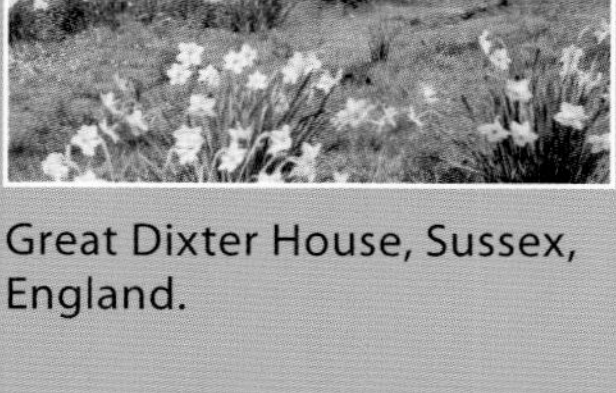

Great Dixter House, Sussex, England.

3

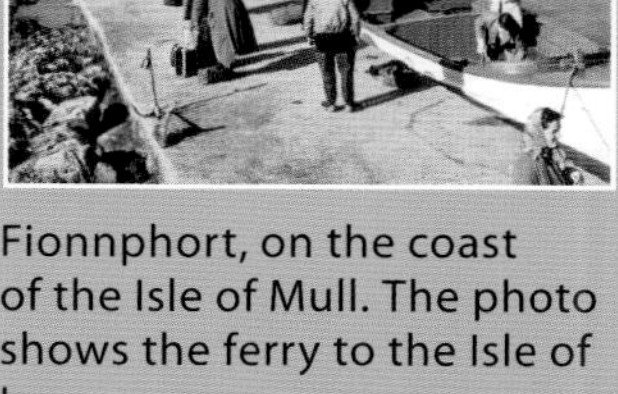

Fionnphort, on the coast of the Isle of Mull. The photo shows the ferry to the Isle of Iona.

4

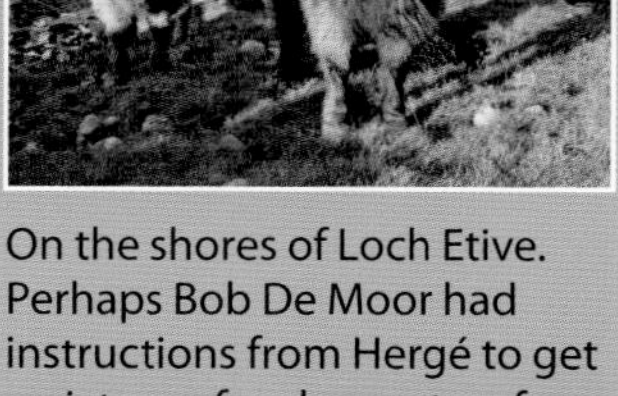

On the shores of Loch Etive. Perhaps Bob De Moor had instructions from Hergé to get a picture of real monsters from the Scottish Highlands!

A busy trip

Bob De Moor traveled from one end of Great Britain to the other, ending up in the Scottish Highlands, just like Tintin! Some funny things happened on the way. A policeman kindly gave him a complete police uniform to sketch, and the Sussex fire brigade even offered to send a fireman to meet De Moor. British Rail, the operator of Great Britain's rail services at the time, was less helpful: officials were so suspicious that they didn't even let him take photographs of their uniforms!

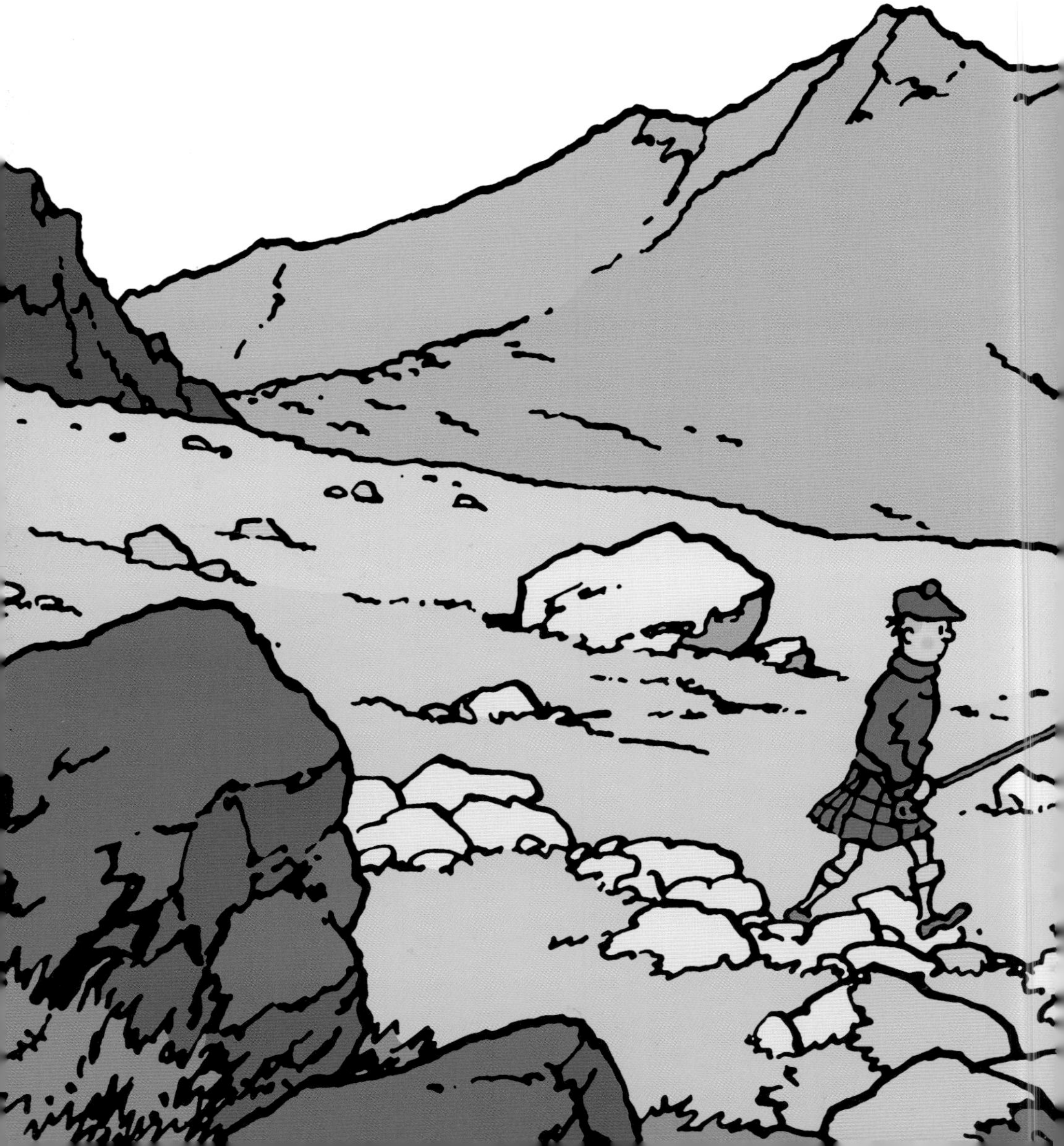

Back home

On October 30, 1961, Bob De Moor returned home to Belgium from his exciting adventure around Great Britain. His sketchbook was full and he brought back many postcards and dozens of photographs, including stock photos that he acquired from a travel agency. Now it was time for De Moor to sit down and update the scenery in *The Black Island*, and now it's time for us to **Explore and Discover!**

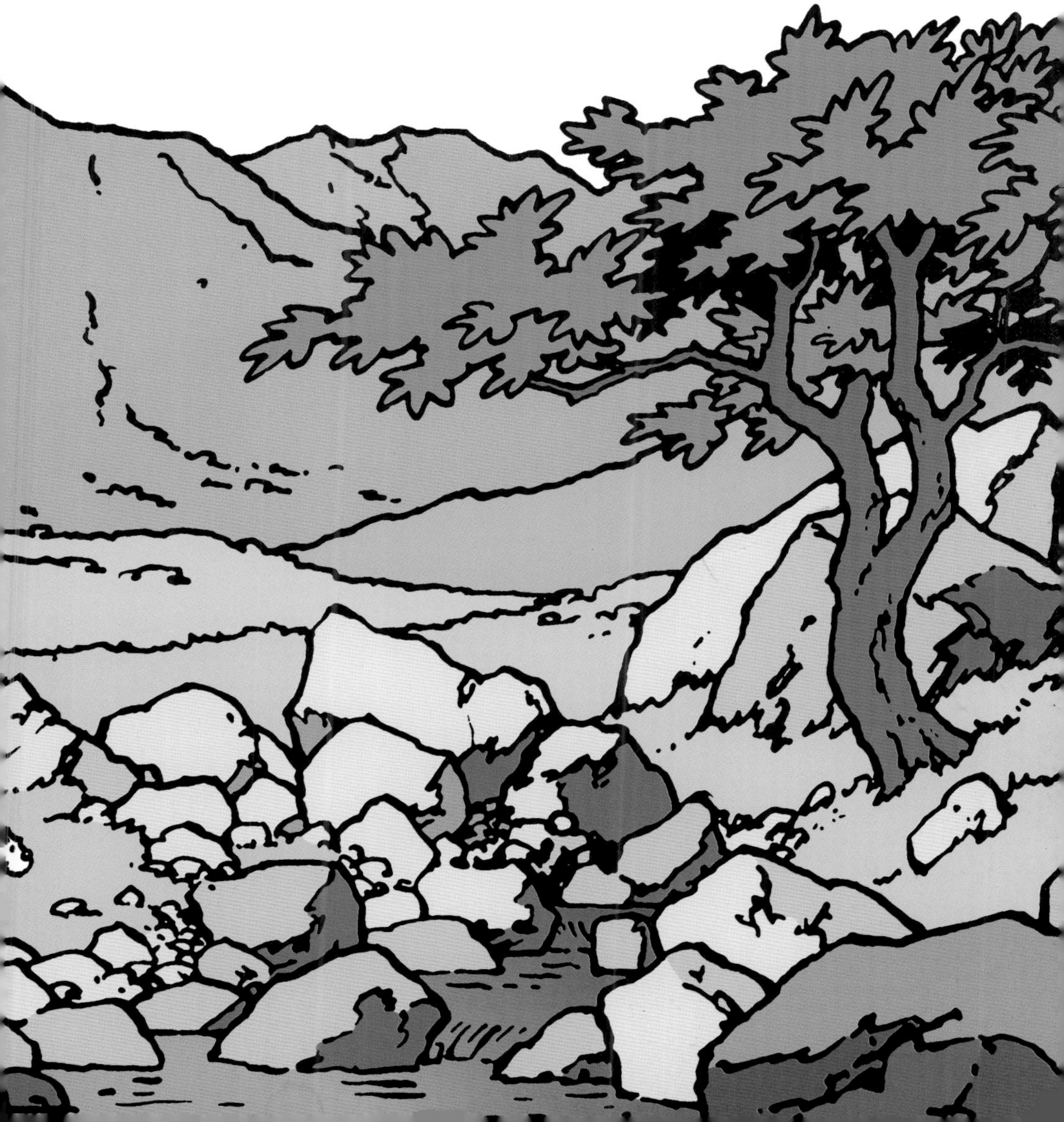

EXPLORE AND DISCOVER

It's the beginning of the story and Tintin is off to England. On this page you can see the first strip from page 3 of the 1943 version of *The Black Island*…

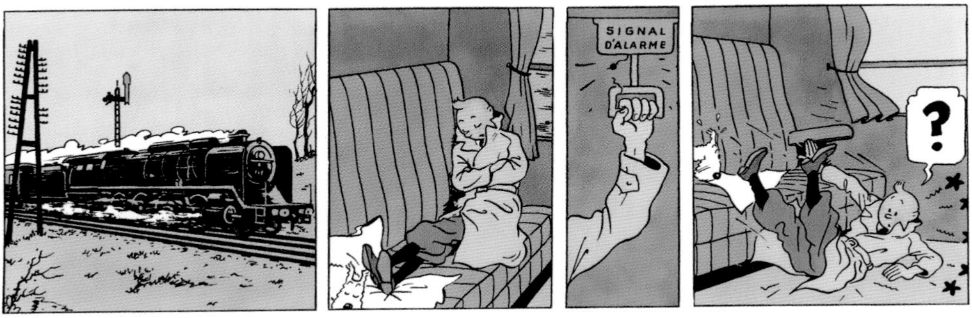
SIGNAL D'ALARME
?

This version shows Hergé's drawing of a Mikado type 141 steam engine. The photo below shows a slightly different model of the same type.

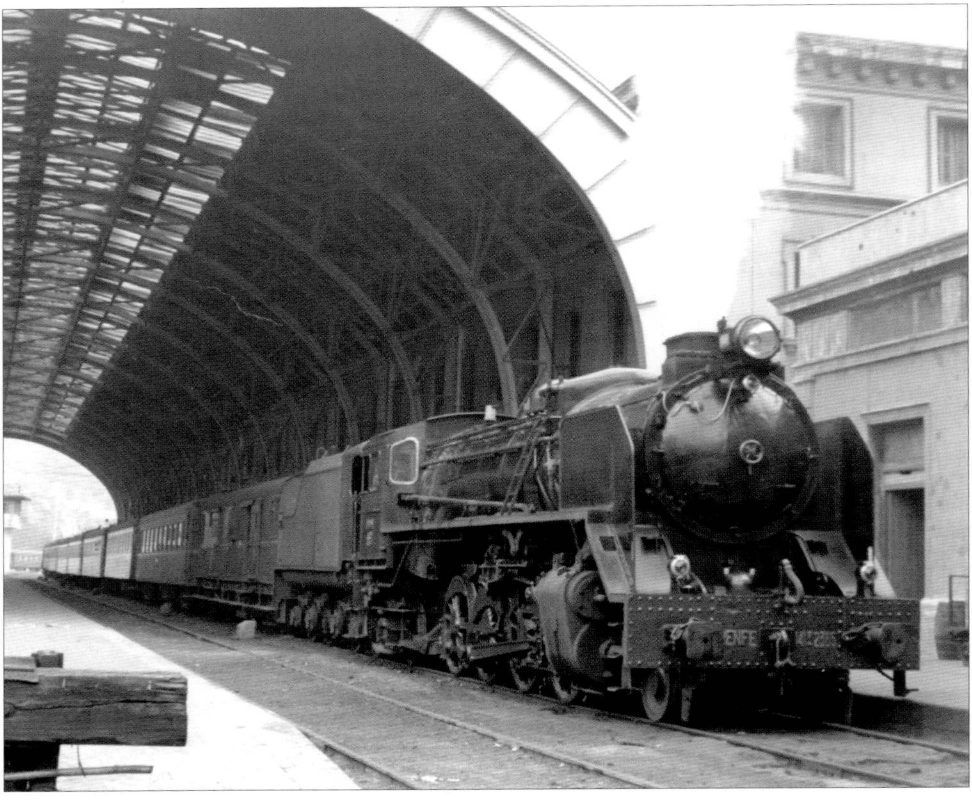

© Werner Soelch

...and on this page you can see the same strip that has been updated for the 1966 version. Can you spot the differences?

Bob De Moor went to great lengths to photograph and sketch vehicles, but Tintin doesn't need to step off the train for us to see De Moor's work: The cartoonist also paid attention to interior furnishings!

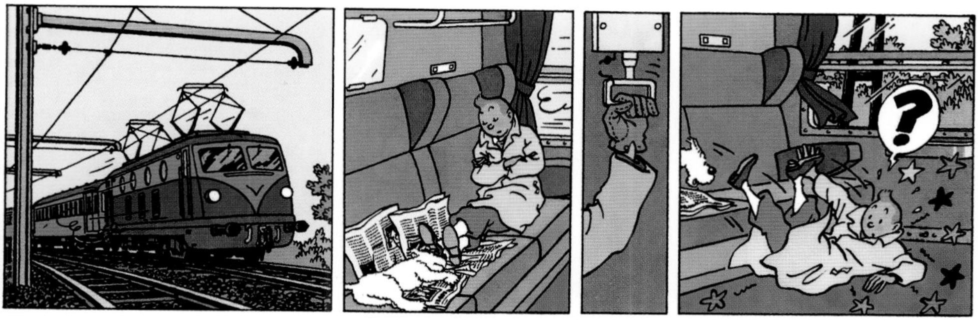
?

In the third version (1966) of *The Black Island*, Bob De Moor updated the steam train to a BB type electric locomotive.

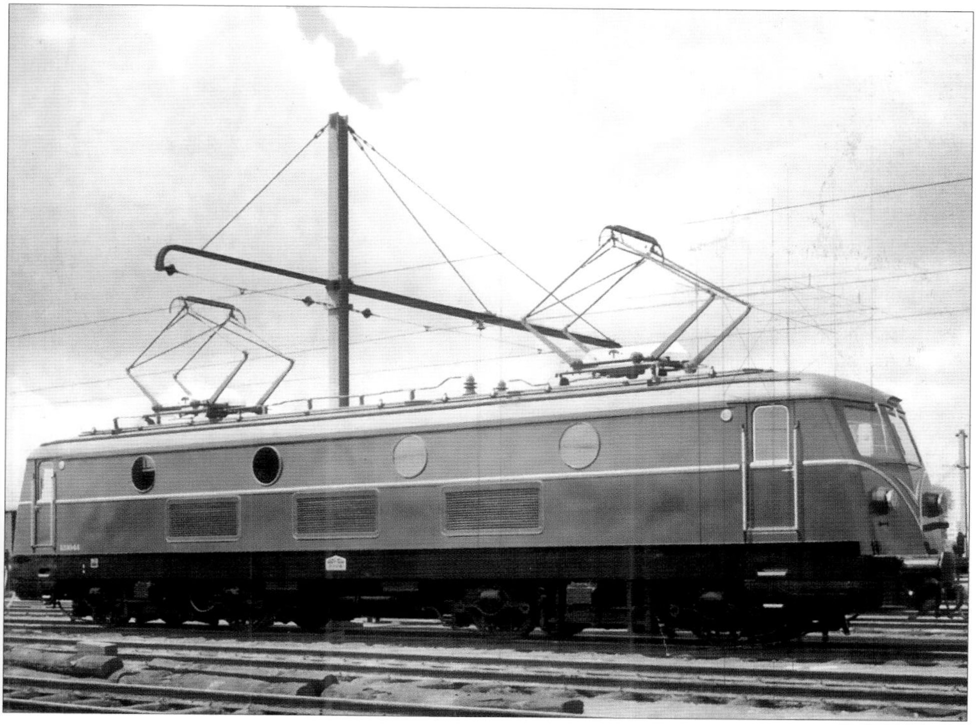

DR. MÜLLER'S COUNTRY HOUSE

While in the English county of Sussex, trying to solve the mystery of the crashed aircraft, Tintin is taken prisoner by the dastardly Dr. Müller. He struggles to escape!

Hergé's assistant Bob De Moor also visited Sussex. He may have come across Great Dixter House (see photo on page 7), the inspiration behind Dr. Müller's country house. The photo on the opposite page, which De Moor brought back from England, was acquired from a travel agency and shows the Solar Room at Great Dixter.

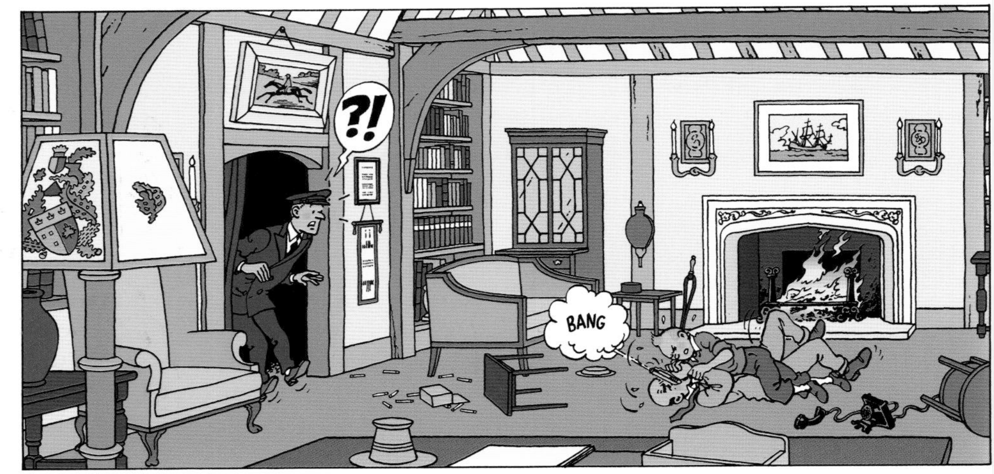
?!
BANG

- ★ **Great Dixter is located in the village of Northiam, East Sussex. It is set back about ten miles from the south coast of England.**
- ★ **Although the manor house of Dixter is first mentioned in records stretching back to the year 1220, the oldest parts of the present building date back to around 1450.**
- ★ **As well as being an important example of historic architecture, Great Dixter is famous for its gardens, which were first opened to the public in 1954 by its owner, horticulturist Christopher Lloyd (1921–2006).**

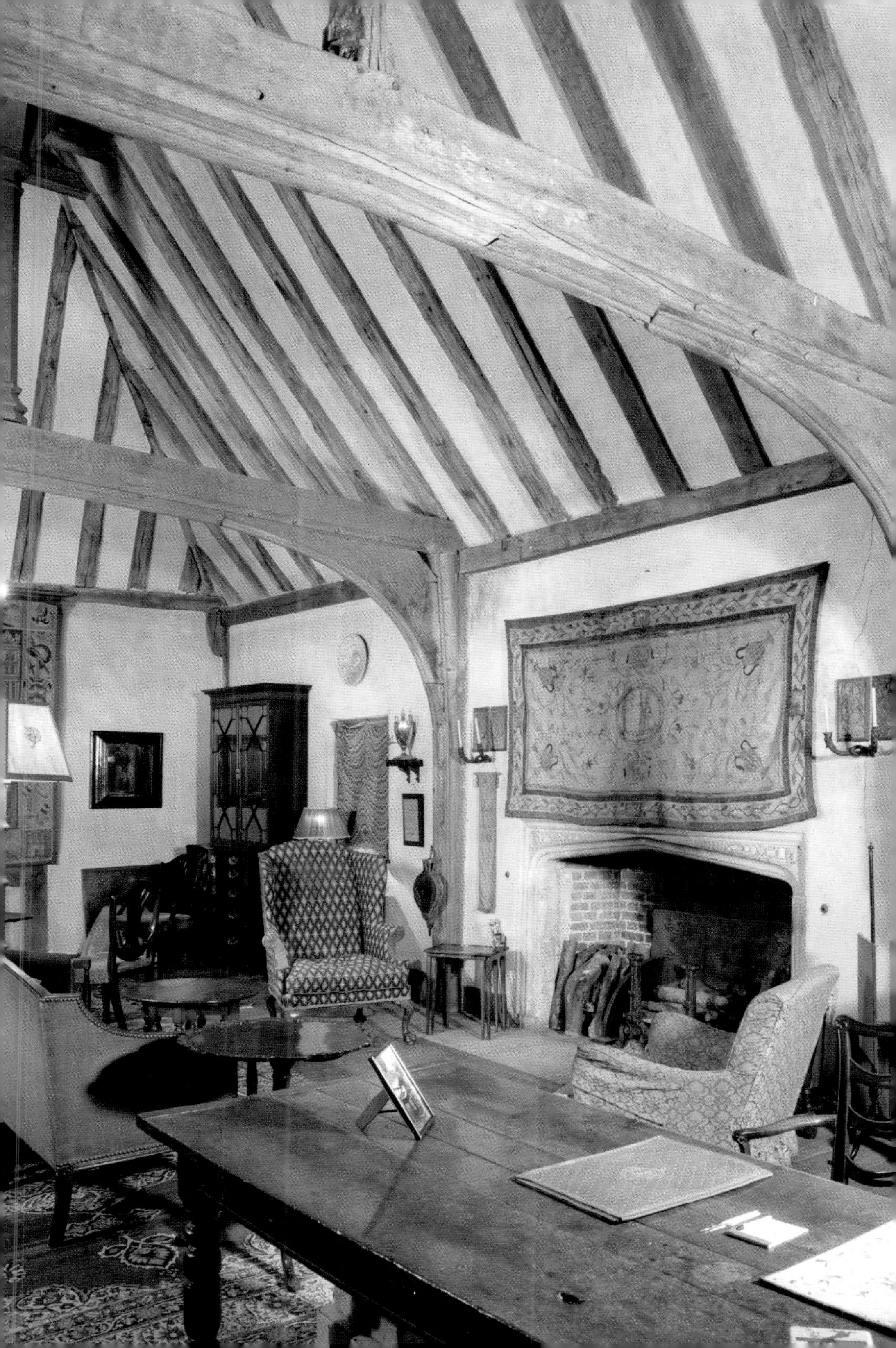

What a marvellous view!

CRAIG DHUI CASTLE

After escaping from the evil Dr. Müller, Tintin's investigation leads him to Craig Dhui Castle on the mysterious Black Island in Scotland. Hergé used several castles for inspiration as he drew Craig Dhui. The tallest tower is based on part of Arundel Castle in Sussex.

Below is a picture of Arundel, created by the British artist Norman Wilkinson, which Hergé kept in his archives. It looks as if there is a small lookout tower on top of the large tower, but this is actually an illusion created by the angle of the picture—it is in fact a tall, thin turret containing a staircase, attached to the far side of the main tower. Perhaps this illusion explains why Hergé drew Craig Dhui's main tower with a smaller tower on top.

As well as copying what he thought was a lookout tower on top of the main tower, Hergé also copied the arrow slits (through which archers fired arrows at the enemy), the battlements (the crown shape on the tower, consisting of a circular wall with regular gaps through which soldiers could shoot arrows and fight), and the machicolations (the row of holes just underneath the battlements, through which stones could be dropped to fend off attacking enemies).

ARUNDEL CASTLE

★ In the year 1066, an army of troops from Normandy, Brittany, France and Flanders defeated the army of King Harold II of England at the Battle of Hastings in Sussex.

★ The leader of the winners, William the Conqueror, became the King of England. He gave a large part of West Sussex to his advisor, Roger de Montgomery.

★ In 1067, Roger de Montgomery began building Arundel Castle on the site of existing fortifications.

★ Arundel Castle was badly damaged during the English Civil War (1642–1651); major restorations were carried out in the eighteenth and nineteenth centuries.

★ Today Arundel Castle, the second largest castle in England, is a popular tourist destination. But be careful if you visit: it is said to be haunted by several ghosts!

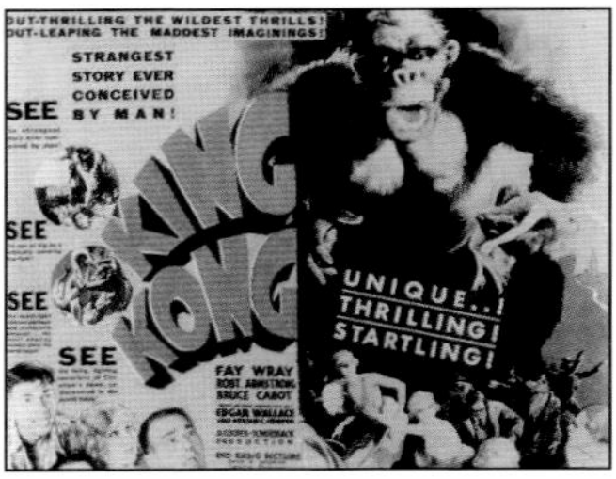
STRANGEST
STORY EVER
CONCEIVED
BY MAN!
SEE
SEE
SEE
SEE
KING KONG
UNIQUE...!
THRILLING!
STARTLING!
FAY WRAY

KING KONG AND...

Just when Tintin is taking a moment to enjoy the view from Craig Dhui Castle, he bumps into the beast of the Black Island! Ranko the gorilla is a bit like the misunderstood giant ape King Kong. The original black-and-white film *King Kong* hit cinemas in 1933, and Hergé certainly would have seen it.

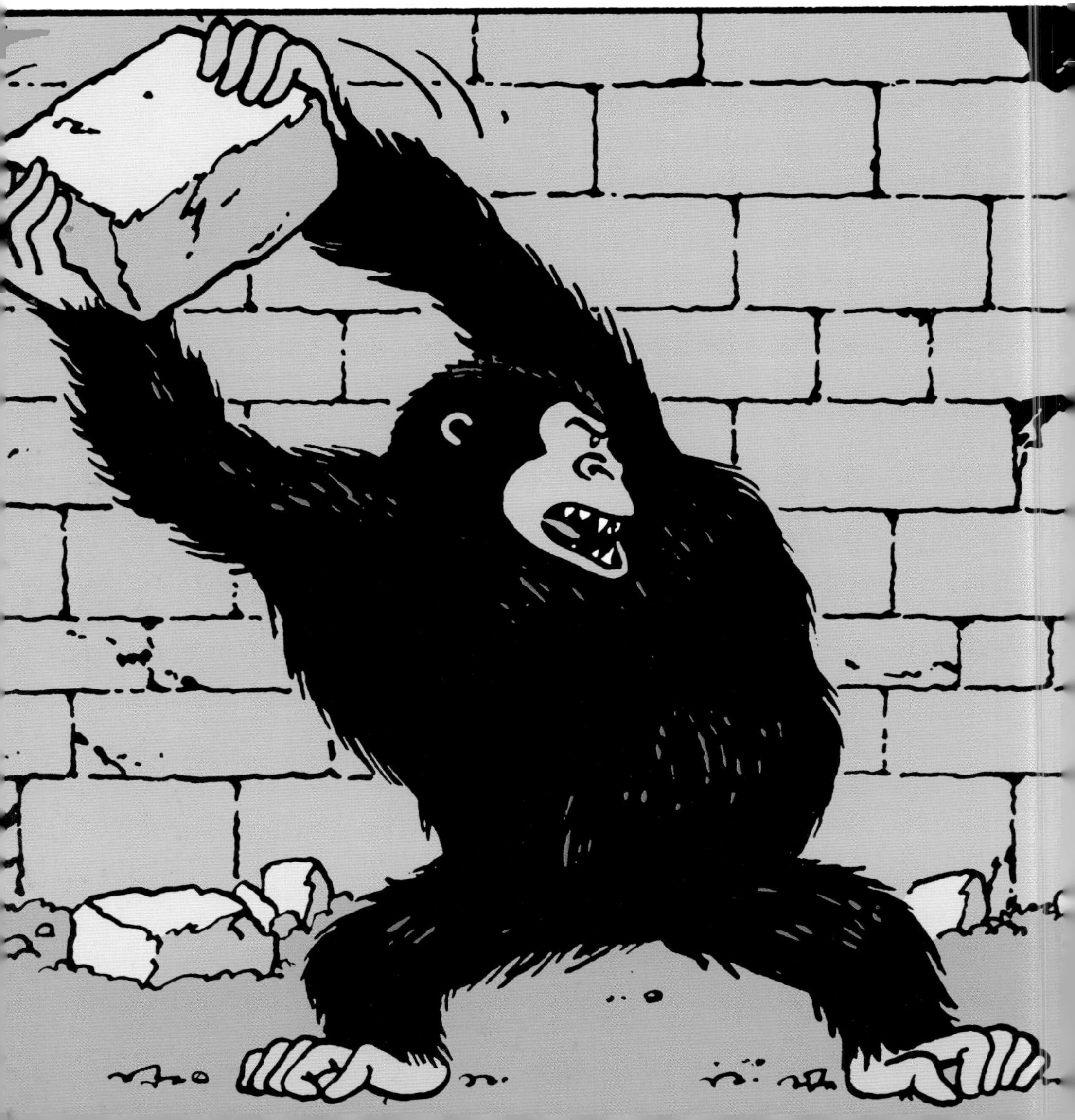

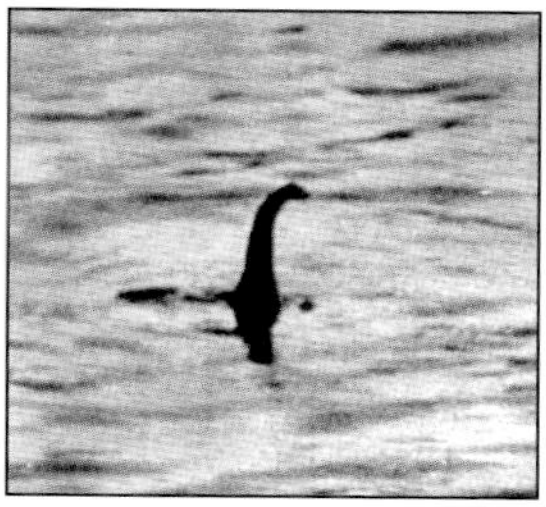

...THE LOCH NESS MONSTER!

The photo on the left supposedly shows the Loch Ness Monster from the Scottish Highlands, and was taken by a doctor in 1934. A year previously there were several reported sightings of the monster. Today the mystery remains: is there a strange, dinosaur-like creature living in Loch Ness, or not?

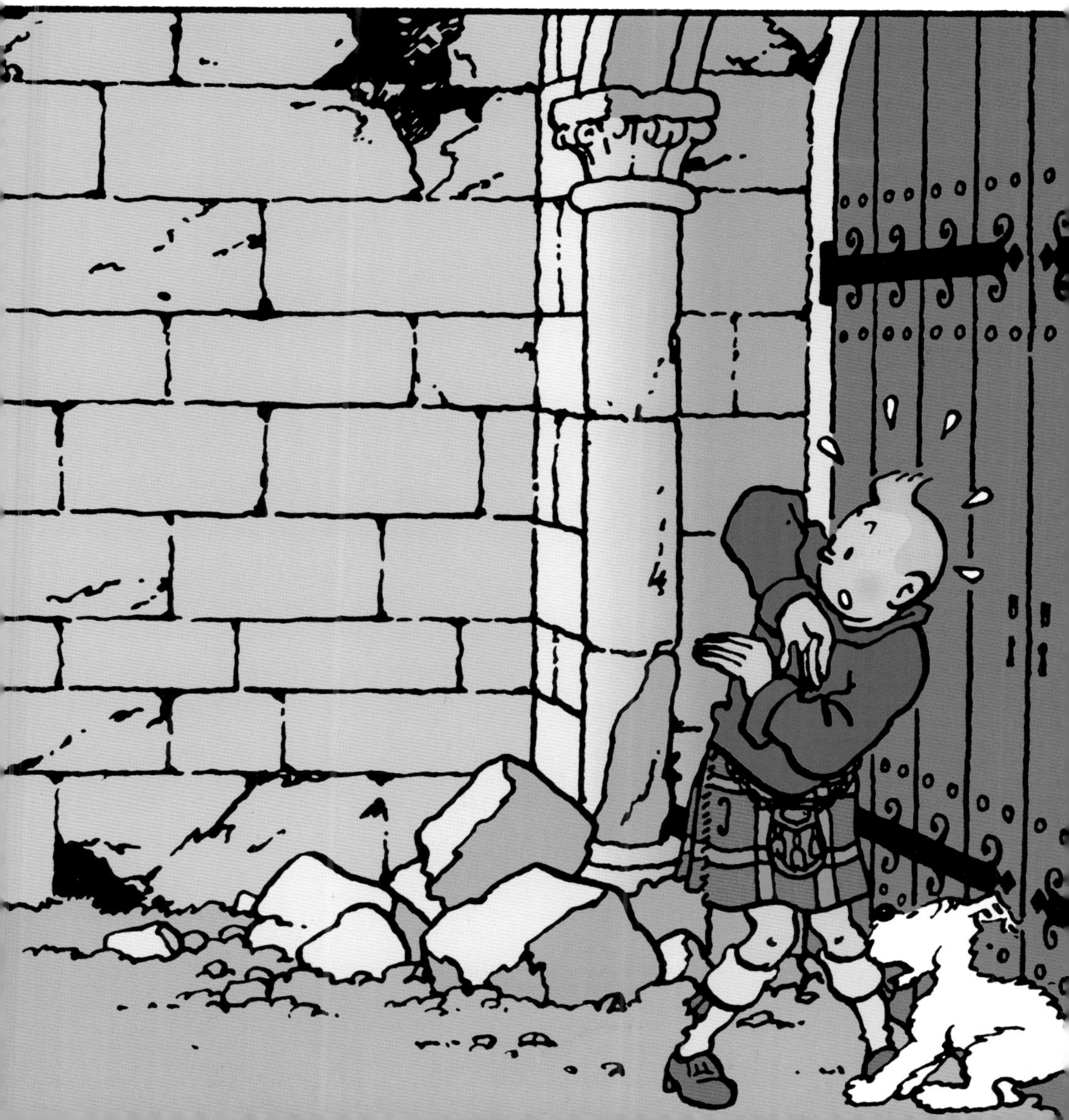

DR. MÜLLER

The Black Island provides the setting for Tintin's meeting with a dastardly villain who returns in later adventures: Dr. J. W. Müller.

In this story, Müller is part of a gang working to forge British banknotes. He is also the medical superintendent of a private mental institution… where patients enter sane and come out insane!

In a later Tintin adventure, *Land of Black Gold*, Dr. Müller appears under the alias of Professor Smith, the aggressive representative of an oil company intent on exploiting oil fields in the fictional Middle Eastern country of Khemed.

Müller really is evil personified! But where did Hergé find the inspiration for this villainous character?

Dr. Müller as "Professor Smith" in *Land of Black Gold*.

DR. GEORG BELL

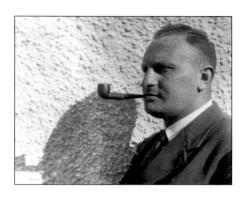

Hergé read all about a shady German man of Scottish descent, Dr. Georg Bell, in the French magazine *Crapouillot* (meaning "little toad," a type of mortar shell used by troops in World War I).

Bell had ties with many high-ranking Nazis as the political party grew in Germany at the beginning of the 1930s. He also acted as an intermediary between Nazi leader Adolf Hitler and the powerful Dutch oil tycoon Henri Deterding.

Dr. Georg Bell was allegedly involved in a plan to destabilize the Soviet economy by counterfeiting Russian rubles and by forging British, American and French banknotes.

Hergé had found the perfect model for the treacherous and cunning Dr. Müller!

DES FAUX-MONNAYEURS !... JE NE PENSAIS PAS ÊTRE SI PRÈS DU BUT !...
ÉPATANT !... ET LE FILIGRANE EST BIEN VISIBLE ....

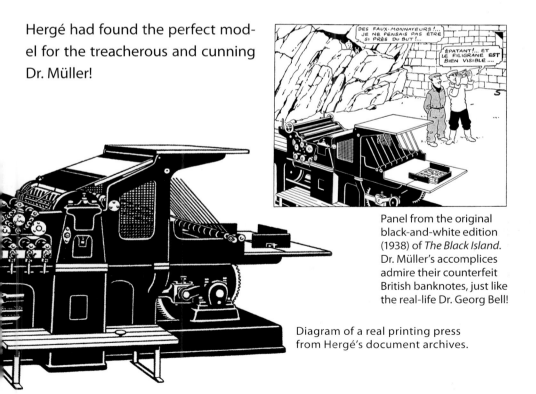

Panel from the original black-and-white edition (1938) of *The Black Island*. Dr. Müller's accomplices admire their counterfeit British banknotes, just like the real-life Dr. Georg Bell!

Diagram of a real printing press from Hergé's document archives.

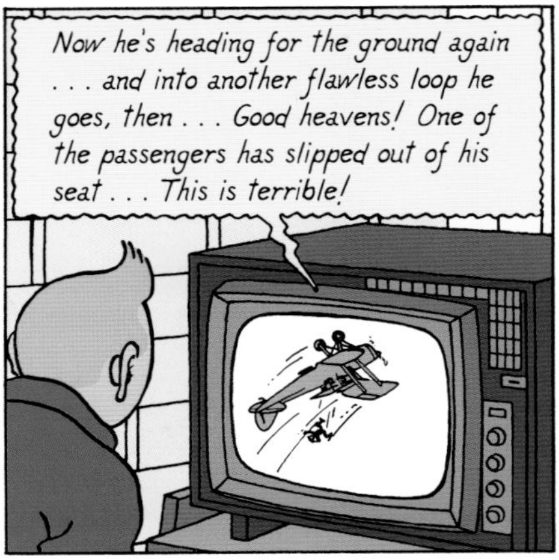
Now he's heading for the ground again . . . and into another flawless loop he goes, then . . . Good heavens! One of the passengers has slipped out of his seat . . . This is terrible!

INVOLUNTARY AEROBATICS!

In the story, Tintin watches in amazement as a daredevil pilot pulls an extraordinary loop-the-loop! Little does he know that the "pilot" has never flown a plane, and that his passengers are...Thomson and Thompson!

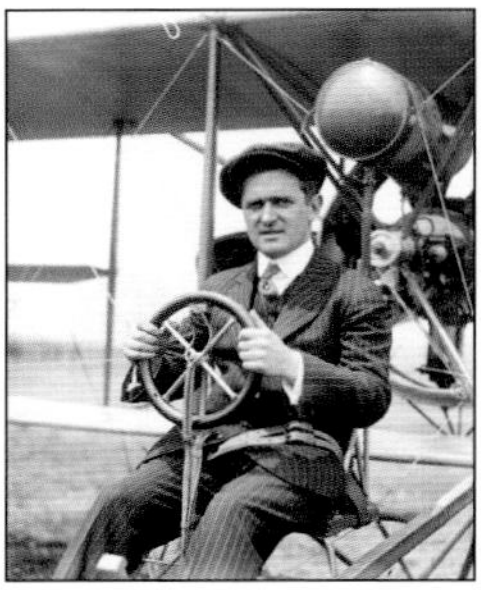

Lincoln Beachley, wearing his trademark suit, prepares for some aerobatics in about 1913.

- ★ **Aerobatics is an extreme sport that developed at the beginning of the twentieth century.**
- ★ **The American pilot Lincoln Beachley (1887–1915) is considered to be the father of aerobatic flying.**
- ★ **Beachley began flying hot air balloons at seventeen years of age. He then learned how to fly planes, crashing several and nearly being expelled from flying school!**
- ★ **Beachley began stunt flying in 1911, racing trains and flying as high as he could before running out of fuel and gliding back down to land.**
- ★ **Unfortunately, in 1915 Beachley was killed while attempting a dangerous stunt to fly upside down.**

Wing-walking daredevils Ivan Unger and Gladys Roy, 1925.

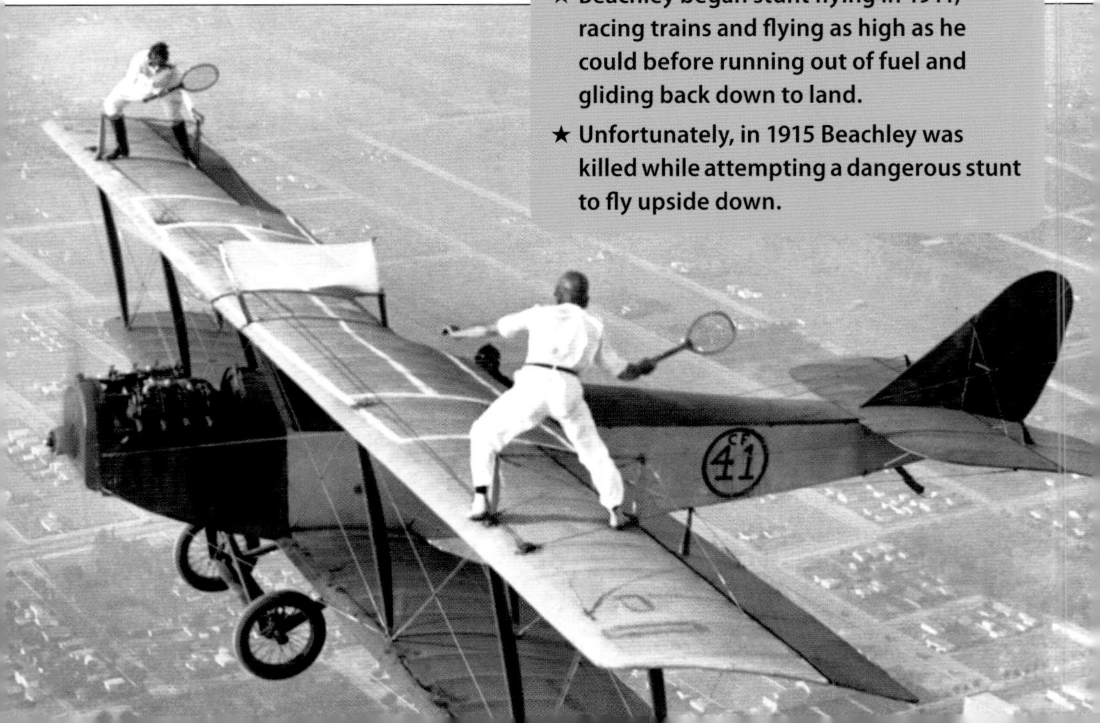
41

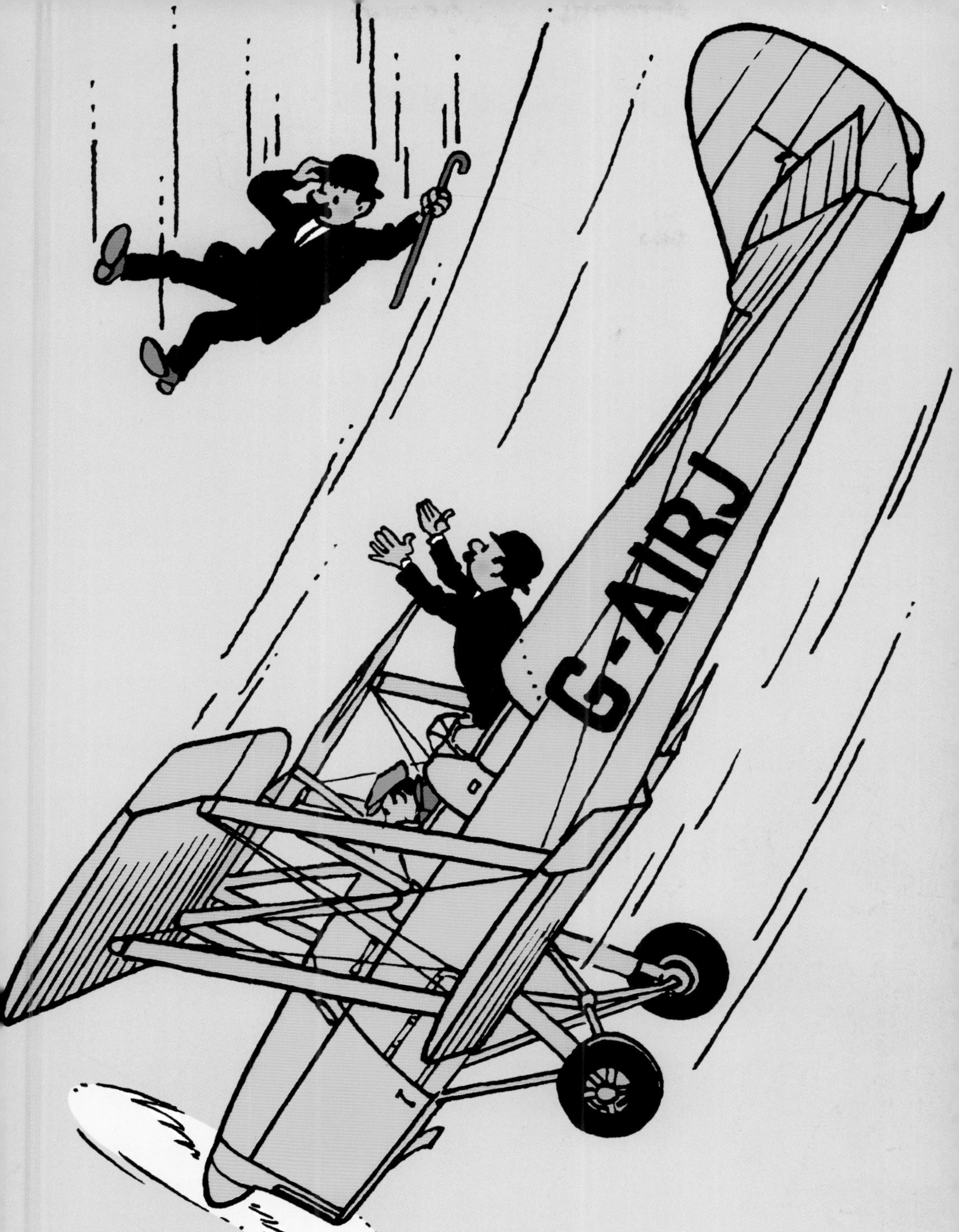
G-AIRJ

LEAVING THE BLACK ISLAND

Tintin and the Thom(p)sons leave the Black Island with their new friend, Ranko the gorilla. Tintin's compassion for the wounded animal has melted its heart, and even Snowy's determined barking may have played a part in taming the "beast"!

With the cunning counterfeiters in police custody, all that remains to be done is to find a new home for Ranko. London Zoo, here they come!

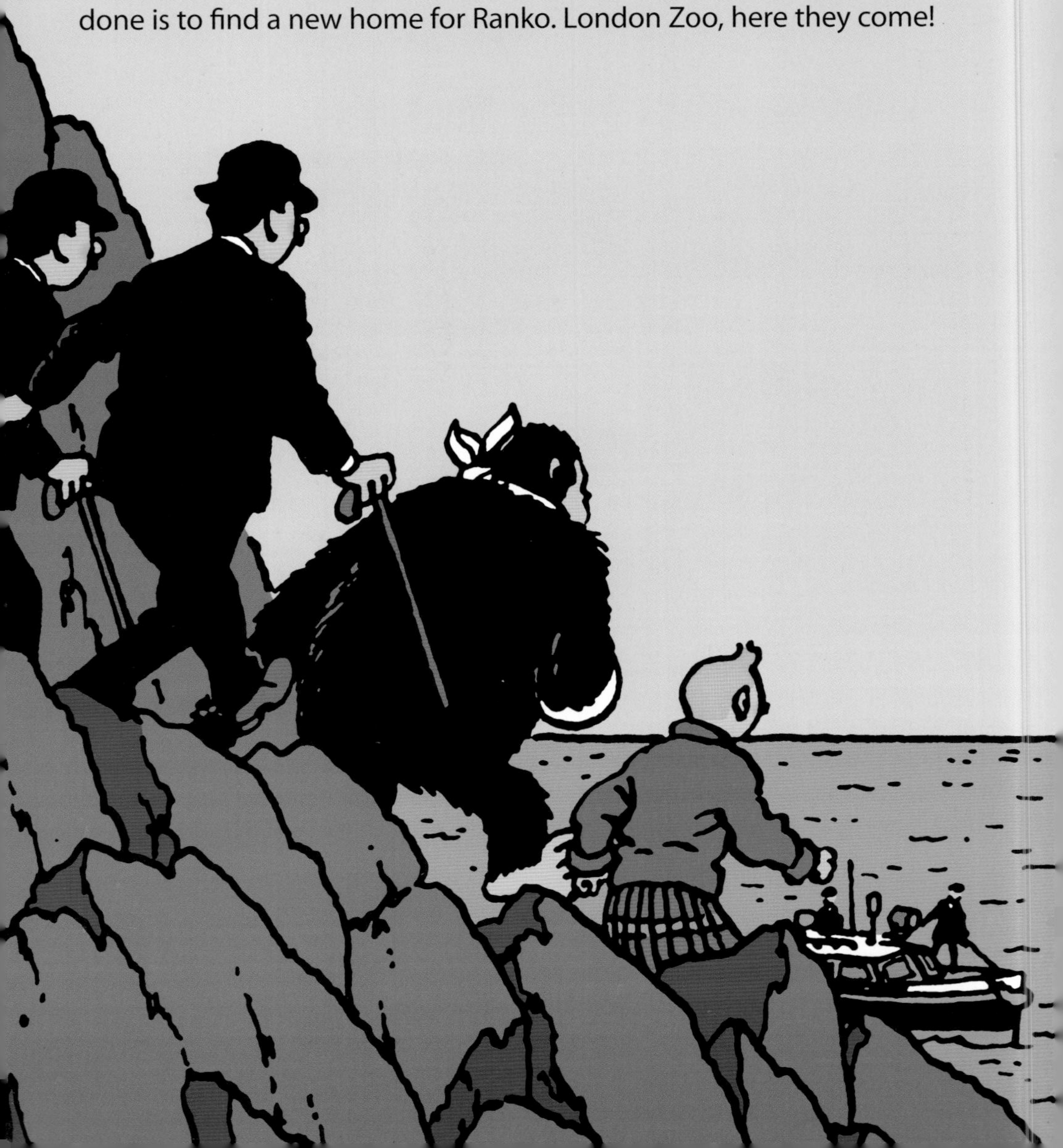

TINTIN'S GRAND ADVENTURE

When Hergé began *The Black Island* in 1937, he was working from home. He was a bit lonely, and this is reflected in Tintin's journey to the desolate Scottish Highlands. By the time the third version of this story was published in 1966, Hergé was surrounded by assistants in his studio. Hergé said that he "much preferred" the 1966 version of *The Black Island*, and noted: "Through the eyes of my assistant, I managed to get a closer look at England."

Trivia: *The Black Island*

When Bob De Moor visited England, he stayed at the house of the English translator Michael Turner in the town of Bishop's Stortford. The bridge Tintin jumps off on page 30 is the bridge at Bishop's Stortford station!

Bob De Moor also created his own comic strips and characters, including Cori le Moussaillon (Cori the ship's apprentice) and Barelli.

Tintin takes a train before catching a ferry to England. If the story were redone again today, no doubt Tintin would stay on the train all the way: today trains run under the seabed between France and England via the Channel Tunnel.

The square tower of Craig Dhui Castle does not appear in the first two versions of The Black Island; Bob De Moor added it for the third version after visiting Brodick Castle on the Isle of Arran, Scotland.

When The Black Island was published, British Rail wrote to Methuen to complain about Tintin jumping on the roof of a train, saying that it set a bad example for children who should be sitting in their seats. They also wanted the "animal" (Snowy) to be on a leash!

When Hergé created the second version of the story (published in 1943), in addition to coloring in the scenery, he colored in the television screen...years before color television was possible! Methuen asked Hergé to make the TV black-and-white again for the third version (1966).

GO ON MORE ADVENTURES WITH TINTIN!

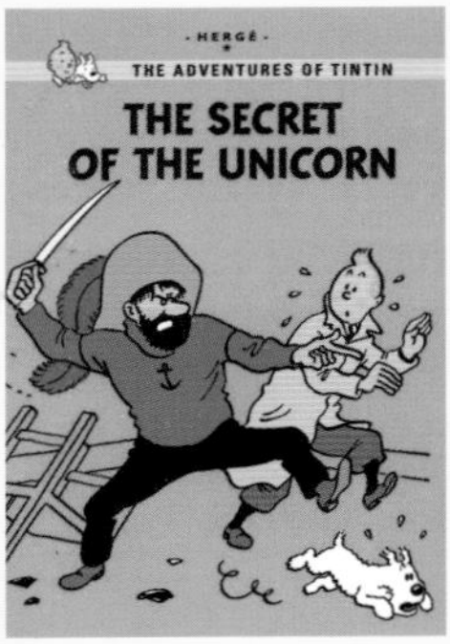
HERGÉ
THE ADVENTURES OF TINTIN
THE SECRET OF THE UNICORN

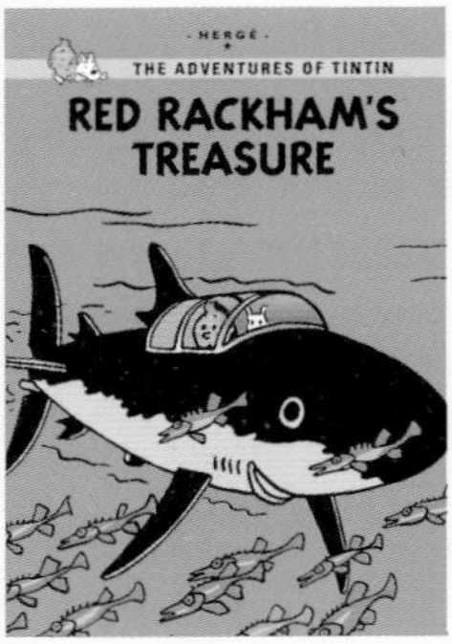
HERGÉ
THE ADVENTURES OF TINTIN
RED RACKHAM'S TREASURE

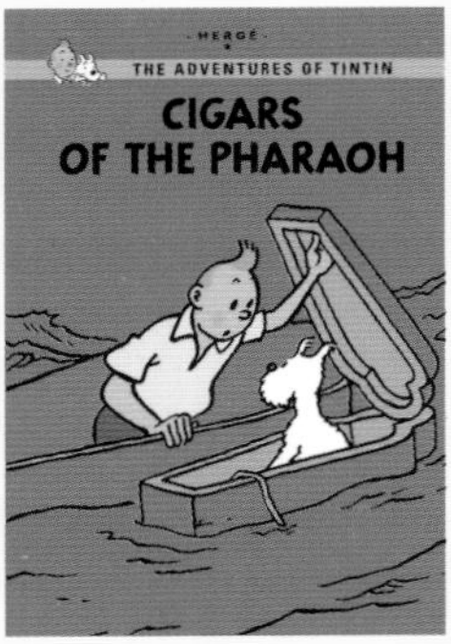
HERGÉ
THE ADVENTURES OF TINTIN
CIGARS OF THE PHARAOH

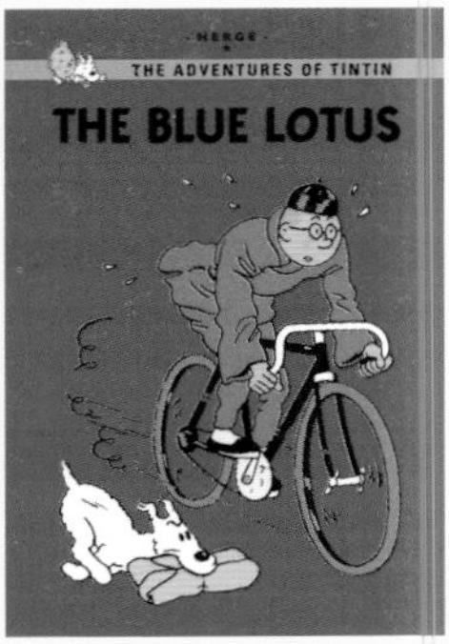
HERGÉ
THE ADVENTURES OF TINTIN
THE BLUE LOTUS

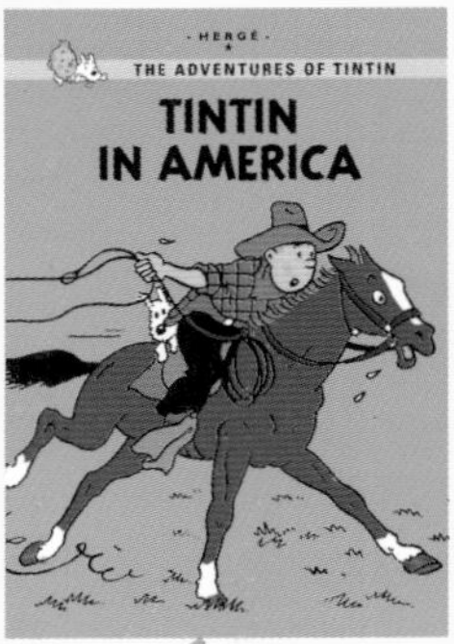
HERGÉ
THE ADVENTURES OF TINTIN
TINTIN IN AMERICA

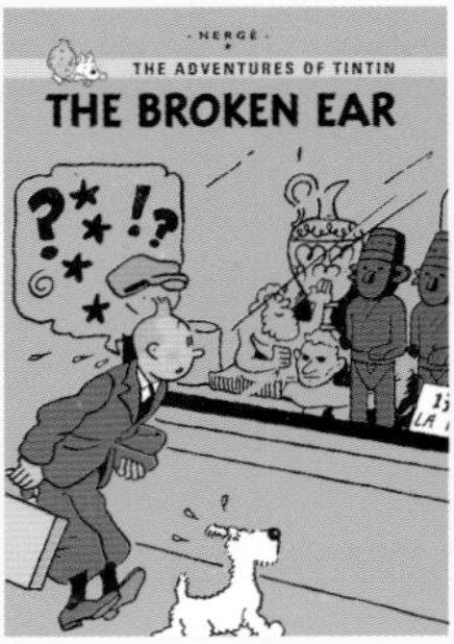
HERGÉ
THE ADVENTURES OF TINTIN
THE BROKEN EAR

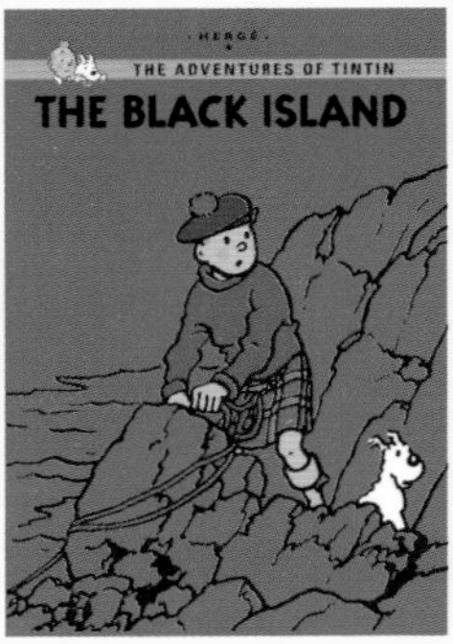
HERGÉ
THE ADVENTURES OF TINTIN
THE BLACK ISLAND

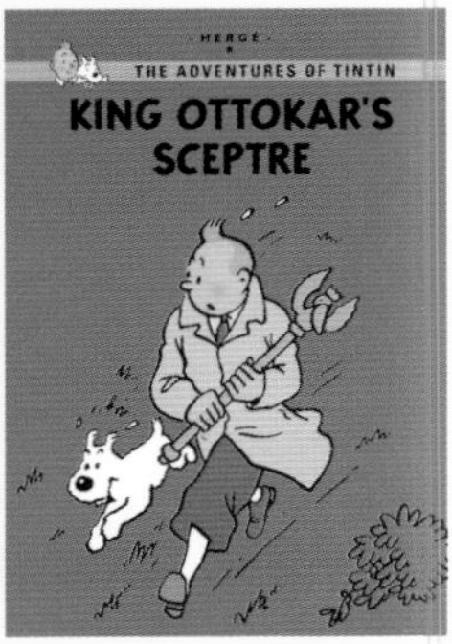
HERGÉ
THE ADVENTURES OF TINTIN
KING OTTOKAR'S SCEPTRE

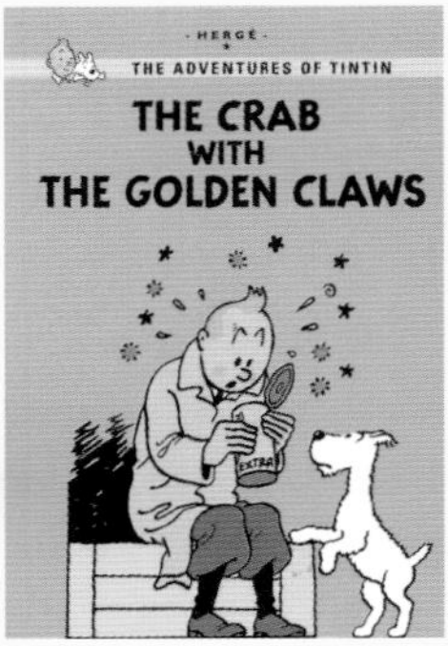
HERGÉ
THE ADVENTURES OF TINTIN
THE CRAB WITH THE GOLDEN CLAWS

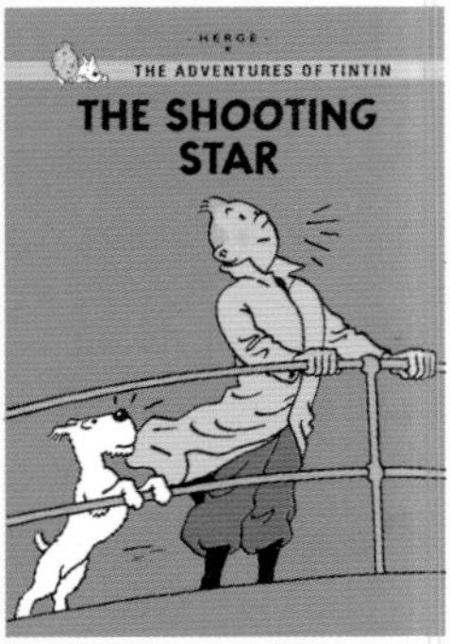
HERGÉ
THE ADVENTURES OF TINTIN
THE SHOOTING STAR

ALSO AVAILABLE

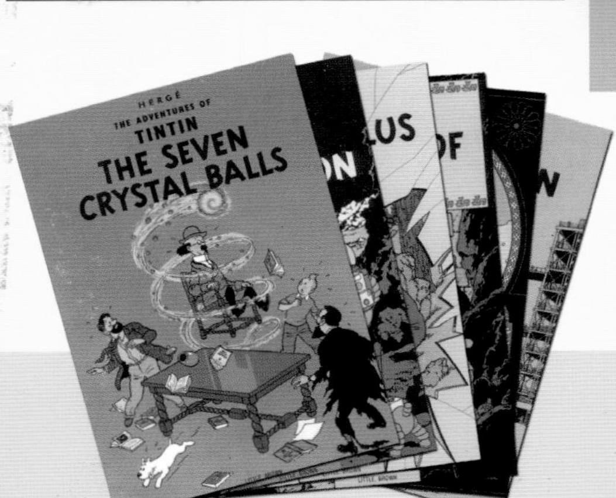
HERGÉ
THE ADVENTURES OF TINTIN
THE SEVEN CRYSTAL BALLS

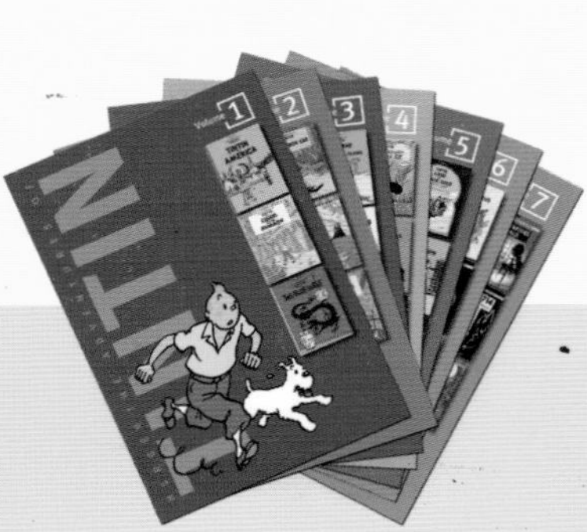
TINTIN

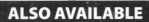